WARPED LINE

AN URBAN FANTASY

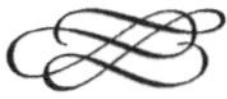

ANN GIMPEL

CONTENTS

An Urban Fantasy

By
Ann Gimpel

Tumble off reality's edge into myth, magic, and Armageddon

Copyright Page

BOOK DESCRIPTION: WARPED LINE

I chose stasis—a long sleep—for me and two of mine. Hard to time these things, but we woke in the eye of a cyclone.

When I went to sleep—to avoid being drained of magic and blood by dark Sorcerers—Vampires weren't exactly on the endangered species list, but not many of us are left. No one ever accepted us. Not mortals and not others with power, either. At least one of those dams has developed a few cracks. Supernaturals aren't quite welcoming, but they'll take help from any quarter.

Mortals have declared war on magic, and they won't rest until we're all sitting in iron-clad prisons. What a bunch of cowards. If they weren't hiding behind false humanitarian walls, they'd be honest about their intentions and do their damnedest to kill us outright.

The world turned into an alien place while I slept. Not

much point returning to my clan house in Italy. It's probably long since disbanded. Besides, fate tossed me squarely in Ariana's path. She's like me, a Vampire, but I hunger for her in a very un-Vampirelike way.

She's tried hard to chase me away, but I'm tough to dissuade. She doesn't know it, but I won't back off until she's mine.

No matter what it takes.

BOOKS IN THE CATACLYSM SERIES

Harsh Line, Book One
Warped Line, Book Two
Cracked Line, Book Three
Broken Line, Book Four

Part of me can scarcely believe I'm writing this series. Vampires have been the bad guys in my Bitter Harvest series and my Gatekeeper series, and several others. Not so in the Cataclysm books.

Maybe I named the series what I did because turning Vampires into heroes was cataclysmic for me. Mortals are a sketchy lot. When the reality of magical beings got a little too close, they banded together and fought back. Silly of them, huh? Even an army of humans isn't a match for a couple of determined magic-wielders, but they're going to have to figure that out on their own.

Ariana is a great heroine. I'm excited to tell you her story. You'll get to know Nickolas much better in this book since he plays a far more major role than he did in book one. And Conan is perfect. He reminds me of my own wolves: noble, principled, and courageous as hell.

I stood in the garage after Ariana's abrupt departure wondering what to do next. I'd clearly trodden on unholy ground when I'd blurted out my question about Mistral. She'd been in the Clan Hawke seethe when he was murdered. At least I knew that much.

Murdered is a bit of a misnomer. As head of Clan Hawke, Mistral was centuries dead, but his Vampiric existence had been cut short—presumably by one of his minions. No one else would have been able to get close enough to a master Vampire to do that level of damage. Back when I was newly made, I'd snuck away from Clan Giovanni more than once, intent on locating the assassin who'd ended Mistral. If I'd found him, I'd have been a hero in Vampire circles. As I hunted, my fantasies vacillated between ending him myself or hauling him in to face justice.

Never did fully decide, and it was a moot point because I never located his killer.

Ariana had done her best to mask her emotions, but she'd been visibly upset when I'd asked about her master. He was probably who'd turned her, which meant she'd have had a special bond with him. I wasn't used to tiptoeing around other Vampires. Most of us lost our reactiveness along with our humanity when we joined the ranks of the Undead.

Ariana was definitely different.

I hadn't realized I'd begun pacing, skirting the rays of daylight filtering around an enormous metal door at one end of what looked like a storage area, but a damned clean one that was absolutely devoid of any contents.

If I was honest with myself, I wasn't the same Vampire who'd chosen stasis to escape dark Sorcerers out for my blood. Literally. Something about Vampire blood bolstered their magic. At the time, I didn't know they also murdered humans, absorbing their psychic energies to strengthen themselves.

For some reason that seems far worse to me than stealing the occasional sip from a willing mortal.

Prior to choosing a long sleep to vanish from sight, I'd been as accommodating as the next Vampire, which is to say, not accommodating at all. It was my way or nothing, and I didn't particularly care whose toes I stomped on. Other magic wielders don't like us because we're at the top of the food chain, and they're jealous of our strength and speed and our genuine give-a-fuck attitudes.

My interpretation.

If you were to ask any Witch or Sorcerer or Fae, they'd label us insufferable, lean closer, and whisper our magic wasn't up to par, either. They're entitled to their opinions.

Now that my views have had a chance to evolve, I can appreciate their line of arguments. We can be pretty damned arrogant, and our brand of magic is different. It's designed to hypnotize prey, so we always have enough to eat.

Beyond that, we don't actually require magic for much. Cheap parlor tricks are a waste of time and energy. I was on my tenth transit of the garage and not one step nearer to figuring out what to do next. Ariana had invited me to her home, but that was before I'd made the mistake of bringing up Mistral. She and Conan, her shapeshifting dire wolf companion, had vanished damned fast after that.

"There you are." Clive, another Clan Giovanni Vampire, trotted into the garage from a door that led into the house. Daylight streamed through the door in the brief moment it was open.

"How'd you manage to transit the kitchen?" I asked.

He blinked owlishly out of bloodshot dark eyes. "Not easily, mate." He examined his hands, the only part of him that wasn't covered. "Don't think I got burned." His accent was pure upper crust British. Blond hair spilled down his shoulders. Like all of us, he was one striking specimen. His tall, broad-shouldered, slim-hipped build was draped in cheap garments we'd stolen from a secondhand clothing store soon after waking from stasis.

Clive's presence settled things. He and I would retreat to the cave where we'd slept a hundred years away and wait out the day. At least I could stop perseverating about whether or not to teleport to Ariana's house.

"Where are Ariana and Conan?" Clive asked me.

"They went home." Something about my tone alerted

him enough to shoot me a curious look, but I outranked him. He knew better than to mine for details. "We've put off the farewell ceremony until tonight."

"For Lorenzo?" He quirked a blond brow.

I nodded. "Too much was going on, and then we lost the night."

"Probably for the best," Clive said. Making a conscious effort, he inhaled and blew out an unneeded breath. "It's all right. The ritual was just to assuage my guilt. We don't have to give him any kind of sendoff. He doesn't really deserve it. Not after how he acted."

I tended to agree. Another member of Clan Giovanni who'd joined me in stasis, Lorenzo had engaged in group sex play with three mortal women. He probably would have gotten off clean, except he'd glommed onto one and drained her. The other two women panicked, and the story blew up all over the place.

"Good for us to remember," I muttered.

"What? To keep our dicks under wraps?" Clive's words were laced with sarcasm.

"I was thinking more about our fangs." I stopped for a moment before adding, "One of the biggest changes while we were asleep is how fast news travels. Computers can broadcast anything around the globe in seconds. It was how the police found out about Lorenzo's swan dive from grace so fast."

"I still think we should go home."

My face must have taken on an odd expression because Clive made come along motions with one hand. "What aren't you saying? I mean I get it we'd have a hell of a time crossing the ocean. I'd need those identification items you just acquired, but we'd figure it out."

"Runs deeper than that. Ariana showed me what Castelrotto looks like today. Sibiu too, which was where she and Conan were before coming to North America."

"You have to say more than that, mate," Clive urged.

"It's not just different," I told him. "It looks a lot like this place, except the buildings are older. If our clan is still in that region, my bet is they've moved out of the city. Not so sure they'd welcome us back. All the woods where we used to find game when we couldn't locate a willing mortal are gone."

Clive took a step away from me. "All of them?" he choked out.

"Most, yes. What trees remain wouldn't offer much in the way of cover."

He frowned. "What do you mean, she showed you?"

"Her computer has pictures from everywhere in the world."

His eyes widened. "We shouldn't have slept so long."

"Hard to second-guess these things." I shrugged. The strips of light oozing around the door were growing. I set a spell in motion and whisked us to the cave that was the closest thing we had to a home here. We're not exactly cold-blooded, but we don't feel the chill like a mortal might.

Once we were back underground, Clive settled on his haunches with his back against a wall. "Is our plan to remain here, then?"

"It's my plan"—I stressed the *my* part—"but if you want to return to Italy, I'll help you finesse managing it."

He was silent for a while, probably running options and prospects through his mind. When he looked up, he said, "I appreciate the freedom, but I'll remain with you. If I return to the clan house alone, I'll have a massive amount of explaining to do. Hell, for all I know, they'll think I did you in just like one of Mistral's minions did to him, and—"

"So long as you brought it up," I cut in, "do not ask Ariana about Mistral. She was there when the incident occurred, and it still upsets her."

Clive cracked a grin. "I'm guessing you already fell into that pothole."

"You'd have guessed right."

"What do you think about Conan?" Clive changed the subject rather abruptly.

It was a reasonable question. What did I think about the shapeshifting dire wolf who wasn't a wolf at all but a guardian?

"It isn't so much a matter of what I think," I began, "but of all the questions I have. His kinsmen clearly want him back, but he has no interest in returning."

"They must have done something," Clive said. "Alienated him somehow."

I nodded. "Beyond that, they didn't look for him very hard."

"We don't know that," Clive said. "His magic is the strongest I've run across. If he didn't want to be found..."

"Presumably the other guardians' magic is on a par with Conan's," I tossed out. My tone was sharp because I don't take to underlings correcting me. I needed to get over that. In the Old Country, I'd outranked Clive, but I had to move past antiquated thought patterns.

"True enough." Clive grinned. "That Ariana. She's really something. Hell, mate, she's as tall as we are. And all that hair is so black, it almost glows blue. Her eyes remind me of blue pearls, and—"

"Enough." I cut him off midsentence before he started in on her high, full breasts and to-die-for ass. As it was, my cock had begun to thicken.

"I get that she's not for me," he said and slitted his eyes my way. "You want her for yourself, don't you?"

I could bluster my way through a lie, but Ariana wasn't someone to lie about. My attraction to her felt almost sacrosanct, not to be trifled with. "Yes, I do, but she and Conan are sufficient unto themselves."

His smile faded. "You're not suggesting they're lovers?" Something about the specter of cross-species breeding—beyond Vampires and mortals—apparently bothered him.

"No. Not at all. They're friends. Companions. He never takes human form. Until we ran into the other guardians, I wasn't sure he even could."

"Mmph. Interesting. Since we're staying here. What happens next?"

It was a reasonable question. For one thing, we needed more clothes. And something beyond this cave so we could clean up. "I'm committed to working off my debt at *Ascent*. Once it's been discharged, I plan to locate lodgings."

"Working there the other night wasn't bad," Clive said. "Never did time in a public house before, but I can wash glasses and buss tables with the best of them. Do you suppose she'd offer me the same deal she did you?"

"She might. You'll have to ask her. And *Ascent* is a nightclub, not a public house or pub."

Clive made a face. "Hate to volunteer for chair time, but maybe you could show me the library where you did all that reading. Soon as I open my mouth, I'm bound to make a mistake, and whomever I'm talking with will figure out quick enough I'm not from here."

"Sure. I can do that. We'll stop by there once it gets dark. And then maybe another quiet visit to Salvation Army once they close. I wouldn't worry so much about idle conversation. Your accent is pronounced. People will just assume things are different where you came from."

"Heh. They don't know the half of it. What happened to your accent, while we're at it?"

"The Scottish brogue disappeared during all the time I spent in Italy. It left my English quite bland."

"Aye, but how'd you get from Scotland to Italy? Were you turned before or after?"

It was a personal question. The old me would have told Clive it was none of his affair. In Vampire circles, I knew everything about those I'd turned, and everyone younger than me in the clan. By contrast, those older than me remained mysteries.

"Sorry," Clive mumbled. "I misspoke."

"Yes and no. If we were still in the clan house, I'd have deigned not to answer. This is the leading edge of a new existence for us, though." I settled onto my favorite flat rock, facing him.

"Our trip to the States to find fresh recruits for Clan Giovanni was far from the first such venture the clan underwrote. Different from the other clans, we've always prided ourselves on our diversity. We've established it by traveling to distant locations and unearthing mortals who were interested and willing to transform themselves."

I leveled my gaze at Clive. "You know this part because you were chosen. Unlike other clans who pick a mortal, drain them, and then offer up a wrist—which the mortal is able to refuse, if they're strong enough—for us, the turning part is a foregone conclusion. We know before we settle in to bleed a mortal to the point of death that they wish to become part of Clan Giovanni.

"I may have been born in the Highlands, but I was conscripted into the English king's army when I was but eleven. By my sixteenth birthday, I'd been knighted. It was what made me attractive to the Clan Giovanni scout."

"So you were selected." Clive nodded slowly. "Just like me."

"In a manner of speaking. Night had fallen after a particularly bloody battle, and I was surrounded by corpses, including my horse. Felt damned bad about losing him. He was the best warhorse I'd ever ridden. My armor had protected me from the worst of things, but that day I'd viewed my future with a clarity that had eluded me before."

"That you'd keep right on fighting," Clive said, something akin to hero-worship shining from his dark eyes.

"Exactly. And sooner or later I'd be killed. Very few knights saw their twenty-fifth year. I was still lying where I'd fallen, not far from my dead destrier, when I heard rustling.

At first, I was concerned it was one of my companions coming out of a period of unconsciousness. Before I rolled over and got to my feet, though, I tried to see what was going on."

"Bet all that armor was heavy as fuck," Clive murmured.

I snorted. "You have no idea. Anyway, I managed to position my helmet so I could see better. Vampires had closed on the field. Not many, only four, but they were systematically moving from corpse to corpse."

I straightened my shoulders. "I wouldn't have admitted it then, but I was scared. Every rumor I'd ever heard about the Undead blasted into my mind, and my heart rate soared. I started panting inside the helmet, and knew I had to get my body under better control.

"If the Undead were feasting on corpses, they'd have a heyday with me. I was quick about quieting my mind and did a decent job pushing my fear to a distant place. My eyes were shut, and I was barely breathing."

"Like that would make you invisible to us," Clive blurted.

"Yes, well, you know, and I know now, but all I had to go on then were myths and legends."

"One of them approached you, didn't he?" Clive leaned toward me, fascinated by my tale.

"Of course, except it turned out to be a woman. She squatted next to me and said, 'I know you're not dead, knight. Sit up so we can talk.'

"I floundered about, making enough racket to wake the dead—probably not the best example under the circumstances. Eventually, I managed a sit. The woman was smiling. Her fangs were on display; blood streaked her chin. I should have been disgusted, but she was so beautiful, I forgot to be terrified."

"She had you in thrall." Clive's words held such certainty, they made me smile.

"She did, indeed. She explained she'd been on the sidelines from dusk onward, watching the tail end of the battle. She complimented me on my bravery, and sketched out the basics about becoming a Vampire. The whole time, she was clear it was my choice. If I decided against the transformation, she'd erase my memory of her, and it would be as if our conversation never happened."

"What decided you?" Clive asked.

"Immortality." I shrugged. "The rest is history. She turned me, and—"

"Did it include fucking?"

He was so direct, I laughed. "It did, indeed. You know her. Roseann was part of the clan when we turned you."

"Ooooh. She's one hot babe. I tried to get into her bed a time or two, but she never gave me the time of day."

My laughter deepened. "She wouldn't have. To her, you were a youngster."

"So were you that night on the battlefield." Clive's statement held defensiveness.

"True enough," I agreed, "except there might have been a fifty year difference in our ages, not a three hundred year one."

"Thank you for trusting me with your origin story," Clive said, his tone formal.

"You're quite welcome. I'm going hunting. I'll bring us back whatever I find."

"Someday, I won't be as sun-sensitive."

"Someday, you won't," I told him. "Rest up. I'll be back before it's time for us to go to the library."

Before he could protest it wouldn't take all those hours to hunt for carcasses we could drain, I got to my feet and launched a teleport spell. At some point during our conversation, I'd decided to drop in on Ariana and Conan. Mostly, I wanted to apologize for upsetting her.

More than that, though, I needed to see her with an intensity that was a physical ache in my guts. Fuck. What was wrong with me? A smarter man would steer well clear unless I was at work.

Fine, I told myself. *I'll apologize, and then I'll leave.*

Even I know a raft of crap when I hear it, and that one was riddled with enough holes to sink itself. I had to be very careful. If I wasn't, I'd throw my arms around Ariana, crush her to me, and bury myself in her body.

Ever enthusiastic, my errant member shot to full attention, readier than ready for action. I'd have to get rid of my hard-on before knocking on her door. A slight alteration in my casting ensured I'd emerge a good league from her cabin. I'd stroke myself into a hasty climax, and then I'd offer my apologies for prying into her private life.

Depending on her reaction, I'd either stay longer, or remain true to my commitment to beat a hasty retreat. We may have won a battle last night, but there was a lot more to do. I couldn't afford to dilute our efforts with a spate of unwelcome advances.

She and I had to work together. With staunch instructions to keep my eye on the bigger picture—the one that included humans who wanted to slaughter every immortal—I emerged into a forest and grappled with the zipper on my trousers.

Clive understood Ariana wasn't for him. She probably wasn't for me, either, but I could fantasize. Imagery of her, head tossed back, neck corded with passion played through my thoughts as I rubbed myself to a mind-bending climax.

CHAPTER TWO, ARIANA

I rattled around my home fueled by nervous energy that refused to abate. My bath had been over with for an hour. I'd folded clothes and moved the next load to the dryer and folded them too. I'd filled up on blood from my freezer. I should be ready to lie down, get some rest, but edginess drove me from task to task. Luckily, Conan was still gone.

The wolf would have been worried about me. Like most Vampires, I'm pretty unflappable 99 percent of the time. Should I go hunting? A glance through a very small, deeply curtained window dissuaded me. It looked like high noon outside. I could wrap myself up like a cut from the local butcher shop, but by the time I'd buried myself in layers of clothing that impeded my freedom of movement, I wouldn't enjoy my outing.

Fighting all the extra clothes wouldn't settle my restless mind. Or body.

Yeah. That was the trouble. My body had come alive with heat and need and hunger. Nickolas was one stunning man, er Vampire. He didn't look anything like Mistral's icy fairness with his tumble of copper curls and cat-green eyes, but he wanted me. He'd shown it by his actions, and with words and old-fashioned courtly gestures that sang to my Undead heart. Despite my best efforts, I'd been drawn in by his interest and the possibilities of what we could be together.

I'd been clear he and I were a no go, but it hadn't even slowed him down.

His attentions reminded me of my early years with Mistral, of months when we'd barely gotten out of bed except to feed. I'd done a fine job burying the sexual part of myself—after I beheaded my maker. Almost as if I didn't deserve to be happy with anyone else since I'd been the instrument of Mistral's destruction, and—

"Stop it," I hissed. The sound of my voice had a mitigating effect, so I kept on talking. "Mistral was done with me. He made it abundantly clear. Even if I hadn't reacted and ended him, I'd still have been alone. Except for the occasional pity fuck. Every time I gave in, I'd have hated myself more."

I inhaled briskly because I wanted air to rattle through my clenched teeth. I'd have been worse than alone watching Mistral fuck Becca's brains out. And whoever came after her in an endless parade of perfect youth, perfect bodies, and oh-so-willing pussies. It was why I'd snuck into the armory and taken a longsword with enough heft to cleave through his neck.

I stopped pacing long enough to drive a fist into the wall. Made of stones and mortar, and reinforced with stout timbers, it didn't so much as creak. Centuries had passed since my misdeed in Clan Hawke. But it may as well have happened last week.

I needed to get a grip, put it behind me once and for all. I hadn't been caught. At the time, I'd taken it as an omen Mistral's days were meant to come to an end. Nothing had risen up to haunt me in the intervening years—until Nickolas and his questions.

Like most Vampires, he'd been outraged by how Mistral's existence had been summarily cut short. Never mind he hadn't even been born as a mortal—let alone a Vampire—the day I'd hefted the blade. Every clan made certain to add Mistral's misfortunes to their list of lessons for all newly made Vampires. I hadn't realized it at the time, but I'd driven a wedge between me and the rest of the Undead. Not that Vampires are especially chummy with one another, but I'd cut off any possibility of true friendships with my own kind.

I'd always hold secrets. Vampires are wonderful at sniffing out hidden dirt. It's how we convince mortals they'd be better off providing us an appetizer or joining our ranks.

I'd resumed pacing. The direction of my thoughts was doing less than nothing to settle me down. I had to figure out a way to bury the past and keep it submerged. The best path was to focus on work.

Mistral wasn't a problem, not really, but a whole raft of other shit was. I forced myself to sit on an overstuffed leather sofa and grabbed a tablet. I'd made the shift to the digital age handily. Clicking the miniature computer on, I brought up the notes section and started typing.

Ascent, my nightclub, had to be my first concern. We'd ended up closing early two nights in a row. First because cops had shown up, except they weren't really cops. The next night, dark mages from another world had broken up my bar party.

If shit like that happened too often, *Ascent* would be finished. Customers liked a place they could let their hair down, not worry about being eaten by giant, poisonous wasps, or jacked up by the law.

Beyond my club, mortals had declared war on everything magical. They were serious this time, and they had the resources to make our lives miserable.

If they caught us.

Therein lay the key. Our magical side had to be invisible to maintain our freedom. Someone had fingered me, but so far I'd been able to deflect law enforcement's attention. It helped that their supernatural special ops force were a pack of clueless nerds.

They wouldn't be forever.

I was vacillating between slotting mortals or dark Sorcerers from another world into my number two position of crap to worry about when I caught a whiff of Vampire.

To me, we smell sweet and musky. Yearning shot through me so intense my hands began to shake. I clasped them together and resisted jumping to my feet. Nickolas was nearby. I had invited him—before he'd launched into asking about Mistral.

Then it was too late to rescind my offer. If I had, it would have looked odd. I'd scooped Conan into a teleport spell and left. The delicious scent unique to Nickolas, piquant aged whiskey, rainswept Highlands, and musk enveloped me. For once, a reason to breathe, and I inhaled like a starving woman. Sure enough, a knock sounded. At least Nick was being respectful, not simply barging inside.

I did get up then and walked to the door. It wasn't locked. I had wards to do my dirty work for me, but they wouldn't have worked on Nickolas. They were keyed to stop mortals, not Vampires.

I could have just yelled, "Come in." But getting the door gave me space to collect my thoughts and wipe the dreamy look off my face from rolling around in his delicious smells. I opened the collection of stout planks that seals my home off from the world. "It was open," I told him.

"Doesn't surprise me all the way out here. Who could even find this place?" He grinned crookedly. It made me want to thread my fingers into his curls and crush my mouth over his, biting and tasting his blood.

I stepped aside and scooped up an armload of his clothes. "Here you go."

He took them, and laid them on a table next to the door. "Thank you. I appreciate it. Once I've paid you back, my next project will be saving money for lodging." His smile widened. "So I'll have access to hot water and a place more commodious than my cave. Clive and I were planning another trip through the Salvation Army after they close. I noticed they have furniture too."

I grinned. Couldn't help myself. Nickolas had an engaging side that was tough to resist. "Two thieves in the night," I quipped.

He made a snorting noise. "Eh, they have so many racks and rows and tables of used items, they'll never miss a few things."

"Be careful," I murmured. "You don't want to get nabbed for burglary, even if it's for low ticket stuff." I waited, wondering why he'd made the trip to my house. If he was thinking I'd tumble him into my bed, he was in for a disappointment.

I wanted him so intensely, a sweet ache throbbed between my thighs. But I was stronger than the idle lust sweeping through me.

Yeah, sweetie. Keep telling yourself that.

He shifted from foot to foot. Silence grew between us. I could invite him to hunt with me. He was old enough to travel in daylight... Eh, not the best idea. The more time we spent together outside of working at *Ascent,* the more attached I'd become. The more attached I was, the tougher it would be not to sleep with him, and the harder it would be to keep my secret.

"The reason I'm here," he began, "is, um, to apologize."

"For what?" I felt genuinely confused.

"When I mentioned your clan and its erstwhile master, it upset you. I'm sorry. I won't bring him up again."

Relief sluiced through me. Apparently, my misdeed was going to remain undetected—yet again. I ginned up a hangdog look. "Thank you. It shouldn't still bother me, but those were difficult days in the seethe. Difficult months, actually. A year afterward, I left. It was when I came across Conan, so perhaps I was meant to leave the clan house when I did."

"Maybe so." He touched my hand briefly, but not so quickly I didn't feel a spark from his touch. Nick shook his head. "That Vampire must have been Houdini since none of you were able to track him down."

Indeed, everyone always thought a male had done Mistral in. It might have been one of the reasons I escaped scrutiny. Chivalry had its uses, one of them being an assumption women couldn't be responsible for dastardly deeds.

The fairer sex and all that rot.

Avoiding Nick's speculation about the entirety of Clan Hawke being out for retribution, which they had been, I murmured, "You were still in the Old Country when Harry Houdini started performing, huh?"

"Yes. He was just getting popular when Clive, Lorenzo, and I booked passage for North America. We caught one of his acts before we left New York City."

"I always wanted to see him, but I was never in the right place. Bet he was spectacular."

Nickolas nodded enthusiastically. "He was. I'd been convinced he was going to cycle through a bunch of mumbo-jumbo tied together with magic, but he didn't have a shred of magic to him. Everything he did was real."

I should have nodded and smiled and told him I'd see him around five at the nightclub. Should have.

"Are you hungry?" The words tumbled from my lips before I could rein them in.

"Yes. Of course. I promised Clive I'd hunt and bring something back for him. Feel like helping? It will go quicker with two."

I wanted to. Not because going outside was attractive but because remaining next to Nick held an undeniable draw. I realized I was looking right at him, drowning in the mossy shade of his eyes. Wrenching my gaze away, I said, "I have bookwork to do."

I jerked my chin in the direction of the couch I'd been sitting on; the tablet's screen was still illuminated.

"You could be back in half an hour." The subtle weave of Vampire persuasion laced into his words.

I should have been angry. Yup. There was another "should." I tried to gin up outrage, but the hard truth was I was thrilled by evidence he wanted me next to him as much as I didn't want him to leave.

I could fight this thing. Or give in to it. It was only a quick hunt. I'd be back here in short order. What was wrong with me? Why was I thinking this to death?

I produced a sunny smile to mask my tumultuous emotions. He didn't know about Mistral. A brief hunt wouldn't reveal my misdeed. Despite my earlier reluctance, maybe getting outside for a while would clear my head.

"Give me a minute," I said and trotted to the tablet so I could shut it down. It had an auto-off feature, but I'd disabled it because it pissed me off when it dropped into sleep mode.

My next stop was for a hooded shawl that I wrapped

around myself. "Do you have something to cover your head?" I asked Nick.

"No. I'll be fine. The trees are thick not far from here. Figured we'd set up a blind and let dinner come to us."

Now that I'd made up my mind, the specter of fresh, hot blood made saliva pool in my mouth. I had bags of blood in my freezer—leftovers from large game either Conan or I had killed—but it wasn't nearly as satisfying.

"Where's Conan?" Nick raised a copper brow.

I shrugged. "This time of day, he's probably gone to ground somewhere." I led the way outside. "I've been thinking about his, um, reunion with his family—for want of a better word."

Nick loped next to me as we hustled deep into the forest. "It was a reunion. What did you come up with?"

"Well, he must have known we'd meet up with his kin near the ley-lines. He could have remained behind. I was worried about him coming with us, but he insisted."

"I remember."

Nick stopped there. I appreciated him for not peppering me with questions and for offering me time to get my impressions in better order. "He must have decided it was time to reveal himself to the other guardians. He's plenty strong enough to stand up for himself."

"Do you suppose it runs deeper than that?" Nick asked.

"Deeper how?" I guided us along familiar paths until we were in the heart of an ancient grove of fir trees. Dark and full of the mystery of all old forests, this spot was perfect for luring game—even midday.

We'd settled on our haunches, backs against tree boles,

before Nick replied. "No love lost between Conan and the other guardians. On his side. They expected him to embrace his rightful spot in their midst."

I thought about Fairclaw, a silver wolf who'd morphed into a silver-haired mage with amber eyes. Conan's refusal to return to the guardians had shocked him. "Go on," I urged, intrigued by Nickolas's take on Conan's long lost family.

"If it weren't for the war with mortals and being under attack from dark Sorcerers from another realm, I don't believe Conan would have exposed himself to the guardians or to us. No reason for him to."

My mouth curved into a soft smile. "Conan has principles," I agreed. "Even when he was a puppy, I felt privileged he'd chosen me to rescue him. The only reason I found him was because he allowed me to."

"Someday, I'd like to hear that story, but we need to hunt. Clive is hungry, and I don't want to make him wait much longer."

Over the next quarter hour, we pumped out vampiric charisma. We're irresistible when we put our minds to it, and soon a bevy of small, furry bodies lay between us. I'd already fed, so I made certain to split our take accordingly.

"Are you certain the rat and those four tiny squirrels will be enough?" Nick asked me. His fangs were down and streaked with blood because we'd eaten as we'd caught the first few rodents.

I thought he looked beautiful. It felt good, right, to have my fangs on display, but my emotions had been ripped wide open because of the hot fresh blood sluicing down my throat.

"I fed before we hunted," I replied. "I'm good."

He tugged a cloth sack out of a pocket and began piling carcasses into it. "Better get these back while they're still on the warmish side." With a wave and a smile, he added, "See you around six at *Ascent*?"

"Perfect."

"Clive was wondering if you could use an extra set of hands."

"Of course. Tell him to find me before we open. He'll need the same type of ID you got, so I can add him to the payroll."

A shadow flickered across Nick's even features, and he retracted his fangs. "Maybe after I've paid you back. It's not fair for you to have to loan us that much money."

"No worries. We're always a bit shorthanded. I'm not concerned about either of you welching on a loan. It's not the Vampire way."

"No," he agreed. "It isn't. We may be the stuff nightmares are made of, but in our own way, we have an honorable core."

After he'd vanished from the small clearing, I sat for a while thinking how much I'd missed the company of my own kind. It was an unexpected revelation because no Vampire worth his salt would admit to neediness of any sort. We lived in clan houses because it was convenient, not because we required one another's company.

Conan faded out of the shadows between two enormous trees and padded to my side. Black and silver, he's half again normal wolf size. Before I could urge him to help himself, he'd snatched up the nice, fat rat and crunched through it in a couple of bites.

It was as good a time as any to test out Nickolas's theory. "You knew you'd see your kinsmen in the space between worlds, didn't you?"

The wolf nailed me with his amber eyes and nodded.

"You could have stayed behind. I came very close to ordering you not to come with us."

He swallowed the last of the rat. "Wouldn't have mattered."

"You'd have come anyway?"

"It was time. We need the guardians. Their magic. If I ask, it will be hard for them to refuse."

Versus me asking and having them snub me. Fairclaw had made it clear he held Vampires in deep distain. I sank a hand into Conan's fur and stroked his side. He'd made a full commitment to my discarded pile of dead squirrels, but he was quick and efficient.

When he looked up, he asked, "Ready to go home?"

Rather than answering, I got to my feet, and we covered the distance to our house in short order. Nothing had been disturbed, but I didn't expect it to be. As Nick had noted, who could find me way out here?

Eh. Anyone with magic, but they respected my privacy. It takes a brave soul to approach a Vampire in their home, and—

A riff of magical notes brushed my ears as a ward fell. Moments later, the smells of Irish whisky and wildflowers surrounded me. "Ruby?" I raised my voice.

She walked out my front door. "Guilty as charged," the

Fae replied jauntily. She hadn't bothered with a glamour. Her red wings were folded behind her back, and her golden eyes with their vertical slit pupils zeroed in on me. She wore her usual dark slacks, white blouse, and leather vest. Her feet were bare. I forced her to wear shoes while she worked, but I had no say over her footwear—or lack thereof—outside of work hours.

"What's wrong?" I charged toward her, worried sick someone had blown up my nightclub.

"Nothing yet," she said, "but we need to talk."

Ruby shared my distrust of electronic messaging, and we knew better than to trust telepathy. Anyone could listen in.

I stopped at the hose bib and splashed water on my face and hands to clean myself up. When I turned the hose toward Conan, he dodged the stream, feinted sideways, and leapt through the open doorway. Dried blood would flake off his paws and muzzle. I'd fuss about it, but he and I both knew blood was no big deal in a Vampire's home.

After turning off the water, I angled toward the door and beckoned to the Fae. Ruby had begun as my employee, but we'd become friends.

"Come on inside," I invited.

"Made myself a cup of tea," she told me. "Hope you don't mind."

"Not at all. Want me to heat more water?"

"That would be nice," she said. "The mint, anise, and goldenseal mixture is what I was drinking."

I left her sitting on a sofa. Curiosity—and worry—thrummed through me, but Ruby would get around to telling me why she'd made the trek out here in her own time. Every brand of magic wielder has their own way of doing things. My respect for each type earned me appreciation in return.

Sure enough, once I'd returned with a tray laden with a teapot, cups, and honey, Ruby folded her pointed ears against her head and began to talk.

this culture. All of it circled back to money, a commodity we were painfully shy of. Clan Giovanni was sitting on a fortune in gold and gems. Technically, a portion belonged to me, but getting my hands on it was another matter entirely.

I had a feeling I couldn't just waltz into the seethe—assuming I could locate it—and demand my share. Not after all this time.

"Cars cost money," I pointed out.

"We could steal one."

I shook my head. "Wrong. They all have license plates. The newer ones can have electronic tracking attached to them. If we're not going to get ourselves into trouble, we have to play by the rules."

"That's not any fun," Clive groused.

"Neither is being tossed in jail."

"We could teleport right out of there."

"Not if there's enough iron in the cells," I told him. It was dirty pool, but I tacked, "Look where flaunting rules got Lorenzo," onto my lecture.

"Point taken." Clive nodded solemnly. "Ariana figured it out. We can too."

"Even if we went to the trouble of returning to the Dolomites," I went on, "everything would be as different there as it is here."

We'd be closer to Clan Giovanni's fortune, but I didn't bother mentioning it.

Clive drew his fair brows together. "Do you suppose with all the new communication methods, we could telephone or email or text? Or maybe send an old-fashioned letter?"

"We could do any of those things. All of them. But where would we send them? I'm certain the clan house has moved."

"Is there some kind of central directory to look up email addresses?"

"I have no idea," I told him, "but even if there were, Italy is full of people with our last name."

"At some point, I am going back to Italy. Maybe not to stay, but to see if anyone is still there." Clive paused for a beat. "You'll have to come with me in case I find the clan house. Otherwise I could end up hung out to dry for what happened to you."

The corners of my mouth twitched from the smile that wanted out. "I have a simpler solution. By then, I'll have a cell phone. You can just give them the number, and they can call me if they're concerned about the state of my health." I dusted my hands together. "Problem solved."

He nodded slowly. "All this is going to take time."

I knew exactly what he meant. Transitioning from the world we'd left to this one required a different mindset. Nothing familiar remained. Vampires are arrogant, certain we're right and the rest of the world is flawed. That attitude had been Lorenzo's undoing. While he'd understood his actions would bring the wrath of mortals down on his head, he couldn't conceive that wrath would spell his downfall.

We passed a promising-looking track between two buildings; the narrow fetid alley stank of urine and garbage. I'd been here long enough to understand not all mortals resided in nice, cushy homes. Many engaged in a hardscrabble existence, living hand to mouth on the streets.

Angling a thumb toward the byway, I ran lightly ahead of Clive. My plan had been to hit the midpoint of the lane and set a teleport spell in motion. I'd have to be careful, ensure we emerged inside *Ascent*. My few hours with Ariana had energized me; an infusion of blood helped too.

No reason I couldn't expect close to full accuracy from my casting.

Clive flanked me. The alleyway was longer than I anticipated. The farther we moved along its length, the worse it stank. Fecal matter and rotten food mingled with piss stench. Large boxes were lined up side by side to our right. I heard the muffled beat of carotids and understood we'd stumbled onto a homeless encampment.

"Maybe not the best choice," I hissed at Clive.

"What do you mean?" he replied in telepathy. *"These are throwaway humans. No one will miss a couple."*

The heat from his interest seared me. It was tempting, but it would place us squarely in league with the dark Sorcerers who'd killed five hapless women and dumped them near a saltwater bay.

Beset by the delicious lure of hot, rushing blood, my newly born compassion did battle with bloodlust. We wouldn't have to kill anyone. We could just drink a little, except it hadn't worked for Lorenzo. Once he'd sunk his fangs into the mortal, he'd been lost. I refused to risk it.

"Well?" Clive's fangs had dropped, but he was waiting for my go-ahead.

Gripping his forearm, I marched us right by the collection of heartbeats. Six, no seven. At first, I thought he was going to fight me. Muscles flexed the length of his arm. If it came to it, I'd drive him to his knees and force him to surrender. It wouldn't be pretty. Worse, it would reveal what we were to the occupants of the boxes. I felt their attention, unseen eyes following our every move as they willed us to walk on by.

Caught up in the throes of brand new emotions, I felt sorry for them.

They had enough troubles without Clive and me adding to them. In the midst of a world where many mortals had too much, this pathetic ragtag crew clung to life by a thin margin.

The tension in Clive's arm lessened as we put distance between us and the vagrants. "It's all right," he said. "I won't do anything stupid."

I let go. A few more steps, and we reached the far side of the alley. It opened onto a street that wasn't nearly as busy as the one marking its other end. This was actually a decent spot to leave from, but Clive and I needed to have a brief chat before we went anywhere.

I was organizing my thoughts, so I didn't come off too much like an officious prick when he took a few steps. Once he faced me, he said, "I know what happened to Lorenzo now."

I suspected I did too, but I held my tongue. This would mean more if it came from Clive.

"Animal blood isn't our preferred food. Once Lorenzo started in on the first mortal he'd tasted since before we went into stasis, his control shattered, and he couldn't stop." Clive shook his head until blond curls danced around his shoulders. "If you hadn't been there just now, I'd have torn into one of those paper boxes and dragged whoever was in it to his feet. I'd probably have totally lost it and drained him dry."

Nothing I could add to his insight by lecturing him, so I asked, "Ready to leave?"

"Soon. How are you managing?"

"If you're looking for closely held secrets, I'm afraid I don't have any."

"Is it because you were turned so much longer ago than me?" he persisted.

I dropped a hand onto his shoulder. "Are you hungry right now?"

He thought about it for a moment before he said, "No." Clive narrowed his eyes. "Shit. That makes this whole thing worse. I wasn't even hungry, and I was about to throw caution to the four winds. If you'd had to wrestle me into submission, those beggars would have figured out what we are."

"Same conclusion I came to. Remind me what you were before we tapped you for Clan Giovanni."

"First apprentice to a blacksmith."

"All right." I nodded and squeezed his shoulder. "How old were you when you joined us?"

"Seventeen."

"Plenty old enough to remember what it felt like to want a woman so bad you'd have dragged her into a private spot, hiked up her skirts, and taken her no matter how loud she screamed."

"Aye, but I never did that." His eyes widened as understanding washed through him. "It's kind of the same."

"It is," I agreed. "With one big difference. Something about being turned wipes out a big chunk of our conscience. We become more self-serving, and guilt drops away. It's worst after we're first turned, but eventually we learn not to dive after every set of beating carotids."

"I appreciate that part, but I was past the worst of it. Had been for a long while. So was Lorenzo…"

How to explain a phenomenon I didn't fully understand yet? Something about this era—or this place—had altered the weave of my Undead being.

I settled for, "We have to be vigilant. And we're also late."

"Sorry. It's all my fault. I'll be sure to let Ariana know."

He was mumbling about still not believing he'd been so rash—and stupid—when I caught us up in a teleport spell that spit us out precisely where I'd chosen: *Ascent's* back room.

Noise from the front suggested the bar was already open. Crap! How late were we? I lacked a timepiece, something I'd have to correct.

Conan slunk from a dark corner, his black-and-silver coat sleek and shiny. He stopped shy of growling, but he didn't look pleased. "You're late."

"Aye, and we're very sorry," Clive said. "It was entirely my fault."

Ariana bustled into the back room. Tonight, she wore a sleeveless blue blouse made of some finely woven material. The color set off her eyes. Dark slacks encased her long legs, and her hair was caught into a queue behind her head. Many small braids cascaded down her back.

"Thanks," she told Conan. To us, she said, "I told him to let me know as soon as you arrived. I was getting worried. What happened?"

Rather than go into our near brush with disaster, I told her, "Tough to find places to teleport from. We went from the library to the secondhand store, but they were still open. It took a while to locate a safe spot to leave from."

"You'll need a car," she said. "And instruction on how to drive it."

"Nick said the same thing," Clive spoke up.

Before he could launch into how he'd suggested stealing one, I said, "Once I've paid you back for the first loan, we'll consider another."

"I'll pay my share too," Clive was quick to add.

Ariana smiled; it sent shivers from my toes to my head. Faithless dog that it was, my cock thickened. "Cars aren't hard to come by, and older ones can be dirt cheap." Turning to Clive, she said, "I've set you up with Rob, the same dude who made identification documents for Nick. Conan will take you there."

The wolf woofed once. He sounded put upon, but before I could offer to escort Nick to Rob's cramped studio a league or so away, the distinct smell of Conan's magic surrounded us. Fur and rain-wet rocks. Before I could blink twice, he and Clive were gone.

Ariana turned to me and crossed her arms beneath her breasts. The effect made her nipples more visible. My cock expanded another few notches until the front of my cheap trousers stood out like a sail in a stiff breeze.

"What really happened?" she asked.

I could have sashayed around the point, made something up, but she'd have known. Vamps possess good lie detectors. "We cut through an alley with a bunch of bums living in it. Clive wanted to feed. I, um, dissuaded him, but we wasted a few minutes talking things out. Even if that wouldn't have happened, we'd still have been late, though."

"Mmph. I see. Was he still hungry?"

I shook my head. "No. It was more of an impulsive reaction. They were there. They were helpless, and so, why not?"

She crinkled her forehead into a somber expression. "This world is so different, it's hard to know where to begin, but a general permissiveness has taken over. Mortals deny themselves little. Their indulgence is addictive and contagious. I've felt it and had to fight against it permeating how I operate."

"Thank you. I sensed something but lacked words to describe it."

"We should get to work, but first I need to tell you about something. Ruby dropped by this afternoon."

Something about Ariana's tone caught my attention. "Is that an unusual occurrence?"

"Very. First time she's used her magic to track me."

My gut tightened in anticipation of unwelcome news.

Ariana's direct blue-eyed gaze bored into me. "It's human nature for people to talk among themselves when they're worried. Well, it's magical nature too. *Ascent* has been a haven for magic wielders, a place they can earn a living and escape notice, fly beneath the radar—although you probably won't fully appreciate that metaphor."

I waited. Was this where she told me extra Vampires weren't helping everyone else's comfort level?

She dropped her hands to her sides. "Two of my staff quit today. You hadn't met them. A bird Shifter and a Druid. The Druid never got along with the Sorcerers, but the false cops and the dark Sorcerers were too much for him and the Shifter."

I wanted to offer comfort, but it would only be words. This could be the leading edge of a very big problem. "Do you believe others will follow their example?"

"If we keep getting busted, yeah, I do. No one wants eyes on them. Not in this environment where they could be dragged off in chains." She twisted her mouth into a sour expression. "The bitch about immortality is we'll outlive mortal generations while they come up with ever more creative ways to make us miserable."

"Maybe we should wait and see before we worry too much," I suggested.

"It was the conclusion I came to, but Ruby wanted to let me know how worried everyone is. They won't come to me directly because they don't want to make my job even harder than it already is."

I stood straighter. At least my dick was behaving itself. Something about prison and punishment drove the blood right out of it. I've never been one to pussyfoot around important issues, so I asked, "Do you need Clive and me to leave? We could find jobs elsewhere with the identification documents, and we'd make certain to pay you back."

"No. You're not the problem."

Her answer was so immediate, it had to be genuine. I

spaded over the relief cascading through me so it wouldn't be quite so obvious. I hadn't wanted to go anywhere, but neither did I want to add to Ariana's staff problems.

I bobbed my head. "I know that, and so do you, but how do the Shifters and Witches and Fae and Sorcerers feel about it?"

She turned her hands palms up. "They're probably grateful there aren't more of us, but they've grown used to me." Thumping my chest with an index finger, she said, "So long as you and Clive behave yourselves, they'll accept you eventually."

"What happened a little bit ago was a wakeup call for Clive. He was certain the worst of the bloodlust was behind him."

"It should have been," Ariana noted.

"I'll be certain to pass on your explanation about permissiveness and self-indulgence rubbing off on us."

"Good." Her gaze skittered to the side. "It was nice hunting together. It's been a long time."

"For me as well." I kept my words—and tone—formal. "Where do you want me to work tonight?"

"Probably the front door along with Percy, but it's just past seven thirty. The Verizon store is open till nine. How about if you run in there and get yourself a phone?" She reached for a scrap of paper that had been sitting on her desk and handed it to me.

I stared at what she'd written on it, but she may as well have scribed the missive in Latin. Except I can read Latin.

Moving to my side, she pointed to the top line. "This is the kind of phone and the amount of data it can store." She moved to the next line. "This is the plan you want. Just give them your driver's license when they ask for it. They shouldn't need anything else."

"They'll require payment, won't they?"

"Use one of the credit cards. There's a small machine where they'll have you insert it. And then a screen where you'll sign your name."

"Sounds simple enough. Which way is the shop?"

"Out the back door, turn right, and then turn left. You'll see the sign."

"On my way. Hopefully, we'll have a quiet night."

She nodded. "Uneventful would be my choice. We need to be busy, I lost a lot of money between last night and the one before."

"Clive and I will pick up the slack for the two who left," I said.

A smile illuminated her face. "I know you will. But I don't have a stash of extras beyond the two of you to tap. The Sorcerers are holding a meeting after the club closes. Everyone will be part of it. They're on the edge of storming the ley-lines and declaring war on their dark kinsmen."

"I don't know enough about other worlds to have any sense if it's a good idea."

"Yeah. Me, either, but I trust Percy's judgment."

"Are Clive and I part of everyone?"

She nodded.

"Where's this meeting?"

"Here. Sorry, I should have mentioned that."

She looked so appealing, wistful and worried overlaid with vampiric confidence, I beat a path out the back door before I curled my arms around her and settled my mouth over hers.

Partway down the alley, headlights split the night. I shaded my eyes with a hand and flattened myself against a wall, waiting for the vehicle to pass. Except it slowed and then stopped. I lowered my arm and recognized the black car —and its occupants.

The two detectives from the city's joke of a paranormal task force sat within.

"Going somewhere?" Detective Riteway asked. Somewhere north of fifty, his face was deeply lined, and his brown eyes were riddled with broken blood vessels that suggested an up-close-and-personal relationship with alcohol. His ultra-short hair was steel-gray.

I nodded. "Sure am. I lost my cell phone. I'm on my way to get a replacement." I opened my mouth to ask him the same question, but good sense jumped into the breach. They could question me, but the privilege didn't extend both ways.

"Run along," Detective Hernandez moved a hand from the steering wheel and made shooing motions. Olive skinned, he had black hair and dark eyes. Younger than his partner, but not by much, he probably outweighed the other cop by twenty kilograms.

Anger shot from my guts like a live thing. If I'd been a dragon, fire would have blasted from my mouth. As if I required his permission to do anything. I'd have won an acting award for the next few seconds when I located a smile, inclined my head, and said, "Thank you, officer."

"That's detective to you, son."

"Apologies, Detective Hernandez."

Before I did something like drive my fist into his face and break every bone in it, I trotted toward the end of the alleyway and raised Ariana. *"The paranormal task force guys are out back."*

"Fuck. Well, I'll just have to go and greet them."

I broke into a trot and smiled. Ariana was more than a match for those two goons. I'd have bet my Undead existence they'd be gone long before I returned.

Nick's transit of the alley was timely. It gave me fair warning. What the fuck were Hernandez and Riteway doing behind *Ascent?* The club was beginning to fill nicely. Soon, the Witches would arrive as promised to provide musical entertainment. Maybe we could quit selling liquor at fire sale prices around eleven or so. I hated to give booze away, but it did pack folks in. Once they got tipsy, their wallets loosened.

I needed an excuse to be in the alley to figure out what Riteway and Hernandez were up to. The paranormal task force dudes were dumb as rocks, but even they'd be able to figure out Nick had somehow warned me if I picked this precise moment to pop out the back door. He'd told yesterday's spate of cops he'd mislaid his phone, or maybe that had happened a couple of days ago.

So that ruled out him calling me. Besides, him letting me

know in any fashion was a dead giveaway we were in full-on guilt mode.

I scanned the storeroom and settled on a full trashcan. It would give me an excuse to be in the alley since recycling bins sat about thirty yards away. Dragging the can to the door, I shouldered it open, still lugging the heavy garbage can.

I knew the cops were there right away. Mortals have a particular smell that's tough to resist. Their car sat in a shadowed alcove; I pretended not to see them and pulled the trashcan onto a dolly. Once I was certain it wouldn't fall off, I strode toward the bins to dump it.

I wasn't certain what I expected, but neither detective emerged from their car. It left me with a problem. Should I go back inside? Or should I peer into the gloom, look surprised, and make a point of greeting them?

I dumped the bottles, separating out a few plastic jugs in the process. By the time I was walking back toward *Ascent's* open back door, the cops had solved my little dilemma. They stood in the doorway, staring inside.

I'd have laughed, but the last thing I wanted was for them to believe I didn't respect them or take their presence seriously. "Evening, Detectives," I called out cheerily. "So far, the evening is going well. What can I do for you?"

I lifted the empty can off the dolly and slid the wheeled contraption where I normally kept it, mostly hidden from view. So far, no one had stolen it, but this wasn't the best neighborhood.

What passed for a paranormal task force turned my way,

fake smiles pasted in place. "Ms. Hawke. What a pleasant surprise."

Yeah. Like you didn't watch me leave the club and traipse to the end of the alley.

I smiled, oozing mesmerism. "Can I stand you gentleman a drink? We have live music tonight. It should start in maybe forty-five minutes."

"No drinking on duty," Hernandez informed me.

I winked and did my best Eve imitation. "I won't tell if you don't."

Neither of them reacted, so I pushed the garbage can back inside the club, followed after it, and turned to face Hernandez and Riteway.

"Where is everyone?" Riteway asked.

I ginned up a confused look. "As in who? My workforce is all in the bar proper. This is just my stockroom."

"Did you leave your dog at home?" Hernandez asked.

I managed an abashed look. "Erm. Nope. He was here, but he gave me the slip. I know there are rules about loose dogs, but I'll make certain to hang onto him better once he returns."

A muted growl sounded from Conan's usual spot behind some shelving. I turned toward it. "You came back, you scoundrel, you." I shook a finger in his direction. "No more unauthorized jaunts, you hear me?"

Another growl was punctuated by a short bark.

I offered a sunny smile at the detectives. "Dog is present and accounted for. He must have snuck in the front door Were you worried about anyone else?"

"So long as you're certain no one is missing." Riteway

leered at me in a way I didn't like at all but figured I could turn to my favor. I bent to flick something off the toe of my boot and undid my blouse a couple of buttons. When I straightened, cleavage had to be on display.

"Um, let's see. Everyone who was supposed to work tonight reported in. Nick went to get a phone replaced. Clive is running an errand for me." I rolled my shoulders back to provide a better view of the girls. "I appreciate your concern, but I really need to get out onto the floor."

Hernandez scrabbled in a coat pocket and withdrew a card. He'd given me one before, but I didn't remind him. Sexual heat sheeted off both cops. Good. My Vampire charm was doing the trick. If I'd have wanted, I could have fed from them both—and then cut a broad swath through their memories.

But they weren't worth it.

I took the card and added saccharine to my smile. "Thanks so much for looking out for me. I appreciate it. Now, if you don't mind—?" I let my words hang and willed them to turn and leave.

"We're as close as that number," Hernandez said. His voice had roughened with desire.

"I'll keep it handy. Right next to my phone just in case." I stopped shy of batting my eyelashes but added a husky suggestive undernote to my words.

I wanted to ask them if they were planning to take up residence in my alley, but I restrained myself. I'd know if they left. A minute dripped past, followed by one more. Finally, the men turned as a unit and trudged in the direction of their cruiser.

I shut the door, engaging both locks, and beat a path to Conan. "Is Clive back too?"

"Not yet," the wolf kept his voice very low, and I reminded myself to scan for electronic surveillance devices. They'd stood in my doorway plenty long enough to have planted something. *"Why are they here?"* Conan switched to telepathy.

"Not sure. It might be because they have nothing better to do, but they probably suspect something isn't right. Before the dark mages broke through from that other world, Percy was certain the paranormal special ops van was on its way here to bust all of us."

"What will it take to make them give up?"

I stroked his rough outer coat. *"Wish I knew, sweetie. I'm going to work. Will you be here?"*

"Part of the time. I have some ideas."

I waited, but Conan didn't add to his statement. Asking for clarification would buy me zip squat nada. *"Alrighty. Be careful."*

"Always."

I turned away from him and sent magic zinging around the stockroom, hunting for something that shouldn't be there. Sure enough, buzzing interrupted my seeking spell. Not one, but two bugs had been cunningly placed under the molding around my door. No wonder the detectives had been standing in my doorway. They'd been busy.

The feel of Conan's power told me he was on his way to wherever. I thought about the surveillance devices. If I removed them, the cops would know I was onto them. Maybe my best bet would be to make certain the door through to *Ascent* remained shut, and then warn everyone not to say anything sensitive in the back room.

I'd have to disable the bugs before the Sorcerers' powwow, but maybe by then Hernandez and Riteway would be home in bed fucking their wives, girlfriends, or boyfriends. Or maybe each other for all I knew.

The evening was busy and, mercifully, uneventful. Cerys kept her word, and a quartet of witches showed up at eight thirty on the dot, instruments in tow. The combination of a guitar, a lyre, a lute, and drums was delightful. I could have listened to them forever, even though I fully understood they tossed magic about shamelessly to imbue their music with an unforgettable patina.

Nick and Clive were long since back, and it was pushing one thirty in the morning. The crowd had loosened up. I'd made a few trips to the storeroom and while I'd expected Hernandez and Riteway to hang out for a while, the fact they were still sitting in the alley at midnight worried me.

If they didn't leave, we'd have to move the Sorcerers' get together elsewhere. I threaded my way across the crowded floor where couples were dancing to the witches' captivating beat. My goal was the front door—and Percy. The tall, burly Sorcerer wore his usual outdated tartan over a linen shirt with long, full sleeves.

He smiled at me. "Pretty decent evening, all in all," he said.

I smiled back. *"Those two detectives are still in the alley."*

"Fuck. That's not good news." Percy turned toward two obviously inebriated men who'd just staggered through the

door. "Closing time is soon, mates. Besides, it's looking as if you've had enough."

"We make that decision," a skinny redhead wearing jeans and a windbreaker announced.

"Of course you do. In your own home," Percy said firmly. "Here, we figure it out for you. If the bartender thinks you're already toasted, she won't serve you. Just fair warning, mate."

"Come on." The other fellow, rotund and blond, tugged on the redhead's arm. "I want to hear that music. I don't care if they serve us."

His buddy took a good look at Percy and decided tangling with the seven-foot-tall Sorcerer was a bad idea. The two newcomers sidled nearer the music.

"Can you move the meeting?" I asked Percy. It was a generic enough question, I didn't bother with telepathy.

Nickolas strode through the front door and offered me a pleased smile. "Nice to see you, Ariana." He turned to Percy. "Everything's good outside except for the problem I mentioned earlier."

"Ari just reminded me," Percy rumbled in his deep voice. "Can you man the door for a bit, Nick? I need to reach out to a few people."

"Sure." Nickolas slid onto the stool Percy had vacated; the Sorcerer walked outside, melting into the night. Even if I followed him, he would have turned to puffs of insubstantial smoke.

"How'd things go at Verizon?" I asked Nick.

In answer, he extracted an iPhone from a pocket. "It's going to take me a while to understand how it works, but everything went smoothly." He aimed a knowing smile my way. "Women love helping men."

I snorted laughter. *"Especially when the men are Vampires."*

He shrugged. "Can't blame a fellow for taking advantage of every opportunity."

An unpleasant jab of something like jealousy curled my stomach into a knot. It was the same reaction I'd had when Mistral showed any interest in other women. I had to get over myself. I would not quiz Nickolas on whether he'd bedded the clerk, no matter how much I wanted to know.

If he had, it wouldn't mean a thing to him. I understood how my kind operated. The problem was it meant something to me. Crap. I didn't own him. We barely knew one another. All we had in common was we were both old and hailed from the far side of the Atlantic.

He circled my arm with a hand. His touch seared me, made me want so much more. "Nothing happened," he murmured. "I told her I was late for work."

"It's none of my affair," I said stiffly and looked away, ready to bolt behind the bar to put some distance between us.

"Maybe I want it to be," he said so low I had to strain to hear him.

I longed to throw my arms around him, but it was a bad idea for all the reasons I'd already identified. I listed them in my head. Again. But they felt forced. Like I'd made them up. Hell, maybe I had. He was looking at me with an odd expression, like he was waiting for me to say something, but I couldn't talk about my convoluted welter of feelings. Not here. And maybe not ever.

"I have to figure out where Conan went," I said and slithered from beneath Nick's touch.

"I didn't know he was gone. When did he leave?"

"Hours ago."

Nick frowned. "Are you worried about him?"

"Eh. Yes and no. He can take care of himself as well as anyone, but he wasn't exactly forthcoming about where he was going."

"Do you have ideas?"

"Not really. And it bothers me."

Percy slipped back through the open door. Cupping his hands around his mouth, he bellowed. "Last call. We close in ten." Leaning near me, he said, "Tell the Witches to quit playing. So long as they're at it, we'll have hell's own time emptying the place out."

"Did you move the meeting?"

He nodded.

I didn't mine for details but made a beeline for the raised dais at the far end of the bar where Cerys and her small group were clearly lost in their own creation. "Time to wrap up," I told them.

The dreamy expression slid from Cerys black eyes, and she dropped a shiny charm down her cleavage. She had the kind of beauty I associated with women from the Caribbean, dark skinned and striking. A sarong painted with runic markings covered her curves tonight. Before, I'd seen her in more Western garb. By contrast, the other Witches in the musical ensemble wore tattered jeans, tight T-shirts, and lots of jangly jewelry. They pocketed their charms too.

Once they'd finished their song, they began packing their instruments away.

"Thanks so much for coming," I told them. "You guys are nine kinds of incredible."

"We had a good time," Cerys said and glanced away.

"Ask her," the drummer, a Witch with blonde dreads, urged.

"Ask me, what?"

"Erm, back in the other place. Where we talked about tonight, you had, um, mentioned something about union wages," Cerys mumbled.

"I'm happy to pay you for tonight. Let me go hit up the cash drawer."

"Not for tonight," the blonde clarified. "But we'd like to do this maybe once a week. If you'll have us."

I held out a hand for her to shake. "Deal. I'm delighted. Thrilled. In love with the idea. And yes, you'd receive union rates. I'm pretty sure they include an extra half hour on each end for setup and takedown."

"They do." The blonde looked pleased I recognized that fact and wasn't negotiating it away.

I joined their circle. "Do you know about the meeting?"

Cerys nodded once. "Yeah. It's here, right?"

I switched to telepathy. *"Not anymore. The two dudes from the paranormal task force have been parked in the alley since about eight."*

The Witches hissed in unison and hooked their fingers into the universal sign against evil.

"Oh yeah, and you cannot talk about anything in the storeroom. They bugged it."

"Bastards," Cerys snarled. "Where'd the meeting get moved to?"

"Not sure. If you hang for a bit, I'll let you know."

I hurried back to Percy and Nickolas, who were herding patrons out the door. Tonight had one good outcome—beyond the obvious that no one had interrupted my customer flow. The witches' music would be a huge draw. We'd have to come up with a name for their group—if they didn't already have one. And then we could advertise.

The last of the night's customers filed outside. Percy dragged the door shut and dropped the bar into place. "We'll be at the guild house," he told me. "Pass it along."

"Does everyone know where it is?" I asked. "Because I don't."

He smiled, displaying very white, very even teeth. "You can track me."

I nodded. "Yup. I can."

Percy looked around. "Where's the wolf?"

"Not sure. He left several hours ago."

"To do what?" Percy raised a dark brow.

I shrugged. "He can find me once he gets back."

I left Nick and Percy piling chairs on tables and went to spread the word about regrouping at the Sorcerer's guild house. Because I'm paranoid as fuck, I used telepathy once I was near the back of the bar. Convinced I'd done a decent job of making certain everyone knew, I strode into the back room intent on getting a jacket, my wallet, and car keys. If

Conan had been here, I'd have ridden him, but his corner was vacant.

I'd known that even before I hit the storeroom, though.

I made myself a note to take inventory the next day. Some of my liquor stocks were getting low. I'd just gathered up my coat and keys when a knock sounded on the back door.

Double fuck.

It didn't take magic to know who wanted in. It was either Riteway or Hernandez. Or both of them. And they knew I was inside because of their nifty surveillance devices.

I created a facsimile of a smile and tugged the door open. Both of the cops leered at me. Great.

"We'll take you up on that drink offer," Riteway said and stepped inside.

"Oh gosh. I'm so sorry. We're closed for the night. But if you boys want to come back tomorrow at seven, we'll be open then."

"You don't get it," Hernandez said. "We want a private drink."

"With you," Riteway chimed in.

I arranged my face into what I hoped was dismay. "Um. I don't think that's a very good idea."

"Why not? You invited us earlier."

"I was offering hospitality, not anything, um, further. If you take my meaning." I tried for friendly but firm. I've had a shit ton of experience dissuading men from pursuing me. I run a bar. It goes with the territory.

Nick must have been listening on the far side of the door leading into the nightclub because he chose that moment to breeze into the back room. "Ready to go, honey?"

He stopped when he saw the two cops. "Evening, fellows. Er, Detectives. Is everything all right?"

"Did you get your phone problem squared away?" Riteway asked.

"Sure did." Nick extracted his phone and showed them before dropping it back into his jacket.

"Evening," Hernandez said in clipped tones before the men turned and walked away.

I pulled the door closed and re-locked it. Nick started to ask me something, but I shook my head and placed a finger over my mouth. Normally, I go out the back, but I gathered up all my things and gestured for him to follow me. It would mean I'd have to risk magic to get the drop bar to seat once we were outside the front of the club, but I did not want to cross paths with the detectives again tonight.

It wasn't until we were in my car and rolling down the road that I said, "Thanks. I owe you. Oh, and you cannot say anything in the stockroom. They planted listening devices in the doorframe."

"Huh?" Nick said, clearly genuinely mystified.

"Tiny electronic bugs that amplify sound. Some have cameras, but they're bigger than these."

"Bastards. What the fuck were they doing when they shoved their way inside?" Nick sounded furious.

"I'd invited them to have a drink on the house earlier. They were there to collect."

"I just bet they were. It explains why they sat in their car all night. Probably whacking off."

I shouldn't have, but I laughed. I was still laughing when we drove around the corner from the Sorcerers' guild house. I'd made certain we weren't followed.

Before we got out of my Toyota, Nick said, "They're going to be a problem."

"Yeah. I know. Eventually, we'll have to deal with them, but I have no idea what it will entail."

Conan padded toward us when we got near the house. "Were you waiting?" I asked him.

"Yes, but not long."

"Are you going to tell me where you went?"

The wolf didn't answer. His silence might mean maybe someday. Or it might simply be a no.

Together, we mounted the steps. The door opened before I had a chance to knock. Something about the three of us together felt right to me, but I shouldn't get too cozy.

Conan and I had done just fine with the two of us. No reason to assume Nick would become part of our merry band. For all I knew he'd head back to Italy at the first opportunity, and—

Get off it, a strident inner voice filled my head.

I might resent the message, but it was spot on. I couldn't let Nick get too close, or close at all. If he did, he'd find out about Mistral. And then, no matter how much I fascinated him, he'd turn me in to Vampire Central. Some things superseded individual interests for our kind. What I'd done sat squarely on top of the heap.

If Mistral had been around, he'd have been laughing his head off. He might be truly dead, but he'd taken a big part of me with him.

CHAPTER FIVE, NICKOLAS

scent had pretty much emptied out. I spent a few minutes with Clive and told him I'd see him at the meeting. Dee trotted up and asked if he wanted to go with her. A Witch, she'd taken Clive under her wing since he'd begun work at the club. At first, she'd clearly been reluctant, but Clive can be a beguiling fellow, and her lack of enthusiasm seemed to have dissipated.

By the time they left, most of the staff had teleported to the Sorcerers' guild house, but a few headed for their cars. I admit I was waiting for Ariana to emerge from the stockroom because I planned on catching a ride with her—or teleporting together. I heard the detectives first knock and then barge inside. Their audacity galled me. How dare they assume they could push Ariana around.

I waited until an opportune moment cropped up and played the same hand I'd displayed a few nights ago in the alley. I breezed in and pretended she and I were a couple. It did the trick. The cops backed off. I knew they would. Men are odd ducks, but they recognize when another man has put his brand on a woman.

I didn't like the looks of either detective. Both stank of lust; my bet was they'd planned on a cozy little threesome. The specter of her fucking anyone infuriated me. Not that I had any rights where she was concerned, but I still wanted her for myself.

It was very unVampirelike, but I'd given up second-guessing my instincts. I longed for her the same way I'd ached for women when I was still human. The bittersweet yearning filled me with joy and hope. I felt certain I could convince her to give us a chance, and I'd put in however much time it took. She was worth it.

Conan returned from wherever he'd gone, and we joined a phalanx of magic wielders inside a rambling multistory home. Its exterior might have been ramshackle, but the inside was tastefully decorated. Dark, polished furniture and inviting overstuffed sofas and chairs graced the common areas. Paintings worth a fortune hung from the walls, and my feet sank into thick Aubusson rugs woven with runic symbols. Crystals in every color, ranging from tiny to a meter tall, were arranged in such a way to presumably maximize their energies. The smell of incense mingled with various mage scents into a pleasing mélange.

A selection of refreshments sat on a side table. I helped myself to a cup of herbal tea, redolent with the rich scents of heather and mint and well-spiked with mead.

In the Old County, I'd been barred from such gatherings,

although I suspected they rarely occurred. No one accepted Vampires, but there was little love lost between the varieties of those with other magics. Each branch of the magical family was convinced they were better than every other branch.

If Ariana's message about mortals going all out to wipe magic off the map was true, we couldn't afford to indulge in our artificial separations any longer. After a while, Percy and a couple of other Sorcerers herded us along a hallway. I figured out quick enough it led somewhere else. As in beyond the house I'd entered.

The flicker and flare of power zapped me as we left Earth for one of the in-between places. Apparently, the Sorcerers had decided not to take any chances one of us had been followed.

Wise of them. It hadn't even occurred to me to check to see if the two randy cops had been just behind us.

Ariana walked by my side with Conan next to her. "I'm not certain if this will make sense, or if these are the right words," I said, "but could those detectives have done the same thing to your car they did to *Ascent*? Plant tiny devices that transmit information?"

Ariana stifled a gasp, interesting since breathing is optional for us. "Goddammit it to hell. I should have thought of that. Of course, they could have. It would have led them here."

"Eh, not here exactly," I pointed out. "They can sit outside the guild house until daybreak, and nothing will happen."

"You're right. I do need to scan the car, though." She

shook her head. "You've spent what? Ten days in this era, and already you're smarter than me."

Her compliment pleased me.

The hallway had ceded to an earthen tunnel. Light flickering at one end suggested we were nearing its terminus. Sure enough, we walked into a generous room with a fireplace at one end. The walls were constructed of mortared stones with no windows.

Intriguing. Had Vampires once been more a part of things than I'd suspected?

Percy gestured everyone to find seats. I counted maybe eighty of us. True to our natures, like sat with like. Maybe at future gatherings—if there were any—we'd be more integrated. As everybody settled in, I took stock of who was here. Mages were decked out in full regalia; no glamours tonight. Witches. Druids. Shifters. Fae. Sidhe. And, of course, Sorcerers and three Vampires. I'd be lying if I didn't admit sharing space with those I've always considered adversaries was uncomfortable.

"Never thought I'd see the day," Clive said softly, right next to my ear.

It made two of us, but I didn't reply. Others with magic could intercept telepathy, and overhear anything I might say out loud too.

Percy stood at the front of the room, flanked by two other Sorcerers, a man and a woman. They could have been twins with long silvery hair shot with bronze highlights and amber eyes. As tall as Percy, but not as robust, they were garbed in robes richly embroidered with runes in Old Gaelic.

I recognized some—wisdom, grace, compassion, strength —but others I'd never seen before.

"Apologies for the obscure location," Percy began. Everyone quieted to listen to him. "First, I wanted to make certain no one mortal could either follow or listen in. But the main reason is others may be joining us presently, and this location was far more convenient for them."

"Where precisely are we?" Dee called from her seat in the center of a group of Witches.

"A spot between worlds where time has no purview," he replied. "Sorcerers have utilized this place as a retreat from the mortal world for longer than my memories."

"Is anything outside this building?" a Druid asked.

"Of course." Percy smiled. "We're on the lower floor of a manor house. Constructed by Sorcerers to meet our needs, it sits on an uninhabited world that's reasonably temperate. Many off-world locales lack air. Or they're too hot or too cold to remain long."

"Thank you for indulging my curiosity." The Druid sat back down.

"We called all of you together for two reasons." The female Sorcerer next to Percy addressed the group. "The first is to decide if it's possible for us to work together. If it's not, we will still need some form of communication so we're not at cross purposes." She stopped to take a measured breath. "The second is to come to agreement whether we are going to stand and fight or adopt a low profile and hope this mess with mortals blows over. Maybe not with this batch, but they don't live very long."

"Regardless of whatever consensus the rest of you come

to," Percy said, "Sorcerers are in full agreement that we will launch an attack on all our kinsmen who have adopted dark ways, whether they reside on Earth or elsewhere. This is our battle, and because we anticipate it will mostly be fought far from Earth, it shouldn't endanger the rest of you should you choose to keep your heads down."

"Back to item one. Can we work with one another?" the woman said, adding, "My name is Mariah."

Percy crooked a finger at Ariana. She walked the length of the room and joined him. "Perhaps the question isn't so much if we can join forces, but if we're willing," Percy clarified and sent a meaningful look at Ariana. "I had my doubts about signing on to work at a business establishment owned by a Vampire, but I swallowed my misgivings and gave it a whirl.

"What I found was someone with an open mind, willing to do whatever was necessary to forge bridges across our differences."

"Thank you," Ariana told him.

"It's true," he replied. "Moving beyond my impressions"—he was talking to the group again—"Ariana's experiment with *Ascent* proved magic wielders can rise above our quarrels, our built-in antipathy and distrust of one another, to form a cohesive whole."

"I began by hiring humans," Ariana said and made a face. "You can imagine how well that went. What a lazy bunch of rotters. Between sick leave and stealing from the till, I had to watch them every minute. Worse, I fired them almost as fast as they signed on. I was determined to make my nightclub work, so I tossed out a net in hopes some of you"—she spread her arms wide—"would take a chance on me."

"Which proves we can work together—if we choose," Percy said.

"Talk among yourselves," Mariah urged. "Take your time. We recognize you cannot speak for all of your kin, but you can serve as emissaries back to your respective guild houses."

"Does it have to be all or none?" Cerys asked.

Mariah drew her silver brows together; twin vertical lines formed between them. "Yes and no. If we vote to launch an all-out war with mortals, it will impact everyone with magic. So even if you have kin who would rather not fight, their quality of life will be altered. They may need to find a location such as this one to sit out the carnage."

"Got it." Cerys nodded somberly.

Ariana made her way back to her seat between Clive and me. Conan padded around the room, stopping to listen to one group or another. Something about his wolf guise was hard to resist; no one shooed him away.

"What do you think?" Ariana asked us.

It was a serious question and deserved more than a cursory reply. Clive and I exchanged glances, and he murmured, "Go ahead, mate."

"We've been at the butt end of the magical pecking order forever," I said, "not because we're weak but because others have looked down on us for our feeding habits."

She nodded. "And?"

"The net impact has been we—or at least I—have become somewhat defensive. Whenever I meet a Witch or a

Fae, I expect they're judging me, so I've avoided confrontations."

"Only somewhat?" She furled a dark brow.

"Eh, maybe more than a little."

"I decided I hated everyone else magical," Clive said. "They made me feel like I was scum, dirty and damaged."

"How deep does it run?" Ariana asked quietly. "Is it something you can lay aside permanently."

Clive frowned. "Why are you different? You're older than me, so you had to have run into the same animosity."

"I didn't start out different." She hesitated. "After an unfortunate incident in my clan, I left the clan house. Soon after that, I found Conan. He and I have been alone for a long while. After we migrated to the States, we didn't find many other Vampires. Nor did we look for them.

"*Ascent* was an experiment. After it became clear mortals weren't the staff I needed, I did some soul-searching —never mind Vampires no longer have such things. I vowed I'd lay my hurt places aside and welcome immortals, if they chose to take a chance and work with me."

"You make it sound so easy," Clive mumbled.

"It wasn't. Not every immortal who came to work has remained, but 90 percent have. I've learned things along the way. About them, and about myself."

"You've been quiet," Clive said to me.

It was true, I had been silent because I was thinking.

"I want to fight," I said. "What mortals have done is wrong. They don't rule the universe, nor should they. They lack both knowledge and restraint. It rankled when I first met Ruby, and she referred to me as, 'Aw crap, another one.'

My usual reaction would have been to toss a barbed comment back her way, but Ariana intervened. And now, Ruby and I are fine. At least on the surface, which is all we need to work as a team."

"So we're decided?" Ariana looked from me to Clive and back. We both nodded. She stood and cupped her hands around her mouth. "Vampires are in."

Perhaps her words spurred—or shamed—the others because soon similar cries rose from the Witches, Fae, Sidhe, and Shifters.

The Druid who'd spoken before rose to his feet. "We are peaceful by nature, but we will help as we can so long as it doesn't involve the actual taking of life, which we hold sacred. No matter who it belongs to."

"Fair enough." Percy nodded.

"Thank you for your open-mindedness," Mariah called in a clear, ringing voice. "To my way of thinking, we have little choice, but I cannot choose for others."

Conan woofed from the far side of the room. It brought my head snapping around. I hadn't forgotten about the wolf, but when I'd last located him, he was in the midst of a group of Fae, all of whom were fawning over him.

A portal took shape behind where Percy stood. Rimmed in pure, shining white, it glowed invitingly.

Ariana smiled. "Aha! I'm pretty sure I know where Conan ran off to earlier."

I was still clueless, but I'd find out soon.

The edges of the gateway pulsed and shimmered. Guardians stepped through. I recognized Fairclaw and Conan's mother from when they'd appeared in the realm of the dead guarding a juncture of ley-lines. They wore their human bodies, naked and adorned with simple gemstones. Hair streamed to their knees.

Conan faced the portal and inclined his head to each of his kin in turn. Five guardians stepped through before the portal winked out behind them.

Percy fell to one knee in front of Fairclaw. "You honor us with your presence."

"Get up," Fairclaw growled sounding a lot like the silver wolf he morphed into. "None of us bow to any other."

Percy stood. "Nonetheless, thank you for heeding Conan's request."

"How could we not?" a mage with white hair and a blue gemstone in the hollow of her throat spoke in a musical voice that reminded me of bells chiming. "My son has asked naught of us since his birth."

Fairclaw squared his broad shoulders. "We acceded to Moonwraith's request—"

"Conan," the wolf interrupted. "My name is Conan."

"Of course," Fairclaw said smoothly. "Apologies, Conan. Your request was reasonable, and we agreed we should be included in any joint endeavor of magic wielders. We stand ready. Has aught been decided yet?"

"Aye. We are in agreement we can lay our differences aside and forge new alliances among ourselves," Percy told him.

Ariana got to her feet and walked closer to the front of the room. Clearly, she had something in mind. Rather than bowing or showing any sign of deference, she planted herself in front of Fairclaw. "When last we met, you were quite clear Vampires weren't welcome in your realm—or your presence. Do you still feel that way?"

I waited, impressed by her courage. Not many would have confronted a guardian. Fairclaw might have told Percy not to kneel, but everyone in the room knew full well the guardians' magic existed in a whole other realm from theirs.

After a pause that stretched long enough I readied myself to spring to Ariana's side in case things got ugly, Fairclaw bowed his head for a scant moment. "I misspoke, Vampire. We are either all a part of this, or none of us are. Your power and strength will be welcome in days to come."

"Thank you." Ariana's tone was formal. Conan stalked to her side and stood next to her while she said, "I cannot vouch for any Vampires beyond the two others in this room. As you know, we have a clan structure, and I walked away from mine a long while ago."

"If each of us does what we can, it will be enough," Fairclaw said and herded the other guardians off to one side. "We shall remain for a short time."

Mariah nodded understanding. "Then we shall make the best of the moments you are with us. We have clarity about burying our differences, our antipathy, because we comprehend the danger mortals pose. My second question was whether we will fight. The Druids are not warriors, but they are willing to play an ancillary role. What about the rest of you? Do we go to war? Or do we adopt a wait-and-see approach? This is a luxury our immortality affords us, so do not choose lightly."

Conversation ebbed and flowed around us. Ariana extended a hand. After a hesitation, Fairclaw shook it. I wondered if it cost him to touch one of the Undead. If so, he didn't flinch. The primary difference between others with magic and us is they're born with their power whereas ours is conferred through a blood-bound ritual.

Immortal and Undead kind of mean the same thing, yet immortal is imbued with a glamorous overtone, while everyone cringes at the mention of Vampires.

Ariana crossed the room again and sank into her chair between Clive and me. "That might have been ill-advised, but I had to do it."

"We understand," Clive said.

I made a chopping motion before Clive launched into calling Fairclaw an insufferable prick. The guardian hadn't been pleasant when we'd first met him, but we had to let it go. Our commitment to amnesty among ourselves had to run more than skin-deep.

Conan joined us.

"No wonder you wouldn't tell me what you were about," Ariana said to him.

"We need their magic," the wolf said. "It could make a big difference."

His words drove home what a rocky road lay ahead.

"Regardless of what everyone else decides," Ariana said, "I told Percy I'd help him deal with the dark mages."

"I'm in," I told her, remembering how they'd slaughtered five innocent women to steal their psychic energies.

"Me too," Clive said.

"Great. I'll let Percy know. We don't require large numbers. In truth, too many of us might be an impediment. Come on, we may as well start strategizing."

She, Clive, Conan, and I formed a small circle with Percy and a few other Sorcerers on one side of the large room. We'd just begun dissecting the fine points when cries of, "Witches will fight," and "Fae are in," and "Shifters will do our part," rang out. In the end, only the Druids chose a less lethal role.

When I gazed around the room, the guardians had moved to the front. Fairclaw still wore a human body, but the resemblance ended there. His amber eyes gleamed with keen, lupine intelligence, and his features had taken on a sharp-edged appearance that made me wonder if he'd employed a glamour earlier.

"Are those here authorized to speak for your people? To enter into binding agreements?" he asked.

Dahlia, mistress of the Witches' guild stood. A large black raven perched on her shoulder. I'd met the bird before. Its name was More Than Never, and it was far more than a raptor. Sentient, and the witch's familiar, it scouted ahead and brough information back to its mistress.

"No," the Witch said, "but it could be remedied. Shall we set a time for our next meeting?" Spiky, red hair stuck out at all angles and hung to the middle of her back. Tall and gaunt, she had eyes the shade of rough emeralds and a sharp face that was all planes and angles. A worn cable-knit sweater hung to hip level, partially covering worn black pants. Scuffed boots hit her mid-calf.

"Done. We shall return in three Earth-days." This time, Fairclaw didn't bother with a portal. Power sweet with the scents of frankincense and myrrh thickened. When it cleared, the guardians were gone.

"What if three days isn't long enough?" Ruby called out.

"Do the best you can," Percy told her and cast a pointed look her way. "You can do a lot with magic in that amount of time."

"True enough." The Fae bobbed her head, and swept her multicolored hair behind her shoulders. "Can we leave from here?" Ruby asked. "Before I blow through a bunch of magic figuring it out."

"You can, but it will be simpler this way. I can part the veils for you if you'll follow me." Mariah ran lightly to the door at the far end of the room, the one leading not to whatever world the manor house sat in, but back to Earth.

I noticed some cross-species conversations as the room cleared. I took it as a sign our commitments to get along were beginning to gel.

Excitement jangled through me. I couldn't wait to get my fangs into those dark mage bastards. One thing about being turned was I'd had to keep most of my power under wraps the vast majority of the time. Running wide open held undeniable appeal.

As soon as Mariah got back, I was ready to roll.

"Crap." Ariana was staring at the face of her phone.

"What?" It didn't seem as if she'd be able to get messages or anything else in this alternate place.

She tapped the display. "I have no idea how we blew through so many hours, but it's time to get *Ascent* open."

"But what about the dark Sorcerers?" I asked.

"They'll still be there after the club closes," she said firmly.

Protests rose to my lips. I'd much rather fight than wash

glasses, but I owed Ariana. She'd been generous to a fault with both Clive and me.

Percy had been slouched against a wall. He straightened. "We'll do everything we can to keep *Ascent* running," he said.

Ariana nodded solemnly. "Thank you. Its days might be numbered, but we'll keep on keeping on until it doesn't make sense any longer."

I wanted to offer comfort, but she didn't require it. In our Undead hearts, Vampires are warriors. She'd sacrifice what she had to, but not until it was necessary. A wave of appreciation and respect shook me to my bones; I buried everything a league deep and returned my attention to a quick spate of plans we'd roll out after the nightclub shut its doors in the early hours of tomorrow morning.

Sometime between now and then, Clive and I needed to feed. Probably Ariana as well, so all of us would be in peak fighting shape, but we'd figure something out.

It hit home I was starting to view us as a unit, along with Conan. Even better, Ariana seemed to be reading from the same script. Seemed to be. I'd do well not to make assumptions.

With that staunch internal reminder, I rounded up the rear as the lot of us hustled through the open door after Mariah and the others.

CHAPTER SIX, ARIANA

The club had filled quickly and remained at peak capacity all evening. Maybe some of the magic from the Witches' music lingered from the previous night. Or perhaps mortals' propensity to live life on the ragged edge prevailed. We'd had enough very public trouble at *Ascent* to either draw the curiosity-seekers or be the death knell for my bar.

I'd been waiting for my two pet detectives to show up: Hernandez and Riteway. But they hadn't made an appearance. Perhaps they had the grace to be embarrassed about the previous evening, but I doubted it. On the way back to *Ascent*, I'd checked the car for bugs and not found anything.

What a lost opportunity. On their side. Men are such odd creatures. Once they fixate on sex, everything else flies out the proverbial window. Turned out to be a good thing for me. I wasn't complaining about their small brain substitution for common sense.

It had been dark when we arrived in *Ascent's* alleyway. Conan had taken off shortly thereafter. For all I knew, he was sleeping in the back room. I hadn't had time to check. Having the guardians on our side seemed like a plus—on the surface. But it could turn into a two-edged sword. I didn't trust Fairclaw as far as I could see him. He viewed Conan as belonging to the guardians and wouldn't yield until he'd chivied the wolf back to his rightful spot.

Not that Conan was a pushover. Far from it. But there was a whole lot more to the story. Things I didn't yet know about why Conan had been running from dark Sorcerers when he'd fled his world long ago. More importantly, why hadn't the other guardians protected their own?

Had he run away?

I filled drink orders with my mind a million miles distant. Conan had principles. My bet was the guardians had done something he disagreed with. Or ordered him to engage in something that rubbed him the wrong way. One of the problems was I knew less than nothing about the guardians. Who they were. What their function was.

Did it run deeper than protecting the ley-lines that carried psychic energies and patrolling the space between the various worlds? Which world had Conan come from? Did the guardians have a role to play there? How many were there? Clearly, they reproduced—unlike Vampires. Unless you counted the whole death and rebirth cycle we're capable of.

Eh. I wasn't getting anywhere. Just digging myself

deeper into a hole where my distrust of Conan's kinsmen was growing larger by the minute. Not a healthy mindset if we were on the verge of heading into battle with them.

I'd been focused on Conan to avoid dwelling on Nickolas. A comfortable place was quickly growing between us, and I couldn't make up my mind whether to welcome or shun it. If I didn't pick a pony—and damned soon—it would be too late. We'd be so much a part of one another's lives, there'd be no going back.

I'd always believed Vampires were never lonely. Yet I'd welcomed Conan's presence in my life. It argued I'd be just as much of a sucker where Nick was concerned. It didn't help that he was hotter than a hooker's doorknob on payday. Every time he brushed against me, my mind turned to mush and all I could think about was ripping his clothes off.

Beyond Nicklas's undeniable physical charm, he and Clive were proving to be excellent additions to *Ascent's* staff. Percy kept Nick busy with security, and Clive had taken up the slack left by one of my servers who'd quit. In between orders, he kept a steady supply of clean glasses on the shelf.

The clock behind the bar chimed one. Only forty-five minutes till closing time. Once we had everybody out of the bar, we'd have a quick war powwow and run with it. Percy and the other Sorcerers would have a game plan in place. I was just going along to add magic and muscle to their effort.

I love a good scrap where I can let my fangs out and get down and dirty, and I hoped to hell the guardians would sit this one out. Almost as if he'd read my mind about fangs and fights, Conan padded out of the back room and walked to where I stood in the drink preparation area behind the bar.

"I found food for us," he told me.

After filling a couple of drink orders, I crouched and wrapped an arm around his shoulders. "Um. Where?"

His thoughtfulness warmed me, at least as much as a Vampire can get fired up about anything. Normally, we're quite the taciturn bunch. But his generosity worried me too. I had visions of carcasses littering the stockroom, which was why I'd asked where the bounty was stashed. *Ascent's* back room wasn't the best location for dead things if I fielded a late visit from the merry detective duo. And then, I remembered their surveillance devices and cringed. Good thing they only transmitted sound and not imagery.

"Not far. Shielded from sight," the wolf reassured me.

Guilt smacked me mid-chest. I felt like a shit for doubting him. Tightening my hold across his back, I murmured, "Thanks. We'll figure out how to get there after closing."

"Hurry. I'm hungry too."

I understood. He'd killed something, or probably more than one something. If he ate them, the blood would go to waste, so he was kindly waiting for me. I took a chance because he hated being questioned. *"Not right now, but at some point, I need to know more than I do about where you came from and why you ran away."*

He shook out from beneath my arm and stalked toward the stockroom, tail swishing. It was as close to a "fuck you" as he ever came.

The electronic ordering system beeped, and I went back to pouring booze into an assortment of glassware. I get into a zone when I work where my mind is mercifully empty.

That's a good thing when I'm hungry. It diverts my attention from all the ready food sources scattered a few feet away. If I home in on the sensation, I can scent and feel blood coursing through carotids and jugulars. Better to ignore the whole mess so saliva didn't pool in my mouth and my fangs stayed put.

It's best if I don't think too long or too hard about how far Vampires have fallen. Not that we were ever revered, but we used to be feared. Respected, even. Now we've turned into some cheap caricature à la *Supernatural's* depiction of us as a bunch of scuzzbags with a mouthful of pointy teeth and the brainpower of a gnat. Sheesh. When that show first aired, it took all my self-discipline not to make an impromptu visit to Hollywood and quietly off the writers and producers.

Would have served the fuckers right.

"Last call," Percy's voice boomed. "Closing in ten."

I'd stopped expecting the detectives to pop in. I hadn't seen the last of them. I felt certain of it. But tonight they were engaged elsewhere. They'd been convinced I and everyone who worked at *Ascent* fit neatly into their wheelhouse. Supernaturals one and all, we'd be prime targets for their joke of a paranormal task force. I'd taken offensive action, deflected their initial certainty about us being immortals, but I wasn't under any particular illusions about my success.

They wouldn't forget about whatever tip had sent them my way the night the dark Sorcerers had broken through. My bet was they were biding their time and trying to gather evidence.

Good luck with that.

Everyone who worked with me was excellent at covering their tracks. Guild houses didn't look any different than any other large home. And there were enough New Age practitioners drifting around that having crystals and herbs—or even robes and old-style garb—was scarcely reason for alarm.

Most of tonight's patrons were on their feet, moving slowing toward the door. The air in the club was relaxed with happy, fuzzy edges. Nearly everyone was comfortably drunk. Probably too intoxicated to drive, but it wasn't my problem if they'd forgotten to assign designated driver status to someone.

A solid *thunk* told me the drop bar was in place across the front door. Once I'd finished filling drink orders, I'd crouched behind the bar to take inventory. I was due for another delivery. I'd have to give Northwest Spirits a call tomorrow to see who'd replaced Roger, the delivery driver Conan had killed.

Roger deserved what he got. He'd been shorting me for months, but I recovered enough money from his stash spot to make up for my losses. I smothered a smile. Worrying about my liquor inventory might be premature. Depending on where tonight took us, we might not be back in time to get the club open tomorrow night.

Or the night after.

"You are back there," Nick called from somewhere above me.

"Yup. Busted."

I straightened and lost myself in his smile and striking green eyes, but not for long. We had a busy night ahead of us. A sharp bark from the stockroom reminded me Conan was still waiting, albeit impatiently, for me to share his kills. I wasn't sure if there was enough for everyone, and the back room was no place to have any conversations since the dynamic detectives were recording my every breath—or lack thereof.

I whistled, and Conan loped to my side. "Is there enough to take care of all of us?" I asked. No need to be delicate. If there wasn't, Nick and Clive would have to do their own hunting.

"Yes. Can we leave now?" The wolf sounded put out, but he was probably just hungry. Like me.

"Conan found food for us," I told Nick.

"Does us include me and Clive?" He addressed the question to Conan.

The wolf bobbed his head. "I'm leaving now," he announced. "If you want to share, come with me."

Nick yelled for Clive. He came at a run, which for us is so fast he turned into a blur crossing the bar. Magic shimmered around Conan, full of the clean scent of fur and rain-wet rocks. "Hold up," I told him and switched to telepathy so I wouldn't have to shout across the bar.

"Percy!"

"Yeah?" He turned my way from where he was battening down the wooden panels that had once been windows.

"We'll be back as soon as we've eaten. Fifteen minutes, tops."

He gave me a thumbs up sign. Conan's magic closed around me like a vise as he launched his travel spell. The club ceded to thick forests in the blink of an eye. Conan didn't have to underplay his magic any longer, and the scope of it stole my nonexistent breath.

A comprehensive sniff told me we were in the woods not far from my home in a clearing sheltered by ancient evergreens. Another blast of power from Conan uncovered two young deer and a pile of raccoons.

"Thank you so much," I told the wolf. "What would you like cleared of blood first?"

"Deer." Saliva spooled from the wolf's jaws.

I didn't make him wait any longer than necessary. I sank my fangs into one of the deer and drank fast. Clive and Nickolas went to work on the other one. Predictably, they finished before me and tossed the carcass to Conan, who dug in making little grunting noises as he ate in record time starting with the guts and moving outward. I carried my deer to Conan and grabbed a raccoon.

There was something comfortable about us sharing food. Nothing was wasted. We drank the blood. Conan finished off muscle and organs. There'd be remains left, but the denizens of the forest would make certain not to waste anything. Nature was helpful like that.

Resourceful and efficient.

It wasn't much more than the quarter hour I'd estimated before all of us were washing blood off ourselves in a nearby stream. The Pacific Northwest is good for streams. Lots of water everywhere.

Clive knelt before the wolf. "Thank you so much for providing food. Perhaps next time, I can return the favor."

Conan laid his big head on the Vampire's shoulder. "I'll hold you to it."

"Shall I take us back?" I asked, not wanting to step on Conan's plans. Or his superior magic.

The wolf straightened and woofed. I took it as agreement and drew a transport spell together. Cautious because I didn't know who we'd run into, I warded us and made certain to bring us out dead center in the bar's main room.

"You weren't kidding about making it snappy," Percy said. He'd traded his spot near the door for one behind the bar where he was draining a bottle of German beer and munching potato chips. My staff had nagged for years about offering food, but I'd never wanted the bother of creating menus or the preparation aspects.

Those were my "out-loud" excuses. I suppose if I'd had any interest in sustenance other than blood, I'd have been more enthusiastic about at least exploring the possibilities. Lots of clubs served food. Most of them. *Ascent* was an anomaly in that regard.

Of course, it was an anomaly on many fronts. Lack of snacks was merely the leading edge of how different we were.

"Where is everyone?" Nickolas asked.

"We're meeting at the guild house," Percy said. "Stayed behind to tell you. I considered leaving a note or texting you, but"—he jumped over the bar and walked to where we stood —"those two jokers know where the house is. They sat outside in their car for a couple of hours last night."

Fuck.

"They must have followed me, but how? I was careful. And I was certain they weren't behind us," I muttered before adding mostly to myself, "My car was clear of bugs."

Percy shrugged. "They wouldn't have had to tail you. Nearly every corner has surveillance cameras. All they'd have to do would be to scan for your license plate."

"Things that take pictures on every corner?" Clive sounded rattled.

"Aye." Percy tossed a pointed look his way. "Inside buildings too. You're damned fortunate a digital image of you wasn't uploaded to every police station in the area after that ménage that was the death of your companion."

Clive made a strangled noise that could have meant anything, but my money was on shock at how difficult it had become to escape detection.

I tapped Percy's shoulder. "I truly am sorry. I should have been smarter and parked a few blocks away."

"Wouldn't have mattered," the Sorcerer told me. "A new Neighborhood Watch group banded together, and they've been ridiculously aggressive about making certain there's not one square yard that doesn't have camera coverage."

"We should teleport everywhere," Nick said. "Just to be on the safe side."

I narrowed my eyes. "That only works if you can absolutely guarantee where you'll pop out. And remain warded. Just in case your calculations didn't pan out. But we can certainly teleport tonight."

"Ready to go?" Percy asked us.

"Almost." I dashed into the storeroom and picked up my wallet and phone, tucking them into pockets in my coat. My keys went into yet one more pocket as I scanned where I knew the bugs were planted. Yup. Still there. It was comforting the detectives hadn't quietly picked my lock and retrieved their electronics. On that cheery note, I made certain the back door was secured and set the alarm.

Percy's spell shimmered around Clive and Nickolas. I hustled to join them. "Where's Conan?"

"He said he'd see us there," Nick said.

Good enough. Conan was changing, or maybe not changing so much as no longer being shy about displaying his power. Not that I'd ever viewed him as lacking in that department, but his skill had entered a whole new class.

Broken the magical sound barrier.

Percy's magic, with its scents of the Scottish Highlands in full bloom mixed with a touch of mead, tightened around us. Part of me, a small leftover part from when I'd been human, missed the rolling moors with their stunted stands of heather and gorse bushes. And mountains towering over pristine lochs. The Cascade Range was in my backyard, but it was nothing like the Highlands. Scotland had history, stories to impart. The Cascades were new and young and raw by comparison.

Percy brought us out not in the guild house but in the meeting room from last night, the one straddling worlds. It was empty save for us. The Sorcerer shut his eyes for a moment and then wove his hands into a complex pattern.

Letters formed in the air, golden and shining before they flamed out.

It was enough. Percy snapped his fingers. "They've gone to Gamma Four."

I blinked a couple of times. "Did I drop into a *Star Trek* episode?"

Nick and Clive looked clueless. Conan was nowhere in sight.

"We renamed all the worlds," Percy said. "To give them an order that made sense. Alpha worlds are nearest Earth, and so on."

"What were they called before?" Nick asked.

"They lacked names," Percy clarified. "It was why developing a nomenclature system was so important."

"We should wait for Conan," I said.

"He said he'd figure it out," Percy reassured me.

"How did the other Sorcerers determine Gamma Four was the correct destination?" I made a face. Probably not the most diplomatic way of phrasing that.

"We're pretty handy at finding our own." Percy didn't sound offended.

Questions batted around in my head, but I figured I'd stop before I totally stuffed my foot into my mouth. Had Conan gone to join the guardians? Would they be sending a troop to the fight? I bit my tongue. I didn't own the wolf, but neither did I trust the other guardians' intentions.

What if they sweetened the pot until Conan rejoined them?

Eh. What if they did? He was a far cry from the scared puppy who'd allowed me to find him so long ago. I should be grateful for the time he'd graced my life, not eaten up with bitterness he might leave my side. We owed one another nothing.

I reminded myself of that as Percy's magic, which had never totally subsided, snapped us into another journey spell. This one would be longer, and I prepped myself to come out swinging at the other end.

Who the fuck knew what we'd find?

Having Nickolas and Clive next to me felt comfortable. I almost told them there was no one I'd rather go into battle with—except Conan, of course—but no one was saying much of anything. We hung suspended in darkness shot with countless points of light. It was eerie and beautiful and threatening rolled into one.

When you've lived as long as I have, new experiences are rare. I cherished this one. And the calm before the storm to come.

CHAPTER SEVEN, NICKOLAS

Finally. We were on our way.

I thought the bar would never close. I'd been champing at the bit for hours to get rolling and kill something. It was thoughtful of Conan to cater dinner for all of us. I hadn't known the shapeshifting wolf very long, but even I noticed distinct changes in his behavior since his origins had been revealed. Where before he'd deferred to Ariana, he'd become far more independent.

Not that he didn't care about her. Their connection appeared stronger than ever, but he'd begun making his own decisions. Perhaps he always had, but they were more visible now. Like him arriving at Gamma Four on his own.

Would he decide to return to the guardians?

A small, selfish part of me thought it was a grand idea. Until I considered how devastated Ariana would be. I might want her to myself, but her happiness was paramount.

Somehow, everything circled back to Mistral's death in the Clan Hawke seethe. Ariana had drowned her horror in caring for the wolf, who'd been naught but a puppy when she found him.

I shook my head, but not hard enough for anyone to notice. More of an internal adjustment. So many things didn't quite add up. Why had Conan chosen a Vampire as his champion? From Fairclaw's initial disgust once he realized Vampires had invaded his domain to his reticence to shake Ariana's extended hand, it was clear the guardians felt the same way about us as everyone else in the magical realm did.

Perhaps they nurtured a grudging admiration for our abilities, but our way of being disgusted them. And I'd always suspected us being dead played a major role as well. Dead, yet not, we inhabited a no-man's land that gave even other magic wielders pause.

Digging deeper, why had Ariana allied herself with what the rest of us would consider a food source? And even deeper than that, her long association with the wolf had changed her, shaped her. Granted I hadn't known her before, but I've known a whole lot of Vampires. We're not warm or fuzzy or compassionate or altruistic. Yet the wolf brought out all those traits in Ariana.

I'd changed too in the brief span of days since I'd wakened.

And Clive had shown more emotion over Lorenzo's death than I imagined him capable of. As we traveled closer to the mysterious Gamma Four, I reined in the part of me that seemed to be shifting back to when I'd been mortal and took a shot at homing in on what lay ahead.

"How many will we be joining?" I asked Percy, followed by, "Any idea how numerous our enemy will be?"

The big Sorcerer slitted his eyes my way. "We kept this project low key because we had no idea what we'd face. If we're badly outnumbered, we may opt to leave and return. At least twenty Sorcerers from our side will be there, along with Conan."

"Is he bringing guardians?" Ariana asked. After Percy nodded, she continued. "I don't need the long version, but what exactly is their role?"

Percy chuckled, but he didn't sound amused. "I believe it was Conan's intent to rustle up some of his kinsmen, but he's never been long on details. As to their role, you're offering me a whole lot of credit, Ms. Hawke. I don't know much more about them than you, other than by reputation."

"Yes, but what do they do beyond patrolling the ley-lines?" I asked.

"And where do they live?" Clive spoke up. "They must have a home somewhere."

"No one knows exactly where they dwell. It could be more than one location," Percy said and turned to me. "To answer your question, legends suggest they are the original magic wielders. That all other magic and magical creatures sprang from them."

If I'd been standing on something—rather than hanging suspended—I'd have taken a step backward. "That's ridiculous," I sputtered. "If they were somehow responsible for Vampires, they wouldn't hate us so much."

"Not necessarily." Percy narrowed his eyes further. "Vampires could have developed from a few strands of magic that escaped their control. You know how it is sometimes. The harder you try to corral something, the worse it gets until you toss your hands in the air and walk away."

"Didn't Fairclaw invoke Anubis at some point?" Ariana asked.

I thought about it. "Yes. I believe so."

"If he's some kind of god to them, they can't be all that ancient," Ariana argued. "Anubis is Egyptian. They called him into service sometime around 6000 B.C. to help them deal with wild dogs who desecrated graves."

"For all we know, Anubis is one of them," Percy said softly.

Ariana shut her mouth with a *clack*. "Eh, you're probably right," she mumbled. "Hadn't considered that angle. How much farther?"

"Not very," Percy replied.

We'd only been traveling for perhaps twenty minutes. I'd expected a longer journey, but teleport magic wasn't linked to prosaic things like distance or time.

"Be ready," Percy cautioned us. "I will do my best to ward us as we emerge, but dark Sorcerers share my style of employing power. It will be simple enough for them to chop through any artifice I pull together to conceal us."

"Any idea who else lives here?" Clive asked.

"Nay. I've given this thought, and we'd have been smarter to send a scouting party, but we didn't. We'll maximize our various skills and do the best we can."

The feel of his magic deepened as he wove a ward. My

fangs dropped—no reason to conceal them. The darkness around us ceded to first gray and then a yellowish tint that made me wonder what this world would hold.

I'd never left Earth before—other than my visit to the realm of the dead and wherever the channel from the Sorcerer's guild house led. Would there be Vampires here? Or were we only found on Earth?

"Fuck." The word ripped from Percy as his spell exploded around us.

It took a moment to register that I was falling, plummeting through a void. I dragged magic around myself to form what cushion I could. And a ward. The latter was an afterthought; I hoped I'd been quick enough. I hunted for Clive and Ariana to include them in my efforts, but they were nowhere close to me.

Neither was Percy.

What in the unholy godhead had happened. Where was I? I had to figure that part out before I could do anything. Once I'd slowed my end-over-end tumbling, I righted myself. The yellow developed green edges, and bones fell past me as if someone had cast them from a point above my head. I might have had an issue with boulders, but bones bounced right off my warding.

"Ariana! Clive! Percy!" I shouted. When that didn't work, I switched to telepathy, repeating myself. Somewhere in the midst of that process, I understood the air had thinned to nearly nonexistent. It wouldn't bother me or the other Vampires. We didn't require any.

I hoped Percy had some way to deal with the problem.

Out of nowhere, the surface raced up to meet me. I hit

hard despite my best efforts to shield myself. Violently enough to rattle my bones, but not so hard anything broke. Vampires are tough. Even if I had broken a bone, it would have healed in just a few minutes. Stumbling upright, I blinked until my surroundings came into focus.

Insight crashed over me. I'd been trapped in someone else's illusion. Falling had been the only real part. All the rest—colors and bones—were the product of a master puppeteer pulling strings. There was plenty of air. It didn't smell all that fresh, but I'd dealt with worse. If Percy's spell had run true, Gamma Four was a damp, cold place pockmarked with deep gullies and crumbling rock formations that looked like limestone with shale outcroppings.

I didn't see any structures.

The sound of water hitting rock suggested a river wasn't far. I called for the others again, using shielded telepathy. No response. Someone knew we were here. The same someone who'd ripped the innards out of Percy's spell. Rain splattered from a yellow-green sky. If this world had a sun, it was nowhere in sight.

Hell, did it even shift from day to night? Or was chartreuse-colored daylight the norm in this place? At least it wasn't burning my skin. I squeezed my eyes tight and pushed myself to focus on the important parts. Who the hell cared what color the sky was? Or whether there was air.

My actions would weaken any cover I'd managed with my warding, but I sent a seeking beam of power outward hunting for my companions. I had to find them before I went scouting for whomever lived here. At first, nothing pinged back, but it wouldn't have. My power is strong, but even it can't drill through wards erected by other Vampires.

I was more worried about Percy, but he's been taking care of himself for a long time. Presumably, he was better suited than the rest of us to second-guess his twisted Sorcerer kin.

I started to leave the spot I'd splatted down but forced myself to wait a few more minutes. If all of us ran off half-cocked, the odds of us ever finding one another would erode sharply—until we were back on Earth. I sharpened the beam of my magic and tried again. This time I thought I might have sensed my missing companions.

Spread in different directions, each was quite a ways distant from me, but not so far they wouldn't have heard my telepathy. If I'd been Conan, hackles would have sprung up the length of my back. As it was, I turned in a slow circle. My hands were balled into fists, and I was ready to jump on whatever felt off to me.

Someone was in charge here. And it wasn't me.

Being helpless isn't my style. Ariana might not need me, but Clive did. Heedless of consequences, I tossed my warding aside and let magic crackle from my fingertips as I cycled through every combination I could think of. I had no idea what the net result would be, but I was done doing nothing.

A resounding crack brought my head spinning around as the world reshaped itself. No more rain. No more crumbled, rocky dirt. No more distant waterfall. Instead I stood on finely ground, uniform dirt in an arena ringed by a series of raised stone platforms, very much like the Colosseum in old

Rome. The sky was still yellow-green. It was the only thing that hadn't changed.

Ariana stood at the far end of the field, facing away from me. Clive was closer. I sped to his side, grabbed an arm, and shook him. Even with physical contact, it might have taken as much as a minute for him to come out of whatever blitzed state had him in thrall.

"Come on," I urged, not bothering to add we could sort this out later.

I repeated my actions with Ariana. She came around faster, fangs out, and spoiling for a fight.

"Gah. Sorry." She yanked her head back from where she'd been poised to sink her teeth into my neck. "What the fuck happened? Where's Percy?"

"Where are all the other Sorcerers who were supposed to be here?" Clive spoke for the first time since I'd jerked on his arm.

It was a good question since the big Sorcerer wasn't in the arena with the rest of us. Perhaps our enemies had segregated us in hopes of harvesting our blood. That was absolutely not going to happen. Not today. Not ever, and definitely not on my watch.

The whole arena scenario was a harbinger of bad tidings. I didn't fancy providing entertainment for a bunch of dark mages. Our enemy had tipped his hand, but I'd take all the clues I could get.

At least Clive and Ariana were losing the dazed look they'd had. My seeking spell hadn't been even close to accurate. If I'd followed its lead, it would have taken me kilometers away from them. Did it mean the same something that was controlling everything else had its claws in my power?

"I'm going to try to move us out of here," I said.

"Won't work," Ariana informed me. "I already tried that. When I couldn't find the rest of you, I tested my magic. Something has it by the short hairs." She screwed her mouth into a snarl. "Good thing you managed to break through the jungle illusion."

"What jungle?" Clive asked. "I thought I was in a frozen wasteland, something like Russia's far north."

"Aye. And it looked like the English countryside to me, but hundreds of years ago," I said and switched to telepathy in hopes of at least slowing our invisible adversary down.

"Waiting around for the next ax to fall won't buy us crap. Let's combine our power into a teleport casting, and—"

Rumbling, grating, and groaning announced our window of opportunity for action had just snapped shut. Holes opened all around us; dirt flew a couple of meters into the air. Reptilian monsters with huge mouths and many rows of teeth lumbered out of subterranean recesses. Their scales were a tired, rust-tinged green and the size of supper plates. They looked impervious to everything. The dirk I habitually carried wouldn't make much of a dent.

I wished I had a broadsword. Something with heft, but I may as well have longed to go back and start this whole ill-conceived charade over again for all the good it did me.

"Showtime," Ariana yelled. If I read her right, she was relieved to have a visible enemy.

"Wait!" I cautioned everyone.

"What for?" Clive's dark gaze skittered my way before returning to the crocodile-esque creatures.

"To see how many. And if they're real."

"Some of them are. It's good enough for me." Ariana charged forward.

I opened my mouth to call her back, but she didn't report to me. Clive ran after Ariana. So far, ten of the things had crawled out of the ground. From the corners of my eyes, the raised platforms were filling with what had to be Sorcerers. I'd been right about one thing. We were in the arena to provide a spectacle.

Their plan. Not mine.

Putting two fingers between my fangs, I whistled and pointed at the growing audience. Only one way to deal with them, and it would take all three of us. "They're the problem," I shouted.

A crocodile waddled closer, jaws snapping. I wove power into a shiny silver rope and looped it around his jaws. He'd work through it, but it would take a while. They had a stink about them that was growing as more converged in the arena. Swampy and rank and rotten.

Clive leapt over two of them. I ran behind him and repeated my trick with the rope. Ariana had flipped one of the nasty creatures over on its back. A quick evaluation showed overlapping discs. Nowhere to drive a fang into. Or my blade. Not easily, anyway.

"Ignore them," I shouted. Easier said than done since their original number had doubled, except many had no substance. It was a waste of magic to test them one by one, though.

Ariana executed a graceful sideways maneuver that shot her clear of the beast she'd been examining and set her square in the path of another. Clive has always been a quick study; he sealed the thing's jaws shut using a variation of my technique.

Boos erupted from our growing audience.

I looped an arm around Ariana's shoulder, another around Clive's. *"Each of you begin at one end,"* I instructed. *"I'll take the middle."*

"Mass hypnosis?" Even in telepathy, Ariana barely breathed the question.

"Exactly," I told her and Clive. *"Won't hold them forever, but long enough for us to get out of here to somewhere we can do some good."*

"No need to be delicate." Ariana sounded positively bloodthirsty.

I approved. Weaving our way around the growing throng of crocodiles—sealing jaws as we went—we closed on the part of the gallery that was occupied. Unlike ancient Rome, this world clearly lacked thousands of feral spectators to fill the stands.

Did the Sorcerers understand enough about Vampiric persuasion to recognize we were more than a match for the fifty or so of them huddled together? Probably not. Most other immortals never bothered to dirty themselves studying Vampires.

About the only thing that was important about us to this crew was our blood. Ironic, since blood is kind of our thing.

It was sinking in that the crocodiles weren't much of an impediment. One of the Sorcerers shot to his feet. I'd gotten used to black lightning forking from their mouths as they crafted their brand of power. Before he got too involved summoning reinforcements that might require more of our attention than the belly-slithering batch milling about the field, I forged a mind link with Clive and Ariana.

Joining our magic to immobilize large groups isn't practiced often. Nor has it been done for a long while. Not that I know of, anyway. Things could have turned upside down after I left the Dolomites. I girded myself. Just because this undertaking wasn't part of my normal repertoire didn't mean it was impossible, or that I'd make a fatal mistake and tip our hand.

As I gathered power from Ariana and Clive, I walked myself through the spell's steps. There were only three, but the whole mess could blow up in my face if I didn't lay the groundwork well for each of them.

A large winged caricature of an eagle popped out of nowhere. Anything with wings could poke holes in my strategy. Big ones if the bird distracted us by driving its beak through something crucial—like an eye. I tossed caution aside and created a carpet of scented violet persuasion, ordering it to flow sure and true. Product of my will and our combined power, it coated the ground. Perhaps the Sorcerers would be stupid enough to believe it was a salvo against the crocodiles.

Ariana threw more magic into mix. Intuiting my intent— perhaps she'd engaged in this same casting herself—she helped me hold the spell at ground level until the last possible moment.

Time for step two. Collectively, the three of us pushed

maximum velocity into the casting and forced it up and over the group of Sorcerers. At the last minute, some of them understood what was happening and tried to lurch upright.

Too late.

We had them precisely where we wanted them. "So far. So good," I ground out. We'd made it to step three. No more pitfalls. The casting had entered bulletproof territory.

"No reason to hold back now." Ariana loped forward until she was right under the group of Sorcerers, all of them sitting slack-jawed.

"Can we annihilate everything?" Clive was grinning.

"Turn their minds to mush," I urged. "Nothing to save them for."

Power pulsed from our raised hands, shading from purple to red. Heads dropped onto chests; Sorcerers fell from their seats and lay in twitching heaps.

"It's enough," I shouted. "Save your magic." No more reason to bother with telepathy. No one left to hear us. I looked around for the eagle, but it had vanished. Maybe it hadn't been real, after all. Just another ruse to distract our awareness.

Clive started climbing toward the nearest of the fallen Sorcerers. "No!" I thundered, understanding he was planning to feed.

Thank the bloody fucking saints he was used to paying attention to me. He halted and yelled, "Why not?"

"Their blood will make you ill," Ariana answered.

"How do you both know that?" Clive wasn't willing to give ground. Not easily.

She grinned, fangs on display. In that moment, she was

the most beautiful thing I'd ever laid eyes on. "Because I drank from such as them—and puked for weeks afterward," she told him.

"When was that?" I asked.

"A long time ago. Mistral warned me, but I figured he was old and full of crap." A closed-off look dropped over her stunning face, and she made a chopping motion. "What comes next? I bet our teleport magic would work now, and—"

A portal blasted into being, shimmering white. I recognized it from the meeting in the place beyond the Sorcerers' guild house. Sure enough, Conan shot through the opening followed by a lot of guardians. More than ten. They wore their human forms. Conan was a wolf.

"I couldn't find you." He bolted to Ariana's side. "I knew you had to be here, but everywhere I sent magic bounced back at me."

She buried a hand in his neck muff, and the two leaned into each other. I looked away. My jealousy had no place here. It wasn't as if they were lovers. I'd gotten over that suspicion a while back. They were friends, companions who'd shared many experiences. Just because I wanted that history with her was no reason to devalue their connection. Or resent it.

Ariana had space in her heart for more than one friend.

Fairclaw faced the comatose bunch of dark mages. After a brisk nod, he raised his arms. The crackle of destructive magic rained from his fingertips, filling the air with the distinctive scents of chemicals I've always associated with morgues. Formaldehyde and grain spirits mingled with an acidic undernote.

Good time to not bother with breathing.

Small smokeless fires broke out. When everything cleared, the only thing left of the black mages was bones.

"Incredible." Clive stood next to me.

I nodded. The guardian's display of raw power had been impressive.

"Do any of you know where Percy and his cohort are?" I asked.

"Back on Earth." Conan shook himself and fluffed out his tail. "We located them easily and sent them home. Other twisted mages are dead, but there are many, many more of them."

Fairclaw turned from watching over the smoldering piles of remains. "Cowards," he pronounced. "They left."

"We should too," I said.

"Indeed." Ariana's tone was crisp. "Time's probably not the same here. I bet we have a bar to open."

Fairclaw laughed. It seemed out of place coming from him. "Funny. But it's the same thing Percy said."

"We had to convince him to depart," another guardian spoke up.

"He didn't want to leave without you," Conan told us.

"He's been a good friend to me." Ariana pulled in her fangs. Her mouth formed a soft smile; a teleport spell built around her. "Getting the bar open is a big job. Let's not make him wait any longer than he has to for help."

The most important part would be him knowing he

hadn't been the cause of our imprisonment on Gamma Four, but Ariana understood as much.

"Come closer." Ariana crooked two fingers our way. "No reason to launch separate castings."

Conan woofed. I took it as instructions to snap to. When I scanned the arena, the other guardians had left. I didn't see how I could have missed their egress, but they were gone.

A mixture of Ariana's and Conan's power surrounded Clive and I. The return trip didn't seem to take as long, but then they never do. We emerged in an alley redolent of urine and feces not far from *Ascent*. It was early evening, not yet nine. A brisk quarter hour walk brought us to familiar streets, and we hurried down the narrow track leading to the nightclub's backdoor.

"Crap on a cracker," Ariana muttered after she rounded a corner.

Sure enough, the goddamned black car I'd come to associate with Hernandez and Riteway sat smack in the center of the road.

Hernandez popped out of the car like a clown. "Where have you been?"

Ariana smiled. Charm oozed from her. I did a quick fang check for myself and Clive.

"Why we went for a walk," she told the detective. "How sweet of you to be concerned about me."

Conan growled.

"Stop that," Ariana admonished him. "These are our friends."

It took considerable effort not to laugh, but I behaved myself and pasted an amiable clueless smile on my face.

By now, the other brainless twit was out of the car. "Where is your vehicle?"

"Out front."

"No. It's not," Riteway sneered.

"Well then"—she ladled compulsion over charm —"someone stole it." Ariana made shooing motions. "Go on. Do your job. Find my Toyota. I'll need it at the end of the evening to get home."

CHAPTER EIGHT, ARIANA

$\mathcal{I}$ was still dithering about Mistral's name slipping from me after Clive had started for the downed Sorcerers, intent on feeding. What in the fuck was wrong with me? My fledgling strategy had been to make Nickolas believe I was still so traumatized by the whole beheading at Clan Hawke, any mention of those days was verboten.

Well. I'd just blown that plan sky high. Way to go.

My problem was I was growing comfortable around Nick, comfortable enough to not be on guard every moment. I'd have to nip my casual attitude in the bud. Before it snaked out and turned into my undoing. Nick liked me, was drawn to me, but I wasn't under any false impressions. If he uncovered the truth, his loyalty to our kind would rise to the fore.

He might not know much about how to navigate the twenty-first century, but he'd embark on a one-man crusade to ensure I was brought to justice. I was certain I'd retracted my fangs, but they were cutting into my lower lip. I concentrated until they were well and truly seated in their slots.

The only one who could knife me in the back was me. There'd been no witnesses. Hundreds of years had passed. So long as I didn't play too many stupid cards, I'd get past this.

But it meant dialing back my emerging relationship with Nick. No more cozy hunting parties. No more visits to my home. From now on, he'd be like any other employee. Valued, but kept at arm's length.

Hernandez and Riteway as a greeting party were icing on the cake. The urge to jump them and wipe their memories was overpowering. My life would be so much better if they forgot my name. Except they wouldn't. Modern cops kept digital logbooks, so even if I carved holes in their recollections of the last month, they wouldn't have to go far to reconstruct everything.

Killing them was the only true solution. Except the police department would assign more to take their place. These two weren't all that bright. Maybe I'd be better served to hang onto them rather than risk unknown quantities. Trying for an upbeat note, I thanked them for caring enough to be worried about me.

Never mind suspicion was rolling off them in a choking cloud of wariness and mistrust. When they informed me my car wasn't in its customary spot, I asked them to look into who might have stolen it. I could give a fuck less about the car, but it seemed like a grand excuse to get rid of the overbearing dickwads. The front of *Ascent* has multiple cameras. Some are owned by the city, but some are mine.

We'd figure out quick enough where the Toyota was. If I got close to where I'd parked it, I could probably sniff out who'd been there, but I had other work to do. The detectives weren't showing any signs of moving, so I nodded briskly and cut a path in front of them while dredging through my pockets for a key.

Ha. Got lucky. I don't always carry keys since I have other ways of opening doors. Once it was ajar, I motioned Clive and Nick inside. Conan stood next to me, keeping a close eye on the cops. He'd never stopped growling, low in the back of his throat. If I'd been Hernandez or Riteway, I'd have been on my guard.

Offering a cheery wave, I said, "If you boys want a drink, come round to the front in a few hours. Just before closing time. If you go inside now, you'll ruin my night's profits."

They weren't in uniform, but I did not want them wandering through *Ascent*. Something about their bearing screamed police. I didn't wait to see what their plans were. Conan followed hard on my heels, and I shut and bolted the door."

"What do you want to—" Nick began.

I shook my head hard and angled it toward the door I'd just secured.

"Oh. Right. Sorry," he mumbled.

Before he could draw me into a dark corner for a private chat, I hustled through into the club. We'd opened a couple of hours before and already had a crowd both milling around and standing at the bar. Nick stuck with me. Clive headed for the wash rack where glassware was piling up. Making a point to catch Percy's eye, I gave him a thumbs-up sign.

"Bet you want to talk with him. Hold up a moment." Nick vaulted across the expanse of floor and tables, clearly intent on taking Percy's spot at the door, checking IDs and making sure nothing smelled like guns or knives. Percy clapped him across the back and skirted the edges of the room. After waving hello to Ruby, Dee, and Selene, I met him near one of the emergency exit doors. We have two of them, per fire department regulations.

"I'm sorry—" he began.

I flapped a hand to quiet further apologies. "It's all right. We made good inroads. Tell you more later." Switching to telepathy, I added, *"The paranormal task force dudes are in the alley. Oh, and my car appears to be missing."*

Breath puffed between Percy's gritted teeth. "I moved it. Sorry. We had a mini riot on Mercy Street earlier. I was afraid you'd lose a window. The Toyota is in the Safeway parking lot."

I grinned, feeling frisky from the success of our mass mesmerism casting and relieved I'd be spared all the DMV and insurance paperwork of reporting the Toyota stolen. "Thanks for looking out for my wheels. Good thing I let Ruby talk me into replacing *Ascent's* windows with decorative wooden panels."

"Pfft. It would be a better thing if the permanent panels ever showed up. I'm tired of looking at plywood. We'll talk after closing. There are a few things you need to know about."

Nodding, I turned away. I should alert the detectives not

to waste time looking for my SUV, but I hated the thought of being in close proximity to them. They made me feel dirty, like I'd taken a bath in goo. I was nearly to one of the swinging doors leading into the drink prep area when I remembered Hernandez had given me a card. Twice.

I could call them.

It was far simpler than making a trip to the alley. If they were still there, it would piss me off. The mood I was in, I might just lose it and decide both of them needed to vanish. Conan would help—if he hadn't already.

He'd been quick enough to deal with other mortals who'd attacked us.

"I'll be back in a minute," I said as I strode past Ruby.

"We're good." She flashed something that might have been a smile. Her glamour was thin tonight, which usually meant she was edgy about something.

A quick grapple through the stacks of paper on my desk failed to turn up the detective's card, but when I opened the top drawer, I found it right on top. After sweeping the paper jungle into a few piles, I vowed to make a full transition to digital.

I'd made that promise to myself before. Maybe this time, I'd follow through.

I tapped the number on the card into my phone, opted for a text message, and typed a few lines.

My car is okay. One of my staff moved it. Wanted to make certain you didn't waste time tracking it down. Guess there was an altercation in front of the bar earlier.

I reread the text a couple of times, decided it was okay as it was. No reason to tell them where the Toyota was. They'd be able to find it easily enough from their network of corner-mounted cameras.

After hitting send, I slipped the phone into a pocket and stared at the spots in the doorframe where the bugs had been concealed. How long did I have to leave them in place? This was private property, for chrissakes. They were violating my rights as a citizen.

Before I realized it, I was on my feet and had covered the distance to the door. A low growl told me Conan lay in his spot behind some shelving. *"Don't,"* reverberated in my head.

I turned to face him. "My little voice of reason."

"I don't like it, either, but if you dig those things out of the wood, they'll know you're onto them."

I dragged the heels of my hands down the sides of my face. It wasn't that I didn't understand the ramifications. It was more I'd quit caring what the Riteway and Hernandez show knew or thought or wanted. A very risky attitude on my part. We had far bigger problems than a couple of pesky mortals, but they could force me out of *Ascent* and into hiding, which would complicate everything unnecessarily.

And put my amazing, loyal staff out of work.

I squatted in front of Conan. He laid his snout on my shoulder for a moment in a show of solidarity. *"Do you think we should close this place for a while?"* I asked.

"No. It would make it appear you have something to hide."

"We might have to close anyway," I said, thinking about the dark mages and the bazillion mortals who were out for magic-laden blood.

"You might miss a few nights"—the wolf shook his fur out—*"but someone will be here to open the doors."*

I opened my mouth to insist I had to be here. *Ascent* had never been open without me being present for at least some of the night. But I closed it before my control issues got the better of me. Pushing upright, I walked into the club. From long habit, I scanned the growing crowd.

They appeared more restive this evening, especially considering how early it was. I remembered Percy's description of a disturbance on Mercy street. Had psychic energy broken loose from some quarter? Humans might not be able to sense power directly, but its presence had a disquieting impact on them. The darker the power, the more it made mortals squirm.

I hurried into the prep area and stood between Ruby and Dee. Clive had shifted to waiting tables. His inherent Vampire charm made him an excellent server.

"Do either of you sense anything off?" I kept my voice very low.

"Hell to the yes." Ruby pursed her full lips into a tight line. "Christa—"

I waited for more, but Ruby had apparently thought better of what she'd been about to say.

Normally, I'd have left it alone. The electronic order system beeped and pinged. I dove in, prepping trays for the servers. After a flurry of orders, I nudged Ruby. "Christa, what?"

The Fae made a snorting sound. "Ha. Didn't think you'd let that one go."

"You don't owe me any explanations," I was quick to insert.

"She's been in a tizzy all evening," Dee said.

Sometimes I'm a bit slow on the uptake. After a quick glance around *Ascent*, boosted by a smidgeon of a magical assist, I asked, "Erm, where is Christa?"

"Guild house," Ruby muttered.

"Is she not feeling well?" I pressed as a work-around to a more direct question, which would have been why she wasn't here.

"It's the dark of the moon," Dee said.

"The dude says he ordered hazy IPA," one of the servers announced and slapped a mug of what looked like amber ale on the bar.

Dee grabbed the tankard and took a long swig. Before I could say anything, she stopped glugging beer and squared her shoulders. "Beats chucking it down the drain."

I filled a clean glass with a reasonable quality IPA from the line of taps behind me and handed it to the server. "Tell him this one is on the house."

The gal, a wolf shifter with a corona of red curls and shining amber eyes, grinned. "Ought to shut him up. I think he tasted the ale and decided he didn't like it, is what I think. I took his order, and I have unusually good hearing."

I chuckled. "I just bet you do."

Once she'd left, I turned back to Dee. The mug was empty; the ale long gone. "Want to say more about it being the dark of the moon?"

"Ideal time for prophecies," Ruby supplied.

The bits of information finally formed a cohesive picture. "Christa is at the guild house tossing runestones."

"And reading crystals, water, and everything else she can get her hands on," Ruby said.

"My, erm, sisters are doing much the same," Dee added. "This moon phase has a strong pull. Can you feel it?" She quit pouring drinks long enough to spread her arms wide.

The din in *Ascent* was loud enough, probably no one could hear, but I switched to telepathy anyway. *"I sense something, but my power isn't constructed like yours. Not especially in tune with the natural world."*

"We figured when we shut the ley-line portal, things would slowly revert to normal," Dee said.

"I'm guessing they haven't?" Ambient evil didn't feel much more pervasive to me than it had before, but like I said, I'm not the best bellwether for shit like that.

Ruby came as close to snarling as she ever does. For half a moment, wings fluttered before she got hold of the magic keeping her glamour in place. "Nope. They grew worse."

"Define worse."

Orders were piling up. After a hasty glance to make certain no one was too close, I switched on Vampiric speed and stacked trays with libations until we'd caught up.

"Ask the trees," Ruby mumbled. "They know. And the birds and the—"

"They don't talk with me," I cut in and laid a finger across my mouth, hoping to return the conversation to silent mode.

"Lots of...those like us are in here tonight," Dee tossed out. "All that energy complicates things."

Those like us, huh? I gazed around the big room. Other than a tinge of ambient weirdness, everyone had done a fine job concealing what they were.

Fuck.

Who the hell knew what manner of being might be masquerading as mortal? It's not as if I had time to inventory the patrons. It was why I stationed someone at the front—and only—door. *"Percy."*

"Yeah," floated back to me.

I hesitated, wondering how to word what I needed to know. *"Any potential problems?"*

"A few firearms and two knives. All are locked away."

It hadn't been what I was after. *"Anyone unusual?"*

"Aye."

"Hold down the fort," I told the women and left the serving area. I needed to hold a private conversation with Percy—or maybe Nick who'd turned into the backup bouncer. Telepathy could be intercepted.

I took my time as I walked the perimeter of the crowd, listening to what I could. Maybe I'd get lucky and overhear something important that would help our side. If the psychic unrest had intensified, it was because we hadn't located all the gateways.

Or because someone had drilled new ones.

Why weren't the guardians on top of the problem? The ley-lines were their purview. They'd fallen down on the job —my interpretation—when they failed to notice the incursion of black sorcery to Earth. Or maybe they had noticed and decided it wasn't their job to fix it.

Who the hell knew how they thought?

Conan would. I could ask him, but it wasn't the kind of question he was likely to answer.

Bits and pieces of conversations buffeted me from various tables. Drug deals. Who's fucking whom. Who skipped out on work and lied through their teeth. Typical bar chatter. No one was talking about witchcraft, or sorcery, or—

If I hadn't been trying for stealth, I'd have slapped my forehead. I was listening with Vampire precision, but I hadn't tuned into anything beyond mortal frequencies. After making a show of gathering empty glasses from a few tables and carting them to the conveyor belt, I altered my perceptions.

The world reshaped itself around me. In case I was sporting a thunderstruck expression, I cloaked myself in shadows. Not exactly invisible, but not far from it. Percy's response about immortals had understated who we served tonight. They were all shrouded, not just from mortals, but from others with power.

The question was why.

My bar has always been open to everyone. But we'd never had numbers anything close to tonight's tally when it came to magic-wielders. Perhaps half the crowd weren't human.

It made me uncomfortable. Enough supernatural creatures were here to start a race war. The newly uncovered snippets of conversation had a common theme. When the moon was dark, it amplified power. How could I not have known that? A closer look beneath glamours convinced me I didn't recognize any of the bar patrons, either.

Where had they come from?

Did Percy know who they were? Sorcerers generally kept tabs on everyone. He must have realized who he was letting into the club. Before my temper exploded into accusations, I finished my circuit of the bar, letting go of the shadows I'd hidden within a piece at a time. Hopefully, no one would notice.

It felt like it took a long time to reach the front door. People were still flowing into the club, but I was viewing them through fresh eyes. The occasional trio or quartet of mortals was eclipsed by sheer numbers of Sidhe, Fae, Witches, and Shifters.

Nick greeted me warmly. Seeing him reminded me of my plan to back away from being overly friendly. It wouldn't be easy. He was damn near irresistible. "Can you manage the door?" I asked.

"Sure thing."

"Figured you'd be up here sooner or later," Percy said and pointed to one of the emergency side doors. It beat swimming upstream against the tide of bodies wanting in.

I nodded and set a brisk course for the door, disabling the alarm. He and I slipped into the alley. "What the fuck is going on?" I sputtered.

"Ssht." His magic wrapped around us, with its scents of mead and the Highlands. Moments later we were somewhere else, a grey empty place not much bigger than a closet. "All right. We can talk here," he said.

"Why is the club full of immortals?" I asked. "You'd have to know. You checked them all in."

He nodded. "I had no idea so many would show up—" he began.

"Start at the beginning, but just hit the important parts," I spoke over him.

"When I got back from G4, Ruby was all over me. Apparently, Christa did a mini-casting, and it was disturbing enough she took it to the guild master. He pulled all the Fae seers together, and they're engaged in some kind of group psychic rabbit hunt."

"So are the Witches."

"Aye. Discovered that part later. Anyway, the condensed version is someone put out the word *Ascent* is a haven for those like us, and—"

"Do you know all these mages?" I interrupted again. "I've never seen a one of them."

"I recognize a few."

"Why are they all here? Is it because of the moon phase? Or the sketchy future seeing?"

"I'm getting to that." He almost smiled. The corners of his mouth twitched.

I reminded myself to shut up and listen. Getting ahead of the curve is one of my less stellar traits.

"The reason you don't know any of the mages in the bar —and why I only know a bare handful—is because they're not from here. From what I can gather, they primarily hail from the West Coast, but..."

Percy was still talking, but I'd stopped listening, mostly because I'd figured things out, and I didn't like the conclusion that emerged. At all.

"Ariana?" He gripped my upper arm.

"Yeah. Sorry." I locked gazes with Percy. "I checked out a while back, but I'm pretty sure I have this. Correct me if I miss something."

"Will do."

"After the last purge, anger's been simmering. Something about the energies associated with the dark moon pushed it into high gear, and everyone's decided they want to fight back. To mow through humans and teach them a lesson. And they picked *Ascent* as their headquarters. Am I close?"

"Very."

I'd balled one hand into a fist. "Well. It's not going to happen. Let them find some other epicenter for their war."

"Isn't that rather akin to stuffing a cat back into a bag?"

Defensiveness raced through me in a scorching tide that made my stomach twist into a tight knot. "I never said they couldn't have their war. But they can leave me and my nightclub out of it."

"How will that work?" Percy's words were soft, nonjudgmental. While I was still sputtering, trying to come up with an answer, he went on, "Wouldn't you rather have the inside track on information? Not be blindsided?"

"I don't want a war at all," I protested. "We won't win."

"Not the prevailing opinion."

I punched the air between us. "Well it's because they're stupid."

"Are they? We control the elements. We can harness wind, hurricanes, tornadoes, floods. We can open sinkholes that will swallow cities."

Understanding smacked me hard. "You're really into this."

"I am. I'm sick of kowtowing to inferiors. When you mentioned the cops earlier. It would have been simple to stop their hearts. I could have done it from my post by the front door."

"Why didn't you?"

"Because someone would have had to clean up the mess, move their car, wipe the digital record of them being anywhere near here."

I smiled grimly. "My reasoning exactly, plus better the devil you know. The next batch might be smarter than Riteway and Hernandez."

"Ariana."

"Yeah?"

"Let everyone have their meeting after the club closes. You get a voice. You can ask them to pick another spot to work out of, but you might change your mind. Once you hear them out."

"Doubtful. Plus, what if the joke of a paranormal task force is still around?"

Percy showed me a mouthful of teeth. "I'll give you a hundred to one someone else takes them out. And wipes away the evidence."

I held out my hand. He shook it. I liked those odds. A lot. While it would be far more satisfying to be the instrument of those two fuckers' deaths, I had the sense to know I couldn't kill willy-nilly.

Yup. Been there. Done that. Got away with it.

Smart Vampires don't press their luck.

"We can go back now," I said.

"Soon. How'd you get out of the trap my twisted kin laid for you?"

My fangs wanted out. I let them drop. "We mesmerized them."

His eyes widened. "All of them? How?"

"We joined our magic. Vamps have a few tricks up our sleeves. Anyway, we'd have called it even after we turned their minds to mush. The guardians showed up and burned them to a cinder with mage fire."

"Nice work. How many?"

"Maybe fifty? A lot of them."

Percy nodded briskly. "Even better. When I realized what had happened, that they'd culled you away from me, I was furious. I did everything I could think of to locate you—and came up crickets. Even when I mind-linked with the other Sorcerers from my guild house, we still didn't unearth any clues. Since we were there—and I was so angry I couldn't see straight—we mowed through a passel of our dark kin. Maybe sixty or seventy."

"And then the guardians showed up?" I furled my brows.

"Yup. And sent me and the other Sorcerers back to Earth. Conan was beside himself, ready to rip the world asunder to find you."

"No one found us until we'd turned the black Sorcerers into drooling idiots. It must have broken the illusion they'd hidden us behind."

"All's well that ends well." Breath whistled from between Percy's teeth.

"It did this time," I said, all too aware "good" endings could turn into two-edged swords.

Percy's magic thickened around us. Before he whisked us back, he said, "Nick is smitten by you."

Frowning, not certain where Percy was heading, I mumbled, "I know. Vampires don't choose mates."

Percy muffled something that might have been a snort. "That might be so, Ariana, but like it or not, he's chosen you."

Before I could protest I didn't want to talk about it, we landed in *Ascent's* back room.

"I'll secure the door we left from," Percy said. "See you in a few."

"Where'd you go?" Conan poked his head out from around a stack of liquor crates.

"Somewhere we could talk." I switched to telepathy and told him the gist of our conversation. Before I was done, his eyes shone with anticipation. Whatever he was, wolf or guardian or something in between, Conan relished the specter of a no-holds-barred war.

What the fuck was the matter with me? Was I the only peacenik in the group? Still dissecting where I'd fallen off the Vampire track, I wandered into the bar and mixed drinks with a vengeance.

I'd grown soft, too human. All that was about to change.

I cursed a blue streak—in Gaelic—but the bar was so loud no one could have heard me. All the shit about change was nothing more than big talk. I needed action to back it up. Put up or shut up. I'd get my chance soon. Very soon. And I'd give the myriad mages who'd landed in my bar—without so much as asking permission—a piece of my mind.

CHAPTER NINE, NICKOLAS

I'd been surprised when Percy mentioned we'd be seeing record numbers of immortals tonight. His warning had been timely. After the first fifty or so, my bent would have been to turn them away, especially after several screwed their faces into disgusted moues once they figured out what I was.

When I'd inquired what the fuck we were doing, Percy told me it would be all right, except I didn't quite believe him. A few of the customers greeted him by name, but it was clear he wasn't acquainted with most of them. I kept my eye on Ariana as she skirted the edges of the club, certain she was up to something.

When she charged over to us and all but ordered me to take over door duty, I sensed uneasiness rolling off her. My first guess was she'd discovered who was in the club, and it made her just as edgy as it made me. For all the Fae and Sidhe and Witches and Shifters who'd marched through the door—along with the odd Druid—I didn't spot a single Vampire.

Ariana had said she was the only one in this part of the country. It was looking as if she might be the only one period. Except for Clive and me, of course. If what was unfolding was a general gathering of magic wielders from distant locales, why hadn't Vampires been included?

I had a lot of questions, but the biggest one was why here and why now?

Percy strode across the floor from the direction of the stockroom. As soon as he was back and perched on his stool, I leaned close. "Why are all of them here?" Whispering wasn't an absolute guarantee I wouldn't be overheard, but it was more discreet than telepathy.

"War council," he mouthed back.

"Ari didn't know, did she?"

Percy shook his head. "Neither did I until I showed up here and someone from my guild house popped in with the news. Not too many spots a bunch of us can congregate and remain relatively invisible."

"Is Ariana all right with this, uh, development?"

"Yes and no. Her first bent was to kick everyone out, and it may still come to that."

"You good here if I go talk with her?"

"Sure." He turned away and gave a couple of mortals the once over before taking their money and allowing them in.

I'd been surprised when I learned Ariana charged admission. It wasn't much. Only five dollars, but it tended to keep deadbeats out of the club.

Ariana was behind the bar mixing drinks along with Dee and Ruby. The Witch and the Fae wore haggard expressions. As if they anticipated the worst from the crowd of supernaturals. Or maybe they were reacting to something I didn't know about.

Aside from the influx of immortals, there'd been something ominous floating about ever since we returned from Gamma Four. I hadn't been able to pinpoint it because it ebbed and flowed. At its zenith, the fine hairs on the back of my neck rose in protest. At one point—not tonight, but a few days earlier—Percy had told me he sensed trouble brewing.

A similar intuition pricked and nagged until I had to pay attention to it. Perhaps it was as simple as all these mages in close proximity, yet my instincts argued it ran deeper than that. Psychic energies had been loosed from somewhere, and they bore down on us.

What it meant remained to be seen.

I could have it all wrong. Wouldn't be the first mistake I'd made since wakening from stasis.

I beckoned to Ariana, expecting she'd leave her post. She didn't, so I went through the swinging gate and walked up behind her. For once, I ignored her alluring musky scent and the lush curves of breasts and ass. They were still amazing, but I couldn't afford to be deflected from my goal, which was a private conversation.

Vampire to Vampire.

"We need to talk," I said close to her ear.

"Why?" She didn't turn around and continued filling glasses with a variety of libations.

I rephrased my request. "I need to talk with you. Now. Before we hit closing time."

She turned toward me, an unreadable expression in her sky-blue eyes. Usually, I'm decent at deciphering other Vampires, but the reactions sluicing from her were a combination of resignation and outright defeat. Anger was there too, but muted.

If I was interpreting her signals correctly, they worried me. In the world I was familiar with, defeat isn't part of the vampiric repertoire. Neither is resignation.

After half a minute had ticked by, she stepped through the gate and bolted for the back room. I'd thought about the surveillance things and had a fix for them if she didn't.

I shut the stockroom door behind me as she was saying. "This is a shit time to talk about anything. Nor is this a good place, but you wouldn't have left things alone."

"No. I wouldn't have." I held up a hand and hastily built a sound screen, wrapping it around us. It wouldn't do much to dissuade anyone with magical skills, but it should be plenty to shield our conversation from the police—if they were even still out there. I'd check on them later.

Maybe they didn't have to be on the other side of the door to listen in on us. I had no idea how the surveillance devices worked.

Ariana took a step nearer to me, and then one more. I tightened the shielding, made the weave smaller still. Conan slithered between us, slicing through my casting and sealing it behind him. He looked at me expectantly, ears pricked forward.

"I'll keep this as short as possible," I said. "Your club is full of magic-wielders who don't like us much."

"Tell me something I don't know. No other Vampires, huh?" The creases cutting through her forehead deepened.

"Nary a one. Whoever organized this tête a tête didn't include us." I stopped for a moment, thinking. "Are there truly no other Vampires in the vicinity?"

"Not here in the Pacific Northwest, but there are a few scattered through Nevada and California. From what I can tell, most of those here, the non-human ones, aren't local, either. Bottom line: we weren't invited."

"So why choose a business owned by a Vampire if they want to exclude us?"

"Maybe it's not so simple," Conan suggested.

"What do you mean?" Ariana's question held jagged edges, hinting she was hanging onto her temper by a thread. It heartened me. Anger is our go-to place. It fits us far better than defeat.

"Could be you're the test case," Conan went on. "They want to see how things go with you before kicking the door open."

I snarled; my fangs dropped. "They can take their titrated charity and shove it up their asses."

"Yeah. Not like we need them. Or their favors," Ariana chimed in. "I wanted to clear all of them out. I might still do that, but I promised Percy I'd at least listen. For a while." She shook her head. "By the time we close, Christa should be back from her scrying session. Cerys will show up here too, along with a few other Witches from a companion effort at their guild house."

"Any particular reason they're looking into the future tonight?" I asked.

Ariana nodded. "The moon phase is auspicious, and we all feel something is off."

"Mmph. I felt it too, whatever 'it' is, but chalked it up to the divergent magics swirling around."

"Runs deeper than that." Ariana set her mouth in a tight line. "It's why Ruby and Dee look as if their closest friend just died. Christa cast her stones, or read tea leaves, or however she does her gig. What she came up with was disturbing enough, she took it to the guild master, who set a phalanx of seers to work analyzing her prophecy."

"Knowledge is never a bad thing," Conan said.

Ariana stared at him. "Whose side are you on?"

"Ours."

"Does that mean any port in a storm so long as we throw the war gates wide open?"

Conan woofed a couple of times. I took it to mean yes.

"I was asking myself earlier why I was so opposed to a full-scale conflict," Ariana said softly. Her gaze skittered away from mine, and she dropped a hand into Conan's neck ruff.

"Did you arrive at any conclusions?" I prodded, taking care not to point out her attitude was antithetical to the core of what makes us Vampires. Beyond feeding and fucking, we live for a healthy scrap. Preferably one with lots of flowing jugulars.

She blew out an unnecessary breath and fastened her gaze on me again, clearly in the grip of an internal struggle. I wanted to hold her, smooth away her uncertain edges, soothe her distress. But those were human needs. Hers and mine. I hadn't done much soothing as a Vampire. The only comfort we needed was a good, quick fuck and plentiful blood.

"I can't back this up with reasons," she said, "but every instinct I have tells me throwing down the gauntlet and announcing a full-scale war is the wrong move. We'll win for a while, but eventually their sheer numbers will drive us underground. And it won't be like it was in the 1800s where we had to be invisible, but when we did surface to feed, no one had the wherewithal to track us.

"Now they do. Eventually, electronics will force us off-world. I don't know about you, but I'm not keen on waiting out my immortality in a garden spot like Gamma Four."

"We didn't actually see very much of it," I murmured in an attempt to lighten her bleak mood.

"Enough to convince me I don't want to return," she said and shut her eyes for a moment. "I want to know why they"—she swung an arm to the side—"chose my bar. Hell, they could have rented a meeting room in a hotel. It would have been just as private."

It wasn't the kind of puzzle we were likely to solve. Neither of us knew enough. I turned my attention to Conan. "What exactly do the Guardians do? And where are they based?"

He shook himself, dislodging Ariana's hand. "Our magic was first, gifted from the gods. Over time, our roles have shifted and altered. During long spans of time, we have done nothing, kept to ourselves."

"But what do your kin do now?" I pressed for

clarification. "Beyond watching over the ley-lines in the realms of the dead."

Conan pinned his ears back. "If they'd actually been doing that, those black mages never would have been able to shape the lines into a portal, now would they?"

"Good point." Ariana clacked her teeth together.

"There is much dissention within their ranks," Conan said.

"Not about you, there isn't," Ariana muttered. "They want you back."

"Only because they consider me theirs, not because they need me for anything," Conan retorted.

It was my fault, since I'd posed the questions, but we were moving away from the reason I'd wanted to talk with Ariana in the first place. While I was curious about the guardians, their internal machinations over who was responsible for what weren't the issue here.

"We need a plan for later," I cut Ariana off. She'd been telling Conan he was right to stand his ground.

She turned her hands palms up. "What kind of plan?"

"First off. Do you suppose Riteway and Hernandez are still out there?" I jerked a thumb toward the outside wall.

"Easy enough to check," Conan said. Power smelling of fur and wet rocks sheeted from him before he said. "The answer is yes." He bared his fangs. "Want me to fix it?"

"Don't tempt me." Ariana made a face. "Aw shit. I invited them to stop in for a drink when we were near closing time."

"No reason to retract it," I said. "Could be an opportunity to educate those sorry jokers."

"Before we kill them." Conan sounded positively gleeful.

"We are not going to kill them," Ariana said sternly. "Turn them into vegetables, sure, but killing cops will bring the wrath of Hell down on *Ascent*."

"How will anyone know where they were?" Conan asked.

"Because they will have checked in with cop-central," Ariana told him. "It's not as simple as purging the digital records in their car."

Time was passing. We still lacked anything as cohesive as a plan. "What would the deciding factor be?" I spoke up.

"About what?" Ariana crooked her brows into question marks. They formed dark wings against her fair skin.

"Working with the bunch who selected *Ascent* as a meeting spot? Or telling them to fuck themselves."

"Depends what they have to say, I guess."

I shook my head. "You have to snatch the upper hand. Right away. Demand explanations. This is your nightclub. They invaded your territory."

"Agreed." Conan punctuated the word with a growl.

"I can do that. Bitch-on-Wheels could be my second name." Ariana smiled. It heightened her unholy beauty—and my desire to crush her into a hot embrace and never let go. Lust prickled through me, and my errant member started to thicken.

"Speaking of upper hands"—Ariana's words dragged me out of fantasies of her body smashed against mine— "I don't like the idea of waiting around for the detectives to mosey into the bar. Let's take a little field trip."

"All of us?" Conan tilted his head.

"Sure. Why not," she told him.

"Where are we going?" I asked.

"Percy moved my car to a parking lot a couple of blocks away. We're going to retrieve it. Once we're inside, we're going to go for a little drive. Diamonds to donuts, they follow us."

Conan barked excitedly. "And then we'll stop. Get out of the car, and take them out."

Ariana laughed. "Love your enthusiasm, bud, but nope."

I snapped my fingers. "How about this? We'll spin a magical facsimile of your car. One they'll waste hours following before they give up. By then, the club will have closed, and we'll have some idea how the crowd is going to react to your ultimatums."

"I like it," Ariana said. "It's simple, elegant, and gets the job done."

Warmed by her compliment, I reeled in my casting, the one cloaking us in silence. Ariana draped a leather bag over one shoulder and led the way out the back door, locking it once we were all through. Sure enough, the black car blocked the alley. We marched right by it. Ariana waved jauntily, so I did the same.

Neither man acknowledged our presence. Just as well. My pleasantness quotient got used up when I waved and smiled. It felt good to be outside in the dark, walking. Night is my time; I welcomed its possibilities.

Ariana's vehicle sat near the front of a vast parking lot. Mostly empty, it was lit by obnoxious bulbs that cast everything in a garish overly white glow. "Is there some reason everything is so bright?" I asked.

"Yup." Ariana withdrew something from her pocket. The car chirped, and its lights flashed. "To dissuade thieves from breaking into cars while their owners are inside shopping. This particular store is open twenty-four hours. Nights are prime time for robbers."

The part about burglars preferring nighttime has always been true, but no one wasted wax or oil holding the night at bay a hundred years ago. Electricity was just becoming popular, but it was expensive and a luxury item. I refocused my wandering mind and got into the car. Conan jumped into the back, and Ariana drove away.

"Ha! They're hot on our trail. Can you handle the spell?" she asked me.

"Absolutely."

"I'll help," Conan said.

"How'd you know they'd follow us?" I asked as I shaped magic to create an illusion.

"Lucky guess. They've been way too interested in me. This should at least slow them down."

"For tonight." Conan snarled, partially obscuring his words.

I put the finishing touches on the duplicate image I'd just made of Ariana's car. "There. I'm done," I said.

"Did you make sure to match up the license plate?" she asked.

What was it with name tags for everything? That was one aspect of the current world I could do without. "No. Missed it. The rectangular piece of metal with numbers and letters on the back. Right?"

"And the front." She flashed me a full-fang grin and then recited a few letters followed by four numbers.

I added it to my illusion. "Done now," I announced. "When I release the spell, you'll drive right out from beneath it."

Conan's power slotted with mine. He was used to working with Ariana, so his assist was seamless. Together, we cloaked the real car until we were a few blocks away from the club. Ariana drove through a back street. I let go of the last of my casting, and we rolled to a stop in front of the club, taking a space with "No Parking" on a sign above it.

"One problem down." She got out of the car. I did too. Conan jumped into the front seat and out my open door.

I'd rather have done away with the swaggering detectives, but her way was probably better. Loud music pounded my ears as we walked inside the club. Percy looked from one to the other of us. "Didn't know you'd left."

"Brought the car back." Ariana glanced at a clock mounted above the bar. I did too. Only about half an hour until closing. I'd done all I could.

Clive dashed to where I stood, a drink tray balanced on an upturned hand. Before words spilled from him, predictable words to alert me we were surrounded by enemy magic wielders, I said, "How about if you deliver those drinks, and then we can talk."

"Sure, mate. Been looking all over for you." Clive hustled toward the center of the bar and offloaded the contents of his tray onto a table with six Sidhe seated at it.

I intercepted him and drew him off to one side. "I know who's here," I told him.

"What's Ariana going to do about it?" he sputtered. "Christ! A Sidhe refused a drink from me. As if I'd contaminated it or something. The others at his table settled him down. Good thing. I was ready to punch him."

Leaning very close to Clive's ear, I covered a lot of territory in very few words. Basically, I let him know we were Ariana's backup. She was going to come out swinging, and we'd be there to enforce her wishes if it came to that."

He smiled, and I caught the glint of the tips of his fangs. "While I fancy kicking some mortal ass, I don't want to work with these bastards any more than they want to work with me."

"We settled this problem once," I reminded him. "When we were in that off-world haven the local Sorcerers keep."

"Aye, but this batch wasn't part of it."

I smothered a grin. The modern terminology was they hadn't gotten the memo, but it wasn't important. "My point," I went on, "is if one group of mages can agree to set their differences aside for a common goal, perhaps another can as well."

"Not looking that way," Clive mumbled.

Percy's ten-minute warning rang out. We were about to discover which way the winds would blow. I had a feeling this would be all over but the mop-up in very little time at all.

And then I could get back to worming my way deeper into Ariana's affections. My cock hadn't totally deflated, but when it threatened to make a full commitment to lust mode, I did my damnedest to quiet it. I needed all my attention on the room, so I'd be ready to spring into action at the first breath of trouble.

CHAPTER TEN, ARIANA

Nick's advice—Conan's too—had been to start at Mach 10. I could do that. It was probably a more viable strategy than my original one, which had been to hang back listening.

Still puzzling over why they'd picked my bar, I got stuck on a line from an old movie, *Casablanca*. It had been playing through my mind for hours, and I could picture Humphrey Bogart saying something like, "Out of all the gin joints in all the towns in all the world, she walks into mine."

Same damned way I felt about the motley collection of supernaturals littering *Ascent*. Ballsy of them to commandeer my club for a scheme I heartily disapproved of.

Percy was shooing the mortals out. Not too many of them were left. Something about the mystical energy floating through the club had chased them away. I waited until I heard the *thunk* of the drop bar and leapt on top of a table right in front of the bar, fangs on full display.

No reason to hide what I was.

Not with this crowd.

"Let me be very clear." I projected my voice. "I did not invite you, and I resent the hell out of you choosing my bar for your war council. I did all of you a favor an hour ago. I lured the paranormal task force cops well away from this location. They've pretty much taken up residence in my alley. So far, they're not certain what I am, but they haven't given up searching for something they can use to hang me out to dry."

I paused for emphasis, not bothering to draw a phony breath. Who cared if these fuckers were comfortable with me or not? "You have ten minutes. Fifteen tops. Why are you here? What are you hoping for? And why in the fuck did you pick my club? Agree on a spokesperson. If you talk over each other, all it will do is waste time."

I glanced at Nick and Clive out of the corners of my eyes. Good. They had my back. Conan jumped to the table next to me and bared his fangs as he eyed the crowd of maybe a hundred assorted mages.

I'm decent at reading body language. It's kept me fed all these years. Surprise rippled through the assemblage. They hadn't anticipated I'd grab the point. Next time Nick and I talked, I'd have to thank him for a needed boot in the ass.

Various magics flickered and flared as telepathic conversations unfolded.

After a while, I said, "You're down to ten minutes. I suggest you get a move on. I was generous. I gave you fifteen."

"What happens after that?" a Sidhe called from the far side of the room. He'd dropped his glamour, and white hair cascaded to midback. I couldn't see his lower body, but his torso was covered by a beat-up leather jacket.

"I ask nicely for you to leave my club. If you fail to comply, I'll back it up."

"Pfft." He rolled silver eyes. "You're outnumbered."

Conan choose that moment to shift to a lion, then a hyena, then an enormous raven. In less than a minute, he was back in his usual form.

"You only think I'm outnumbered," I pointed out.

The Sidhe was on his feet. Medium height with red-brown wings, he closed the distance to Conan, power sparking from him. "What are you?"

"I don't answer to you," Conan replied.

A Witch with cropped gray hair and dark eyes stood. Short and so thin the bones in her face stood out, she extended a hand, palm outward. "Forgive us," she began. "We have been unspeakably rude. We had no idea our visit would come as a surprise to you. We sent emissaries. They said you were in agreement with hosting us."

I know a lie when I hear it, and she was telling the truth. My eyebrows shot up. "Really? How long ago, and who did they talk with?"

"You're bungling things, as usual," a bald Shifter not much taller than the Witch got up and sprang lightly forward, covering about half the distance to where I stood with my hands extended, ready to rain ruin down on everyone in my bar.

"I was the emissary," he went on. "And I spoke with a middle-aged fellow. Short gray hair. Brown eyes. Spiffy clothes. I explained what we were up to, and he assured me there'd be no problem with us congregating here." Looking pleased with himself, he dusted his hands together before adding, "The only mystery is why you're so put out. Why having us here is quite the honor, and—"

Conan barked long and loud, cutting him off before he could launch into how I, a lowly Vampire, should be delighted so many august mages deigned to enter my humble abode.

I shushed Conan, and Ruby stepped from behind the bar. "You stupid twit," she shouted at the Shifter. "You talked with a cop. A cop, for chrissakes. And not just any cop. One of what passes for a paranormal task force here."

"I did not," the Shifter sputtered. For a moment, an outline of the raven he turned into shimmered around him.

"Yeah. You did," I reinforced Ruby's message. "At least it explains why he and Hernandez have been sticking to me like glue." Anger surged, simmering at a boiling point. "You've fucked me and fucked me good. Once the detectives surface from the wild goose chase I led them on, I fully expect you to pretend to be a hopeless drunk, one who hallucinates. Maybe if they chuck you in the drunk tank for twenty-four hours, believing you will turn into a harder act to follow."

"I'll do no such thing." The Shifter narrowed his eyes.

"Fine. Then you come up with something that will neutralize whatever you told them."

"Killing them is simpler," someone I couldn't see shouted from the back of the club.

"And pointless and short-sighted," I shot back. "If you think they didn't dutifully report everything numbnuts here spouted, you're mistaken. Everything is digitized. And backed up. It's impossible to erase shit like that." Since I was on a roll, I kept talking. "I am not in favor of a balls-out war. It's stupid and ill-conceived. We have to come up with something subtle and ingenious that serves our purposes and doesn't end with large numbers of us imprisoned forever."

Before we left the topic of the bird shifter who could well spell my ruin, I turned back to him. "Fix this. Fix it first thing tomorrow morning."

"But I verified his identity," he sputtered. "The guy you think is a cop wasn't human."

My mouth might have fallen open, but I recovered quick. "What was he?"

The Shifter shrugged. "I wasn't certain, but he registered as one of us. And I did check. I'm not that irresponsible."

Dee emerged from behind the bar. "It was a charm," she hissed. "Similar to the one that false cop from the other dimension had when he showed up here a few nights ago demanding you admit to being a Vampire. Except this one was designed to hide the detective's humanity."

"Oberon's balls. I'm sorry." The Shifter turned bright red. "I'll figure something out. I'll adopt a hangdog look and tell them the whole thing was a joke, that I'd done it on a dare to fuck with you. Eh, maybe I can say you jilted me or something. Give it a personal vendetta touch."

"What exactly did you say to him?" I probed for details.

He narrowed chocolate-brown eyes. "I've been trying to reconstruct the conversation. People were walking by, so I made a good-faith effort to be discreet. It was midmorning. I asked if he worked here. It was a logical question since he was standing right outside your back door. When he said he did, I asked if it would be all right if we had a meeting at the club two nights hence.

"He asked what kind. I gave him the old nod-nod, wink-wink and called it even. When he asked how many would show up, I said not more than a hundred representing all the guilds." The Shifter screwed his face into a grimace. "Might not have been so bad if I'd stopped there, but when he asked which guilds, I blithely listed them. He smiled, reassured me it would be fine, and I left."

"Any reason you didn't ask if I was available?" I spun one hand in a come-along gesture.

His face grew redder still. "I, erm, figured you'd be in your coffin. Or something."

"We do not sleep in coffins."

Fuck.

Side conversations had bloomed all around me. "Shut up!" I shouted. Maybe because I was still standing on a table, the crowd obeyed me.

"It appears the paranormal task force has informers within our ranks," I said. "Dark magic practitioners who are more than willing to trade talismans for money or perks or get-out-of-prison-free cards."

"They might not all be dark magic wielders," Nick called from his vantage point not far from the front door.

"Moldering in an iron-lined cell for months, watching your magic wither and die, can be quite the incentive."

"Damn it. That's even worse," I snarled. Before everyone started talking again, I took advantage of the relative silence to pound home my point. "This is why war won't work in our favor. Not an overt, in-your-face one." I held up one finger. "First off, some of our enemies are internal."

My second finger was accompanied by a meaningful glance around the room. "This is a hastily patched-together alliance. Admit it. Until very recently, every group represented here hated each other. And Vampires. We're at the tippy-top of everyone's hate list." I was still pissed about the Shifter's coffin comment, but I let it be. We had bigger problems than misconceptions about Vampires.

"I've been alive for a long time," I went on, "and wars waged by reluctant collaborators rarely do well."

"We have to do something," the too-thin Witch said. Her tone suggested an inner strength not apparent from looking at her. "My coven has lost half its members. They've all disappeared. One day, they don't come home, and they're gone without a trace. I've cast seeking spells, crafted charms. None of it does any good."

"Our guild has been decimated too," a Sidhe concurred. Blonde, she had cherry-colored wings and a cherubic face. Sans glamour, she appeared about fifteen. After striding across the room, high-heeled black boots clicking on the wooden floor, she hugged the Witch.

A flash of power spun my head around in time to see a portal form. Christa tumbled through along with three other Fae I didn't know. Two men. One woman. She stopped dead and stared at the mix of mages. "What the hell?" she sputtered.

"Didn't want to bother you while you were working," Ruby told her.

"But this mirrors our scrying," one of the newly arrived male Fae said. He tried for a level tone, but he sounded unnerved. Silver wings were folded across his back. Burlier than most Fae, he might have been six feet tall with ice-blond hair and Christa's white eyes. Blind to Earth sights, he found his way by reading psychic emanations.

I've never been big on portents; all that hand-wringing goes against the grain. Before I could herd the group in a direction that made sense to me, Ruby asked, "What did you see, Hal?"

"This." The blond Fae swept an arm wide. "Mages from all the disciplines in the same place." He slitted his eyes. "You're plotting war. All the signs point that way. Don't bother to deny it."

"Why would we?" a Witch asked.

"Because the runestones suggested as much. Stubborn mages spawning destruction. All at cross purposes and lying through their teeth. We saw darkness, unending darkness and the death of all magic," Hal intoned.

It was as solid an entry as I was likely to get. "There will not be a war. Not the way you're envisioning it, which is slash and burn and mow down every human who crosses your path."

"You can't stop us," the same Sidhe who'd told me I was outnumbered announced.

"You're right, I can't. But I'm hoping you'll listen to

reason. Vampires have an ace up our sleeves. We can go into stasis for long periods of time. If things get unpleasant for those with power, we'll check out and resurface in a hundred years. Or two hundred. Or five hundred."

The din in the bar was growing. Nick joined Conan and me on the table, which groaned alarmingly. Good thing I'd put out big bucks for sturdy furniture. "Mind if I say something?" he asked me.

"Go ahead. I'm fresh out of ideas and damned close to booting the lot of them out of here."

Conan howled—eerie, mournful, it brought everyone to heel. Nick jumped into the slice of silence. "An overt war is a last resort. Since you're all here, and have presumably buried your differences—or at least glossed over them—how about selecting two delegates from each guild house?"

"Does that mean four Fae?" Ruby asked. "Since we have at least two Fae guild houses represented here?"

"If you want it to," Nick said smoothly.

I had to hand it to him. He had more patience than I did. I'd have cut it at two delegates from each discipline and let the mages duke it out for who'd represent them.

"Once you've chosen representatives," Nick went on, "set up a meeting schedule. Ariana believes we can develop something subtle that trips mortals up and forces them to back off."

I thought of something and spoke up. "Before you decide, I have two questions. I understand full well you believed you'd cleared *Ascent* as a meeting place, but why did you select my club? Second question is why are no other Vampires represented in your ranks?"

"Good points," Nick said softly.

I waited. Their response would dictate if I was part of their think-tank or if Vampires—and presumably guardians—would sit this one out. On the one hand, sitting things out was fine with me. Vampires have never been team players. On the other hand, we have control issues. The specter of someone else dictating my fortunes and me not having a say in the outcome rankled.

The Witch who'd offered up the apology squared her thin shoulders. "As you may have inferred, we come from many locales. Guild houses from California to Nevada to Canada traveled here. The Seattle area was reasonably centrally located. Nevada might have worked if we'd stuck to the uninhabited regions. Scanners that test for magic are being installed on every major highway."

"What?" the word burst from me. I'd expected something like that, but not until years in the future.

The Witch gave a curt nod in my direction. "The developers of the technology have tried to keep it secret, which is why you don't know about it. Nevada was a perfect crucible. Not many cities. Few major highways. The pilot's been underway for maybe six months now."

"Why didn't someone say something?" Conan asked.

"We've had our hands full mapping out routes that are still safe," the Witch replied and shook her head sadly. "Those from my guild house who are here with me understood full well this was a one-way trip. We will have to rely on the goodwill of the local guild to take us in."

"No worries on that front," Dee called out. "You're most welcome. We have plenty of space."

"What about the other Witches?" I asked, surprised I'd be concerned about a batch of mages I'd never met. Ones who'd dislike me on sight because of what I was.

"Only five remained behind. They were waiting until I let them know we were well and truly away, and then they were going to attempt to follow our same route out of Las Vegas."

"Are they coming here?" Nick asked.

She shook her head. "Arizona, but it doesn't matter. The rollout of the magic scanner is nearly complete. I've been hacking into their computer network for months; it's the only reason I know anything. The plan is to market it to every state and the federal government. The machines take a while to build, and they're expensive to maintain, but once they're in place throughout the country, nowhere will be safe for us."

She stopped long enough to blow out a noisy breath. "We selected *Ascent* because we assumed any establishment owned and operated by a Vampire had built-in safeguards."

"And my second question?" I folded my arms beneath my breasts. My only safeguards to date had been making nice with mortals by pretending to be one of them. And keeping a very low profile.

I'll hand it to the Witch, she looked me right in the eye and said, "You're different from the rest of us."

"We are," I agreed. "We're made, not born."

"This next is our own fault," she went on. "None of us know anything about you. Like the Shifter who offended you with his coffin comment. Because you're an unknown quantity, we agreed it would be wise to start with one of you to assess if you'd even want to work with the rest of us."

"We were surprised to find three Vampires," a Shifter said, "plus whatever he is." He pointed at Conan.

"Vampire champion," Conan spoke more clearly than he usually did, perhaps so there'd be no mistaking his meaning. And then he jumped off the table and ran to Christa, who buried her hands in his neck ruff.

"What did your future seeking reveal?" he asked her.

I wanted to know too. I considered walking over to her, but I wasn't quite ready to cede my power position where I looked down on the crowd.

Christa drew her dark brows into a thin line, creating two vertical furrows between them. Usually, the goth garb she favored looked jaunty, but tonight it hung on her tall, thin frame. Even her silver wings dappled with jewel tones drooped.

It took her a long time to respond. Maybe she was searching for a better spin on the impossible. Finally, she said, "It's a damned-if-we-do damned-if-we-don't proposition."

I waited, certain she had more to add. She didn't disappoint me. "While we didn't come up with anything as concrete as the scanners the Witch alluded to, what we did see was darkness spreading everywhere, eating up everything magical in its path."

"We altered our casting, again and again," Hal tossed out. "Hoping we'd made a mistake and different images would emerge."

"Except no matter what we did, the situation only grew

worse," Christa said. She stopped petting Conan and turned so she faced the room more fully, hands clasped behind her back. Her milky eyes were pinched at their corners. "At the point we gave up, not much was left."

"Do you mean to say all of us were dead?" a Sidhe asked.

"Dead or gone to ground or imprisoned, but sure and 'tis far worse than that." The Irish brogue that added a lilt to Christa's speech when she was upset was out in full bloom. "Magic is an integral part of the warp and weft of all life on this world. If we die out, the mortals will not be far behind."

Conan woofed. If I read him right, he'd known that little tidbit. I hadn't, and it surprised me.

"There's our angle," I said loud enough for my voice to carry.

"They'll never believe us," Christa said dolefully.

"Are there source materials?" I pressed for details, hoping for ancient tomes we could offer up as proof.

"Sure," Ruby said. "But like anything written a millennium ago, they're open to interpretation."

"'And mired in mysticism," Christa added. "Not something most mortals have bothered with for at least a century."

Ruby reached behind the bar, grabbed a bottle of something, and took a deep swig from it. I didn't blame her. This was one of the few times I wished liquor affected me. It doesn't. I enjoy its taste, but Vampires don't get drunk. Except on blood.

She set the bottle down on the bar and said, "Well, that's a pisser. Clerics might believe the lore, but they view us as anathema. Getting close enough to convince one to listen would be a neat trick."

"Wouldn't matter, even if they did believe us." Percy jumped into the conversation. "Mortals have no faith in them, and they don't shape policies—or laws."

It was time to abandon my post. The group was talking about alternatives. My job might not be done, not by a long shot, but I'd accomplished my first task.

Nick hooked a hand beneath my arm. "Nicely done," he said softly.

"Eh, we barely scratched the surface." My current top-of-the-heap concern was the two detectives. They were parleying with mages, using charms they had no business employing, and were out for my blood.

Nick spun me to face him. Having him this close would have stolen my breath—if I'd had any to steal. The press of his palms against my upper arms felt delicious; I leaned toward him. My nipples formed peaks, and pheromones must have been spilling from me.

Alarm bells tolled, but quenching my arousal on command was about as likely to happen as stuffing feathers back into a ruptured pillow.

Nick skewered me with his gorgeous eyes. "You're amazing, but we have to do something about those two detectives, and night is slipping away."

Interesting he'd come to the same conclusion I had, but that didn't make it a smart move. "Nah. If we end them, it will just make more problems."

"Maybe not. Didn't you tell me mortals aren't supposed to have any dealings with us?"

I nodded. I had, indeed, said as much.

"So, maybe, their transaction with whomever gave them the charm to make them appear immortal isn't written down anywhere. In those electronic records you're always referring to. We can make certain whoever finds their car also finds evidence of their wrongdoing."

I rolled the idea around but couldn't find anything amiss with it. "You might be right," I mumbled. Hope flared, along with a crushing need to do away with those bastards once and for all. We could feed them to the same cougar pack who'd deal with the last humans I wanted out of the way. After we relieved them of their blood.

"We know where to find them," Nick went on. "They're still chasing my illusion. We can trade it for your real car and lead them to an out-of-the-way spot."

If my fangs hadn't already been out, they'd have dropped in anticipation. A hunt. With human bait. Life didn't get any sweeter. "Hang on a moment," I told Nick, "and then we'll leave."

I located the Shifter who'd been duped and quietly told him I'd be taking care of the problem. He trained his brown eyes on me and said, "I want in."

"Thanks, but we have it handled." I winked. "Vampire style."

He chuckled. "I like you. I didn't think I would, but I do."

I patted his arm and trotted to Ruby. "Nick and I are leaving to do a bit of cleanup work. Make sure everyone's out of here before dawn."

"Will do." Ruby dipped her chin my way. "I'll also fill you in on whatever they decide about their next steps."

"Perfect. Thanks."

Nick was already at the front door. Conan stood next to him. "Couldn't keep you away if I tried, huh?" I said to the wolf.

He snorted what might have been lupine laughter, and the three of us hoofed it into the night.

CHAPTER ELEVEN, NICKOLAS

My fingertips still tingled from where I'd touched Ariana. I'd have to be careful. There'd come a time when I'd toss restraint to the winds and kiss her. Once I did that, I wasn't at all certain I'd be able to stop. She wanted me. The tang of her arousal had been sharp and sweet in my nose. Yet something still stood between us. Maybe I'd come out and ask about her reservations.

Maybe I wouldn't.

My relationship with her was complex, delicate. I felt her move toward me, check herself, and bounce back out of reach. Almost as if she was in love with someone else. Except Vampires didn't fall in love. In lust, maybe, but not in love.

If that was true, though, the love part, what was happening to me? I hadn't yearned for a woman the way I longed for Ariana since I'd been turned. And that had happened so long ago, I was surprised I could still remember what it felt like to be mortal.

Had she caught me in a weak moment as I emerged from stasis?

Maybe so.

Still, it made no sense that a hundred years of waiting out the clock would have altered the bones of who I was. Once we were in the car, I hunted for my spell. It hadn't moved too far from where we'd left the detectives driving in large circles through a residential neighborhood a few miles away.

"I'm surprised they haven't given up," I muttered.

"Me too," Ariana concurred. "They have reason to suspect the mother lode is at *Ascent*. I'd think they'd want to be there rather than tailing me."

"That's my doing," Conan woofed from behind the seats.

"Planted a few seeds?" Ariana glanced over the divider at the wolf.

"More than a few, but I timed my intervention to play out around dawn."

"What, exactly, did you do?" I asked Conan.

"A little of this, a little of that. I effectively blinded them to everything except tracking Ariana. If I hadn't, eventually it would have sunk in something wasn't right, and they'd have shown up at *Ascent*, furious at being duped."

"That would have happened anyway," Ariana said.

"Indeed, but by then, the club would have been long since empty," Conan replied.

"You'll tell the other guardians about tonight's various events. Right?" I asked him.

"Most of it."

"But you made a point of making sure they came to the

last all-mage meeting. The one hosted by the Sorcerers," I reminded the wolf.

He woofed again but didn't offer clues regarding his rationale.

Ariana pulled over to the curb, and we waited for a couple of minutes. Sure enough, the black car whizzed past, following something only the detectives could see. I linked to my illusion and primed myself to dismantle the magic holding it together. "Get ready," I told Ariana.

"Tell me when to hit it," she said.

Some of her terms weren't familiar, but it was simple enough to figure out what she meant. "Three. Two. One. Now," I said.

The car rocketed forward. For maybe half a second, there were two vehicles, but the intrepid detectives didn't miss a beat. As soon as she was certain they'd made the transition, Ariana guided the car to a roadway where she could drive faster. "How are you doing releasing their minds?" she asked Conan.

"It's done. They're thinking again," the wolf responded.

"I'm going to pull off in maybe five miles," Ariana said, "and take to the back roads. If I go too far, they might run out of fuel. They've been driving for hours. This is one time I don't give a fuck about fair. We mesmerize them, drain them, and feed them to the cougars. They may be stupid bastards, but I'll give you better-than-even odds their guns are loaded with silver-laced bullets. We do not want to give them a chance to fire at us."

"What about me?" Conan asked.

"You can eat your fill, and then the cougars get them,"

Ariana said and smiled indulgently. "We'll have to get rid of their car, which won't be easy. All those bloody cop cars have tracking devices. If we remove the damned thing, the car will go dark down at cop central, which is bound to alarm someone."

"Can't we drive it far away, leave it, and teleport back?" I asked.

"I'm not sure. It could have cameras inside. We won't know until we look at it."

Saliva pooled beneath my tongue. First things first. Anticipation of human blood was heady, intoxicating. The car swung around, tires skidding as gravel splattered the sides. Ariana didn't even bother to shut off the engine before leaping from the car. I joined her, moving far quicker than anyone who was merely human could have followed me.

Supernatural strength and speed come in handy.

I reached deep, pumping out magic designed to stop the detectives in their tracks. Their shiny black car slewed to a halt. It didn't seem as maneuverable as Ariana's. Sure enough, both doors flew open; Riteway and Hernandez barreled out.

"You're under arrest," Hernandez barked. "For evading peace officers." His weapon, a large bore handgun, was trained on me. Riteway's revolver was pointed right at Ariana.

I used a variation of the same hypnotic spell I'd levied at a different detective, one named Bryce, in the alleyway behind *Ascent*. Then it had worked perfectly. So well, Bryce-baby had walked toward me, neck angled to provide stellar access for my feeding preferences.

These two seemed impervious to the spell spilling from me and coating them with what should have been slam-dunk cooperation.

"Whatever are you talking about?" Ariana said. "Nick and I went out for a drive after the club closed. We were, erm, looking for a private spot because we couldn't wait until we got all the way home. I stopped the car, and there you were."

"Bullshit," Hernandez snapped, and took a few steps closer. "We've been tailing you for hours."

"Not possible," I said. "We've been at *Ascent* all evening. Many can attest to our presence at the club."

"Yup. If you don't trust us, check the surveillance cameras. My Toyota's been in front of the club for hours. Before that, it was in the Safeway lot." Vampiric persuasion shimmered around Ariana. She must be as flummoxed as me at their lack of response.

Where in the hell was Conan? I hadn't seen him since we jumped out of the car.

"You're coming with us." Riteway unclipped handcuffs from his belt.

"No. We're not," Ariana insisted. "We've done nothing wrong. This is America. You can't just run around arresting citizens for no cause."

"We'll sort the 'no cause' part out down at the station," Hernandez said. "Are we going to do this nicely?"

"We're not doing it at all," I said and judged the distance between him and me. I could take him down, but maybe not before he fired his weapon.

He narrowed his eyes and flashed a light in my direction.

"Aha. Knew it. Fangs. You're both Vampires, just like we were—"

Conan came out of nowhere, silent as a wraith and knocked Hernandez facedown in the dirt. His gun went off, but the bullet went wide, vanishing into the night. Taking a page out of the wolf's playbook, I sprinted behind Riteway and dealt him a deathblow to the base of the skull before he knew what hit him. His blood wouldn't be ruined. Not if I drained him right away.

His finger must have spasmed over the trigger because bullets sprayed wildly. I heard Ariana scream. Fury and pain punctuated her howls. I forgot all about feeding. Riteway was dead. Hernandez too. I covered the distance to Ariana in less time than it takes to tell about it.

She was still on her feet, but her face was contorted into a rictus of agony.

"Where is it?" I shouted. Time was critical. I had to get the bullet out of her before it did permanent damage.

"Shoulder," she ground out.

I sliced through her jacket with the knife I always carry; it fell to the ground. Before I got her shirt out of the way, Conan stood next to us, muzzle coated in blood. "What is it? Did that bastard shoot her?"

"Aye. Help me." I cut through the thick fabric of her top and saw an alarmingly large hole in front of her right shoulder. A quick check didn't reveal an exit wound. Meant the bullet was lodged in the bones and sinews. I sucked on the wound, hoping to dislodge the bullet. No dice. Silver residue burned my lips and mouth, but I didn't care. Ariana sagged against me; the silver was doing its insidious work. It's the only deadly poison that can bring us down. Iron is an irritant, but silver chomps through our magic.

Conan dug a claw into the wound. Ariana screamed but didn't fight him. I waited anxiously, willing him to succeed. I had my dirk in hand, ready to hack into her shoulder. Anything to get that bullet out.

I cursed the cops up one side and down the other.

Conan withdrew his claw. "Almost." The wolf was panting. "I touched it, but I fear I drove it in deeper." Power rained from him as he shifted forms to something that looked like a cross between a beetle and a spider. I understood and lifted him in front of the wound. Black-edged blisters were developing around the hole as tissue died.

Ariana had passed out. The only thing holding her upright was my arm around her back. I positioned my dirk, in case Conan's current form couldn't dislodge the bullet. Ariana moaned. I was glad she'd moved beyond where she could feel pain.

The edges of the raw, jagged opening pulsed alarmingly. With no warning or fanfare, the bullet shot through, followed by Conan. He was back to wolf form before it registered he'd succeeded.

"Good man," I said.

"Why isn't she better?" Conan demanded and pushed his snout against her side.

I was afraid to answer him. Almost as if saying the words would seal her fate. We'd been fast, but maybe not quick enough. Silver executed its insidious destruction on our bodies without regard to anyone's timetable.

Scooping her into my arms, I carried her to the corpse

that was still intact. "Flip him so his neck is easy to get to," I told Conan. As soon as he did, I bent and nicked a carotid. They're bigger than jugulars, and the guy was dead, so we didn't risk blood geysering all over everything.

To be on the safe side, in case whatever charm had made him impervious to our mesmerism, had also tainted him blood, I took a quick taste.

"That's for Ariana." Conan head butted me out of the way.

I met his unrelenting amber gaze and answered telepathically since my mouth was full of blood. *"Yes. But not if it's been poisoned in some way."*

The wolf glared at me as I rolled the blood around in my mouth, testing it and ready to spit it out if need be. "It's all right," I told the wolf and settled Ariana so her mouth rested above the torn vessel.

Conan nudged her gently. "Drink," he urged. "Grow strong."

She lay so still, I feared she might have passed over, but her body was still intact. If she'd died, it would have begun a hasty retreat to decomposition.

"Different approach," I told Conan. "Lie close and let me prop her against you."

Once she was settled, head lolling, I bent and took another mouthful of blood. Once I had it, I pried Ariana's jaws open with one hand and let the blood in my mouth flow into hers. She gagged. Some of it slopped out, but she swallowed too. Once, and then again.

I tried not to hope too hard.

Moving fast, I repeated my actions. On the fifth transfer,

her eyes flicked open. She batted me away and crawled to the corpse, fastening her mouth over the same spot I'd been feeding her from.

I sank onto my haunches next to the wolf, too overcome by relief to feed myself. I should. The other body still had blood in it. Conan had taken care to eat both lower legs, after bending them at an angle to keep the blood from pouring out of mangled vessels.

"We did it," I told Conan. "She'll recover, and damned fast."

"*Thank you,*" the wolf spoke into my mind.

"Thanks back," I told him. "We make a good team."

Ariana repositioned herself, coming to her knees to improve her angle of attack. It would be dawn soon. I'd see her home and then worry about disposing of the bodies. I had no idea what to do about the black car. Even if I knew how to drive, where would I take it? Ariana had said it had a tracking something-or-other built in or added on or some such thing.

"You should feed." Conan nudged me with his snout.

It was sound advice. This might be the last meal I saw for a while. Wasting it would be stupid. I'm quick and efficient. I drained what was left in the other detective in less than five minutes. Once I was done, I searched through his garments, hunting for whatever charm had made him impervious to my magic.

I knew I'd found it the second my fingertips brushed an inside pocket. They tingled and burned, but I drew the offending bit of hair and bloody bone out anyway, dropping it into the dirt to get a closer look. It stank of witchcraft.

"At least we know for certain who's been helping them," Conan said and growled.

I looked around for something I could wrap it in to quiet the noxious waves cascading from it, but didn't find any candidates so I propped it against a tree bole.

Ariana rolled to her feet, mouth and fangs streaked with blood. Nodding grimly, she looked from me to Conan. "You two saved me. Thank you."

For the first time, I noticed she was naked from the waist up. I'd been so frantic to save her life, I hadn't paid any attention to her breasts. How could I have been so unmoved at the sight? High and full and tipped with golden-brown nipples, they were lovely. Enticing. Alluring.

"Apologies about your wrecked clothing," I blurted as my cock shot to attention.

She smiled crookedly and glanced down, as if she was just now noticing her missing garments. "I forgive you. Extenuating circumstances and all that." Ariana made a quick trip to her car and retrieved a sweater that she pulled over her head. She also shut off the engine that had been idling all this time. After a quick glance skyward, she said, "We have to hurry. Dawn's not far off."

"I'll move the bodies," Conan said. "Somewhere no one will ever find them."

"Off world?" Ariana raised both dark brows.

Conan didn't bother with words. The ground beneath both detectives formed sinkholes, absorbing them. The wolf's brand of power turned the air a delicate blue. By the time the scents of fur and wet rocks subsided, Riteway and Hernandez were gone.

"Sorry you didn't get to eat more of them," I told Conan.

"I had enough. I can hunt later." He planted himself next to Ariana and nuzzled her side. She stroked his rough coat.

"Their car is a problem," she said.

I waited. This was one spot I was out of my depth. A crackling sounded from inside their car, followed by, "Report Three-Niner-Three." Whatever that meant.

"Fuck," Ariana muttered. "Means they know where the detectives are."

"We're running out of time." I pointed at the sky.

She nodded. "Desperate times require desperate solutions. I'm going to move my car a few miles from here and teleport back. Once I'm gone, get rid of my tire tracks as far back as where we turned onto this sideroad. Before I leave, though, I'll add a few incriminating notes to whatever they have in the way of digitized tablets in their car. Then I'll give it time for someone at the station to be sure to read my additions."

I started to tell her I'd do that, except I wouldn't have had the first idea how to access their electronic recordkeeping systems.

Ariana was in and out of the detective's car in short order. The Toyota's engine roared to life, and she took off through the woods. Conan and I traced its tracks, smoothing the dirt as we went. By the time we returned to the clearing, Ariana was back, arms outstretched, power glinting from her fingertips as she torched something inside the detectives' car.

I remembered the charm I'd lifted from the dead cop. It

was right where I'd left it, and I once again hunted for something to wrap around it that would mute its toxins.

Pops, crackles, and smoke rolled from the black car. For good measure, Conan sliced through tires with a claw. After a brisk swoosh, the collection of metal and glass sank lower to the ground.

"Done," Ariana said. "I destroyed everything electronic. It's bound to get someone's attention at the station, along with the incriminating notes about paying Witch informants and dicking around with Witch magic."

"I found out why they didn't react to our persuasion," I told her and pointed at the charm I'd left on the ground.

She stood over it, hands on hips. "Damn. We really should bring it back to the Witches so they can examine it for clues about who made it."

"I'll take it," Conan said. "It doesn't bother me." He snatched up the charm in his mouth.

"Good enough." Ariana turned in a circle, checking the area. When she stopped, she was facing me. "You're coming home with us."

I wasn't about to argue. Clive wouldn't worry about me. I'd explain things when I saw him tonight.

Before I could protest it was too much too soon and she should conserve her strength, Ariana wove power around us. She brought us out next to her car and then drove to her house. The sun had just crested the horizon when she pulled into a graveled area near her front porch. I opened my door, but she grabbed my arm. "Get out of your shoes right away. We left tracks all around the detectives' car. We can't wear these anymore."

"It's my only pair, but I can get more." After the day was done, I could. But by then, I'd be at *Ascent*, working and barefoot. Eh. I'd figure things out.

"Going hunting," Conan told us. *"I'll leave the charm with Dee."*

"Thank you again for saving my life," Ariana told the wolf and exited the car, standing right next to it.

I got out on the same side as her to minimize our footprints in the dirt.

Conan jumped out the open hatch, dropped the charm, and rose up, placing his paws on Ariana's shoulders. "We must survive, you and me. We are instrumental in what is to come."

"If you know something, tell me," Ariana closed her teeth, fangs still on full display, over her lower lip.

"If I knew more than that, I would. For now, believe in me. In us."

"I do," she said, her tone solemn.

He dropped easily to the ground and picked up the charm. Once he had it in his mouth, he turned and walked through a gateway that hadn't been there before. When it cleared, he was gone.

A place in my mind that had been shuttered popped open, perhaps jarred by the wolf's prediction. Memories of Christa telling me Ariana was a lynchpin surfaced. "The Fae think so too," I said.

"Think what?" She stood so close, her musky scent enveloped me, teasing and heady.

"That you're a key element in whatever is playing out."

Ariana snorted. "Shit. I feel like I just dropped onto a Ouija board. As a major player."

Even I recognized what that was: a metaphysical parlor game introduced in the late 1800s. A ray of sunlight jabbed my back; I jumped sideways.

"Shoes," Ariana urged.

I bent to unlace them, and she removed hers as well. Once they were off, she smoothed the dirt, but with a pine bough rather than magic. Dropping the branch, she surveyed her work. "Good enough," she said. "Come in. We need to generate a credible story about where we went after we left the club. And then you can fill me in on whatever Ruby told you."

"Christa," I corrected her.

Ariana rolled her blue eyes. "Crap. That's even worse. I've never assumed destiny had jack shit to do with anything. Vampires are a practical bunch. Maybe because we started out human. But I've never believed all that precognitive crapola."

I grinned.

"What's so funny?"

"Sometimes I need a dictionary to translate your phrases. What happens with the shoes? Can we maybe not wear them for a while?"

"Nope. We're going to either burn them or hide them in my basement."

It was growing uncomfortably bright as I followed her up the stairs and into her house. Unlike my last visit, I felt more at my ease, less desperate to ravish her. Desire swelled through me, sweet and hot and urgent, but we could talk first.

About anything she wanted.

Maybe I should wait until she was more rested before I filled my hands with her unbelievable breasts. She'd come within a hairsbreadth of dying, after all. Thoughts tumbling every which way, body on fire with lust, I shut the door behind me.

"Grab a seat," Ariana called over one shoulder. "I'll make us some tea."

"I can make the tea if you're still recovering," I offered.

"Nah. I'm maybe seventy percent," she said. "I'll catch a nap after we talk."

I settled on a plush, leather sofa in front of a fireplace with candles on the mantle. I'd barely noticed her house my last trip here, but it was comfortable. Furnished with ornate dark wooden furniture and loaded with bookshelves of every variety, it exuded a homey charm. One large room ran the length of the house. I remembered the bathroom at the far end where I'd showered. It and presumably a bedroom were closed off by doors.

My fangs were still out. I retracted them so they wouldn't chip the tea mug. A ringing phone brought my head snapping around. Ariana sprinted for her ruined jacket. She'd carried it into the house with her.

Her phone was joined by a second summons. It took me far longer than it should have to understand my phone was ringing too.

My shoulder still ached from where the bullet had lodged. I'd always wondered what it would feel like to die as a Vampire. Now I knew. It was an excruciating process where my body felt like it was being shredded from within. The pain had begun in my shoulder, but it hadn't remained there. In ridiculously short order, it had spread to every corner of my body until the ripping, tearing, hot-knives sensation grew unbearable. I'd checked out, but a corner of my mind stood off to one side watching. I'd heard Nick and Conan talking, seen Conan shift to insect form, and felt him go after the bullet with his scuttling legs and sharp pincers.

Humans can have easy deaths where they go to sleep and don't wake up. Apparently, there's no gentle way out for Vampires.

Naturally, Mistral rose to taunt me. Again. I felt like

screeching at his image in my head. Telling him his death had been quick, at least, and his suffering minimal.

Once the bullet was out, I expected everything to snap back into place. It didn't. I couldn't move, and I was still watching myself from a vantage point above the clearing with both cars and the two dead detectives. The look on Nick's face seared me. He cared about me, genuinely cared in a way that ran far deeper than the lust I'd felt spilling from him.

He looked at me with a tenderness I'd longed to see in Mistral's icy eyes, but never had. Mistral had loved my youth, my body, my enthusiasm for blood, but he'd never bothered to figure out who I was. At the end of the day, he was like most Vampires, out for number one.

When I wasn't able to feed—because I was still paralyzed from the silver residue—Nick transferred blood from the corpse and let it drip into my mouth. If I'd had control of my body, I'd have cried. He was so loving, so caring, so worried about me it touched my Undead soul to its roots.

He'd accused me of not being very Vampire-like. Well, neither was he. My excuse was my long tenure among mortals. Perhaps his was a hundred years in stasis. Regardless, neither of us would do well in a seethe or clan house without a drastic attitude adjustment.

Not that returning to a group-living situation with a phalanx of other Vampires was on the horizon. Depending on the outcome of the rest of last night's discussion after I'd left the club, I might float the argument we needed to include more Vampires before adopting a final strategy. We have different strengths than other mages.

Very different.

I'd always thought we'd be unstoppable if we teamed up with the rest of the magical world, but the prospect had seemed so remote, I'd never pushed the theory. Plus, once Conan and I relocated to the northwestern part of the States, there hadn't been enough Vampires to worry about. There still weren't, but I was fairly certain I could appeal to a few in California to join forces with us. Surely, they weren't thrilled with the status quo. We're hunters, not prey.

My thoughts ranged wide as I blew up the electronics in the cops' vehicle, teleported us back to my car, and drove home. Luckily, no one seemed interested in conversation. It would take me a while to fully recover. The sun was up—never a good thing—and I couldn't stop thinking about Nickolas.

The expression on his face after Conan asked why I wasn't getting better had been laced with anguish. He'd done everything he could and was frightened it wasn't enough. I recognized the problem because I've been there.

Helpless and Vampire are oxymorons. We pride ourselves on being on top. In control. Of everything. But the raw pain carved into Nick's high forehead and the squinched areas around his eyes said he was fresh out of ideas more clearly than any words would have.

The sun burned where it filtered through the windshield, and I was happy when I turned down the long, rutted road that ended at my house. It would have been simpler to teleport, but I didn't want my car anywhere near the ruins of the detectives' vehicle.

Someone would be deployed to hunt for them. That order had probably gone out the minute I'd spilled the beans about their alliance with Witches. If not then, surely when I'd decimated their electronic toys. Even though my body still hurt, and weariness racked me, it was better this way. We could wait out the day here and show up at *Ascent* around the usual time.

Having Nick so close was problematic, but I shoved my worries to a distant spot. Now that I knew how much he truly cared about me—hell, he'd put off feeding to make certain I got badly needed blood—keeping my distance would be much more difficult.

He was magnificent. I longed for him, craved him. When I'd realized I was half naked in that clearing, part of me had been proud to show off my breasts. I know how perfect they are. It's one of the perks of being a Vampire. Our beauty puts humans to shame. But a bigger part of me had been mortified. Naked led to touching. Touching led to fucking.

Restraint plays zero role in any Vampire's lexicon. We have no moral issues around sexuality. If we want someone, we go after them. If I'd gotten the memo—and absorbed it— Mistral's attraction to others wouldn't have ruffled my feathers. But that part of Vampirism passed me by. From the moment I laid eyes on Mistral when I was still mortal, I'd had one goal in life.

To make him mine.

One of my arguments against getting closer to Nickolas

had been he'd be just like Mistral. A player who'd consider me another notch on his metaphorical bedpost...

The sound of Nick's door opening snapped me out of my musings. I grabbed his arm, trying not to think about how good he felt beneath my fingertips, and told him to get rid of his shoes. I didn't see how any of us had left other physical evidence at the scene, but we'd sure as fuck left footprints. I'd sprawled on top of the cop I'd fed from, but his body would never be found.

Conan went hunting, and I suggested Nick hang out in my living room while I made tea. I was just pouring mead in the bottom of two mugs when my phone trilled. Normally, I ignore the damned thing, but I was worried something had happened at the club.

I retrieved the phone and tapped the display, grateful I'd gotten to it before the "private caller" hung up. "Yes?"

"Fuck me. You are there. Been trying to get hold of you for hours." Ruby's gravelly voice blasted me. I turned the volume down.

"Yeah. What's up?"

"You know better than to ask. I'll be there in a bit. Christa too. And maybe one of the Wit—er Dahlia or Dee."

"I'll be here. If you want snacks, bring them with you."

Ruby started to laugh. She was still laughing when the line went dead.

The sound of Nickolas's voice brought me around. He held his brand-new phone awkwardly. I crossed the space to the sofa and mouthed, "Who is it?"

"Clive. He's still at the club. Can I set this so both of us can hear him?"

Alarm hustled through me. I tapped the display, put the phone on speaker, and said, "Ariana here. Anything said over the cellular network can be hacked."

"Huh?" Clive's deep voice rumbled through the phone's audio system.

"Overheard," I clarified.

"Bloody good to know," he muttered. "How can I let Nick know what happened after all of you left, then?"

Since we'd have company soon anyway, I said, "You're welcome to join us here. Ruby's on her way. Maybe you could piggyback onto her—" I'd begun to say spell, but caught myself. "Erm, maybe you could catch a lift with her."

"I'll figure it out."

Since the conversation seemed to be over, I tapped the red circle while telling Nick, "This is how you end calls."

He set the phone on the coffee table in front of the sofa and circled my wrist with his fingers. "Is there an instruction book for that thing? I figured it had to be Clive since he's the only one who has the number—except for you."

"We'll see if there's a PDF we can download." Liquid heat shimmered through me, flowing from the spot where his fingertips brushed my wrist.

The corners of his generous, chiseled lips twitched. "I think I might have a vague understanding of download, but PDF is beyond me." Lifting his other hand, he stroked strands of hair away from my face. "You're so beautiful. I haven't been able to think about much else since the day I met you."

My heart gave a funny little double flip. Now was the time to smile pretty and finish making the tea. I tried, honestly I did, but my legs refused to obey me. Instead, I sank onto the couch next to him. "Was that why you came back to my club that next night after I chased you away?"

The twitching yielded to a soft smile. "It wasn't the reason I told myself, but yes, you were why I returned." He shrugged self-consciously. "I couldn't stay away."

His mini confession thrilled me. Every gate I'd erected to keep him at arm's length fell, and I laid a hand over the one he'd cupped around the side of my face. He leaned close, so close I'd have felt his breath on my skin—if we had a need to breathe. I still could have made good on my escape to the kitchen. He was moving slowly, taking his time, giving me choices.

Except my choice was him. Deep in my mind a voice was shrieking no. If I booted the gates wide open, sooner or later Nick would discover my secret about Mistral, and then I'd be doomed. I tried to care, to resurrect my barriers, but I failed miserably.

It's just a kiss, I argued with my inner maven.

Yeah, sure, bitch. Keep telling yourself that, it snarked back.

Nickolas snaked out his tongue and licked the seam between my lips. Need and heat and lust shot through me like high voltage electricity. Christ. I was pathetic. One swipe of his tongue, and I was lost. My nipples hardened beneath my sweater, and every drop of moisture in my body headed south, slicking my thighs with musky desire.

No hiding that scent. Not to another Vampire.

He settled his mouth on mine, slow, lazy, as if we had all the time in the world. Except we didn't. He'd heard me say

Ruby was on her way here—and invite Clive to join her—but I hadn't given a timeframe. Because I didn't have one, not exactly.

The press of his mouth was hot and delicious. I realized I was kissing him back, and the moment I reached around and sank my fingers in his lush hair, I was lost. He licked me, kissed me, brushed my mouth with his fangs. They'd been hidden, but his lust drew them out. I pressed my tongue inside his mouth. When he sucked hard on it, I swear I almost came. My entire body had turned into a raw nerve ending, primed for sexual pleasure.

Low moans rocked me. Some mine, some his, except he sounded like a big jungle cat on the prowl. Not exactly purring, more of a guttural noise that told me I was his. Somehow, I ended up in his lap, breasts pressed against his chest. The swell of his erection jabbed me in the stomach. If we weren't living on borrowed time, I'd have reached down and undone his trousers, taken the delicious length of him into my mouth.

He slipped a hand beneath my sweater and settled it over a breast, tweaking and twirling the nipple. Sensation cascaded through me, and much like I'd done in Mistral's hallway all those long years ago, I stuffed a hand between my legs. This time, Nick moved it, replacing it with his own. The simple pressure of his palm against my sex made me howl with delight.

His tongue was inside my mouth now. I sparred with it and pretended it was his cock. Sexual images bombarded me. Erections spurting semen. Beautiful men. Muscled chests. Shapely legs. Fangs dripping blood. Hair cascading around me as a man took me. Eyes wide open, I drank Nickolas in. Every detail from his lush, coppery curls to his green eyes. Eyes that had deepened to emerald as his desire grew more urgent.

I slipped my hand between us and curved my fingers around the jut of his cock. All Vampires are hung like there's no tomorrow, but I didn't care about the rest of them. I only cared about Nick. He thrust into my hand as I squeezed the length of him through the rough fabric of his jeans.

Time stuttered to a standstill as we grappled with one another, mouths glued together, fingers teasing each other's sensitive places. He'd begun rubbing me, alternating small circles with a back-and-forth motion that drove me crazy. My world narrowed until the only things in it were him and me and the crazily sweet music our bodies made grinding together.

The world could have come to a standstill. The Russians could have dropped an atomic bomb. The paranormal task force could have sprayed silver powder around my house. Nothing mattered except coming. If Ruby and the others showed up, they'd have the good sense to stay outside.

I hoped.

Even if they didn't, I didn't care. Vampires aren't shy about sex or being naked. The unique feel of Nickolas's magic added spice to what he was doing to my clit. Sensation had been so staggeringly intense before I almost couldn't stand it. When he gave me an extra push with his magic, I shot skyward like a rocket. Ripping my mouth from his, I yelped and cried out as delight hit every nerve in my body.

"Just keep on coming, darling," he crooned and poured on more mesmerism.

Sure enough, a second climax seeded itself from the dregs of the first until I almost passed out from pleasure. Before he could urge me to a third peak, I undid the fastenings on his pants, slid downward, and plunged my mouth over his harder-than-hard cock.

He was even bigger than I'd imagined. Not just in length, but in girth. Imagining what he'd feel like inside me, stretching me, plumbing me heated my blood all over again, but I didn't want to be greedy. We shouldn't be doing this. We should be plotting our next moves, getting an airtight alibi in place in case the cops showed up at *Ascent* tonight with a warrant.

I shut my mind off and concentrated on the luscious taste and feel of Nick's cock in my mouth. He'd threaded his hands into my hair, and his head was thrown back, neck corded with ecstasy. I had a finger pressing the base of his balls, so I felt them tighten, snug against his body, and sent boatloads of magic to heighten his release.

Semen painted the inside of my mouth. Hot. Bitter. Salty. Vampire jism tastes different. I like it better. It goes down like nectar. I was still licking and sucking and urging him to give me more when he rasped, "Wonderful. So wonderful, but we should stop."

I lifted my head and locked gazes with him. He was right. We'd been damned lucky no one had simply teleported inside. Or maybe they had. I wouldn't have noticed, and neither would he, probably.

Warmth and caring were reflected in the depths of his

eyes. Beyond that, I also caught a flicker of possessiveness, of pure male Vampire having branded a new woman. Except Vamps never hung around for very long. Christ. I hoped I was right about Nick, that I'd read him right. Possessiveness was a two-way street. He was mine now.

Mine.

Until he finds out about Mistral... My implacable inner critic was back.

I'd work things out, find a path through the wreckage. Mistral had been a selfish asshole. I refused to let him ruin my life for any longer than he already had. Big words. Time would reveal what my follow-through looked like.

Nick tapped my forehead. "Your mind is busy. What are you thinking about?"

I shook my head. "How wonderful everything was. But you're right. We need to set ourselves to rights. The others will be here soon. Must be something serious, or Ruby wouldn't be making the trek out here."

Nick nodded. "For Clive to figure out how to call me means whatever's going on couldn't wait until tonight."

I hated to leave my spot right next to Nickolas, but I pushed myself to my feet, straightening clothes as I went. Snatching a towel off a hook, I tossed it to him so he could clean himself up.

He joined me in the kitchen as I was finishing our tea and wrapped his arms around me from behind as he nuzzled my neck. "You are one hot number, darling. No matter what happens next, I'll always cherish those few moments we just shared."

Something about his tone alarmed me. Before I could

demand what the hell that was supposed to mean, as in did he have some foreknowledge of what might unfold that would get in the way of him and me, power blasted through my house.

Ruby, Christa, Clive, and Dahlia shimmered into corporeality in front of the hearth. Dahlia's raven, More Than Never, perched on her shoulder. I hadn't realized familiars could teleport. Still reeling from Nick's statement, which might have meant nothing, I dragged my full attention to the new arrivals. They all looked as if someone near and dear to them had died.

"Spill it," I said.

Ruby nodded. "We'd just gotten everyone out of the bar, around 4 a.m., when I heard a bunch of pounding out front. At first, I thought it was one of the mages wanting back inside, so of course I opened the door."

"And?" I spun one hand in a come-along motion.

"It was a bloke in a uniform," Clive said, "nailing a sign to the front door. Except he had to stop after Ruby opened it."

"What kind of sign?" Nick sounded furious.

"They're closing the club by orders of the paranormal task force for suspicious activity."

I shook my head hard, not certain I'd heard right. "But they can't do that. They have no evidence. This isn't the Old Country where they could jail you if you didn't smell right."

"Yeah, well, they're trying to," Dahlia said. Her bird squawked, clearly as put out by the turn of events as I was.

"Piss on that," I said. "I'll call that attorney I use. He can figure out some kind of stay, maybe file a lawsuit for unlawful something-or-other."

"Lawsuits are the American way of life," Christa agreed.

"So did he just tack up the sign and drive off?" I asked.

"Pretty much," Dahlia said.

I picked up my mug, changed my mind, and went for the mead bottle. I really wanted to blot everything out for a while, but wanting and having were two wildly divergent things.

"Won't work," Nick said and pried the bottle out of my hands after I'd swallowed a quarter of what was left in it.

"Yeah. Don't I know it," I muttered. "There's not enough booze in the world to make this better. Even if it affected me."

"What are we going to do?" Ruby asked.

"It's why we're here," Clive said, "so we can figure something out."

"How about if you start at the beginning," I suggested. "What happened with the mages and their meeting. Once I've heard about that, maybe my head will be a little clearer."

Ruby started talking. Focusing my attention was a struggle. Barely restrained fury scoured me until I felt raw. We'd get through this. Somehow. I'd save my club, and my reputation, goddammit.

No one, particularly not Riteway and Hernandez, would have the last laugh. I was glad they were dead. And sorry they hadn't suffered more.

"Ariana?" Ruby tapped my arm.

"Yeah. Sorry. My attention was elsewhere. Go on."

CHAPTER THIRTEEN, NICKOLAS

I still couldn't believe Ariana hadn't batted me away when I kissed her. I took it slow, gave her plenty of time to slide out of my arms, but when she closed hers around me and looped her fingers into my hair, no force on earth could have gotten in my way. The feel of her skin against my hands and her musky arousal still clung to me. I found myself inhaling just to breathe her in, keep her close for a little bit longer. We were off to what I hoped was the beginning of immortality lived together, but pairing up wasn't exactly the Vampire way.

Still treading gently, not wanting to make any assumptions, I told her how precious our few stolen moments had been to me, no matter what the future held. My intent had been to set her at ease, reassure her I wasn't jumping to any conclusions about what kisses and shared ecstasy meant over the long haul. The oddest look crossed her face after I said that. I'd have followed up to make certain

I hadn't inadvertently offended her, but Ruby and Clive and a couple of others showed up.

They didn't have to say much before I understood we had a huge problem. My first guess was the detectives had issued orders to shutter *Ascent* at some point when they were chasing the illusion of Ariana's car. Damn it. Maybe my bright idea hadn't been all that inspired, after all.

Back in the Middle Ages, what had passed for officialdom had closed the occasional public house, mostly because of plague or hints of heretical activity. In those days, suspicious proprietors had been run through with swords and burned in the public square. By the time I'd entered stasis, judges and juries had come into vogue. Mortals congratulated themselves on becoming more enlightened, less brutal.

One of my biggest drawbacks was how little I knew about the world I'd wakened to. While I joked with Ariana about not understanding some of her verbiage, the unpleasant truth was I picked up perhaps half of what she said and filled in the missing links via inference. If I'd been sharper, more attuned to whatever year this was, I might have chosen a different path than forcing the detectives to chase a mirage.

The front door opened, admitting Conan, and then swished shut behind him. Blood flaked off his snout, and he looked as if he'd had fun killing something. I could easily see where Vampires and wolves would make good bedfellows. Born hunters, we rise to the thrill of the chase. And we wouldn't be tripping over each other fighting for the spoils.

The wolf's nostrils twitched as he glanced from me to

Ariana. No hiding sex smells from a wolf. His gaze tracked through the rest of the room's occupants. Ears pricked forward, he rumbled, "What happened?"

"The cops are trying to shut the club." Ruby squatted next to the wolf and rubbed her hands through his fur.

"Why? What did we do?" A growl punctuated Conan's words.

"Nothing that I can see," Ariana sputtered.

"It could be my fault"—I pushed my shoulders back, ready to take full responsibility—"because I'm who sent Riteway and Hernandez on that wild goose chase. I bet they got angrier and angrier."

Conan shook Ruby's hands away. "They shouldn't have been able to do anything except follow Ariana's car. No talking and very little thinking."

"Well, the bloke was most explicit," Clive said. "Shuttered by orders of the paranormal task force."

"Impossible," Conan woofed. "I had their puny minds in thrall. They wouldn't have been able to talk with each other, let alone issue orders."

My mind raced as one possibility after another presented itself. "We had one spate of false policemen," I said carefully, treading gently in case I'd misinterpreted things. "Is it possible this was another one? As in not a cop at all?"

Ruby's eyes widened. Ariana fisted a hand and punched the air. Damn it. She needed rest. And I wanted to take another look at her wound to make certain no silver residue remained.

"Entirely possibly," Dahlia muttered. "Did any of you get a good look at his car?"

"Sure," Clive said. "It was black, just like the other one."

"It shouldn't have been," Dahlia was quick to say. "They'd have sent a drone out to post a notice like that, so he should have been in a Kirkland PD car—black and white with shields on it."

"Brother am I slow on the uptake," Ruby groused. "I should have noticed the discrepancy."

"Fuck!" Power glistened around Ariana.

"What are you doing?" I asked, alarmed. She should be conserving her magic, not blowing through what was left of it.

"To *Ascent* to get the goddamned notice. I want to look at it."

"I'll do that," I told her. "You rest."

Christa extended an arm; a shining length of Fae-imbued power circled Ariana. Christa scrunched her forehead into a mass of lines. "You were injured. How?"

"Awk. Is that why I couldn't get hold of you?" Ruby narrowed her golden eyes with their odd pupils.

"For fuck's sake," Ariana sputtered. "I'm all right."

"Aye, but you very nearly weren't," the Fae pressed, her Irish brogue back to its maximum.

"You have to tell us what happened," Ruby said. "We'll find out sooner or later, anyway."

I took the diversion as license to fetch the document nailed to *Ascent's* door and prepped my own journey spell. Before I launched it, Ariana had begun detailing our fight with the detectives. She wasn't able to get more than a few words out without being bombarded with questions. The raven flew around the room before settling on Conan's shoulders. The two of them had met before, and seemingly liked each other.

If it had been night, I'd have taken my chances with one of the side streets linking to the alleyway behind *Ascent*, but it was midday. I planned things so I'd emerge in the stockroom. Its single window had slats covering it. The club had no windows. I could hustle the door open, grab the paper, and be gone quickly enough to avoid the nasty bite of the sun.

My spell ran true, but then I'm decent with things like that so long as I concentrate. *Ascent's* storeroom formed around me. I hadn't thought to ward myself because I wasn't expecting anyone to be here. The cleaning crew had like as not seen the sign and not come inside.

I may not have lived in this era long, but I'd been here for sufficient time to fully understand that anything tagged by the paranormal task force scared the fuck out of mortals. It was almost as if they thought magic was contagious, and they could catch it if they got too close to us. The thought made me smile sourly because their fear only came close to hitting the mark when the proximity involved Vampires.

Even then, we had to like a particular human well enough to turn them, a rare occurrence all in all. And one that had grown ever less frequent with the passage of time. I started for the door leading into the club but stopped dead. Someone had been here. Ariana's desk was in disarray, as if someone had riffled through the stacks of paper on it. Drawers stood open.

Suddenly cautious, I warded myself and listened intently for movement elsewhere in the building. Had I gotten lucky and materialized in the storeroom in between visitors? The thought of anyone violating Ariana's private domain infuriated me. No matter what I might have said about not having any expectations regarding her and me and what we meant to one another, it had been an outright lie.

She was mine.

If I'd had any doubts about it, they'd been washed away by our kisses, by the way her back arched when I made her come. By the hot vacuum her mouth made around my cock. The mere thought of her tongue and teeth made me hard all over again.

I ripped the erotic imagery out at its roots before it had a chance to develop a life of its own and went back to carefully assessing if I was truly alone. If anyone was here—anyone at all snooping through Ariana's club—it would be the last thing they did, by god.

Killing the detective had felt good. He was our enemy, and now he wouldn't bother us any longer. Ariana preached caution, but in this instance she was wrong. In the Old Country, mortals might have been disgusted by Vampires, but they also offered us grudging respect. They knew when they were outmatched. They never put out offerings, like they did for the Fae and Sidhe, but neither did they make the mistake of pitting themselves against us. The majority of them, anyway. The occasional band of self-professed Vampire hunters always came to unfortunate ends.

We saw to it. And then things would settle down for a decade or two before the next batch of stupid had to be taught a lesson.

The modern version of human had an entirely different

mindset. The new rulebook taught them they sat at the top of the food chain and could run roughshod through their world, any animals that got in their way, and magical creatures. It hadn't taken too many hours in the library to infuriate me.

Maybe we wouldn't win in an all-out war, but we'd sure as fuck pound the haughty humans down a notch or two. It wouldn't take much for them to realize how weak and ineffectual they were.

Nearly done with my assessment, I was satisfied no one else was here. Still warded, I walked quietly to the door leading into the club and pulled it open a crack. I'm not restrained by nature, but I had no idea what I'd find. The neat bar area had been ransacked. Broken bottles littered the floor, and the stench of spirits was strong.

Damn it. Whoever had vandalized Ariana's desk hadn't stopped there. Had they taken anything? Before I submerged myself too deeply in that bottomless pit, I refocused my attention. It didn't make any difference what some nameless batch of thugs had taken.

What was more important was who had been here.

I scuttled across the floor, crunching through broken glass and sticky spilled liquor. And I cursed my lack of footwear soundly as I plucked a sliver of glass out of the bottom of one foot. Snatching the notice was simple. Crumpling it, I stuck it in a pocket. I got one small burn on my hand, but it was healing before I slammed and bolted the door, dropping the latch bar into place. The door had been unlocked; whoever had been here had left it like that.

Did it mean they were on their way back?

Was a group outside watching the bar?

I'd accomplished what I'd come for. Before I left, though, I sent magic far afield scouring the vast room as I crossed to the back portion, taking care to avoid the broken glass. Mortals had been here recently, but so had dark Sorcerers and Witches, presumably the black magic variety.

Where had they come from? We'd shut their portal. Presumably, the guardians were keeping a close eye on the ley-lines and the realm of the dead. I'd reached the bar. Every instinct I had was alert, on edge. I didn't see why. No one was here.

Or maybe they were and had carefully shielded themselves.

This wasn't the time to dig deeper. My warrior side was deeply disappointed when I took the prudent path and kindled a teleport spell. For a count of maybe two when my magic was slower to respond than I expected, I prepared to fight my way out of *Ascent*.

It didn't come to that. Something was definitely stirring beneath the floorboards, but my hasty egress must have surprised whatever was down there. Fuck. The last incursion of Sorcerers and their pets had come from beneath a big, fancy house. It argued another channel had been forced open.

Where were Conan's kinsmen? Obviously not patrolling what they claimed was their territory. I still didn't fully understand their role. Maybe I never would. I took care to cover my tracks as I teleported. A skilled mage could have followed me, otherwise, and our cache of safe spots to hide was shrinking fast.

Because I was distracted, I popped out in the woods perhaps half a league from Ariana's house. Good. My miscalculation would give me a chance to make double damn certain I hadn't been followed. Still warded, I leaned against a tree, doing what I could to keep daylight at bay. It was well-shaded where I was, but the sun pricked the exposed backs of my hands and the top of my head. I tugged my jacket sleeves as low as I could. Not much I could do about my scalp. My hair is thick; it offered some protection.

I let minutes slide past. When I got to five, I let go of my ward. No reason to waste magic keeping it in place. Even if someone did show up, I'd kill them. Wouldn't matter a whit if they saw me. My fangs had dropped, a sure sign I was heartily sick of mortals and dark mages and everyone else standing in Ariana's way. And mine.

For the first time, I grasped the desperation of the assembled group of mages from early this morning. Their survival was on the line. I didn't fancy living out the next several millennia in a cave, emerging at night to skulk in shadows and lure what animals I could to feed from.

News articles from my library sessions bombarded me. If they were correct, Earth didn't have millennia. It was on a collision course with disaster, if no one intervened.

Fuck mortals. The more I knew about them, the less I liked them. But we couldn't fight both them and the resurgence of twisted sorcery. An unpleasant thought intruded. Judging from the mortals masquerading as cops who'd stormed *Ascent* a while back, the Sorcerers from Gamma Four weren't working alone.

They'd co-opted mortals from their dimension as stooges,

agents to do their dirty work for them. Even if we returned to Gamma Four, I was fairly certain the dark Sorcerers had moved on. We'd killed enough of them to get their attention. Knowledge slapped me hard. The destruction at *Ascent* was payback for what we'd done.

It was the likeliest explanation.

Satisfied I hadn't been followed, I put my head down and covered the distance to Ariana's at a run. Didn't take long. I can move quickly when I set my mind to it.

The door opened of its own accord when I got close, and I skidded to a halt inside. Escaping the weight of daylight was welcome. I spun to pull the door closed, but it was already well on its way to the stops. When I'd left, everyone had been standing. They'd moved to the collection of soft chairs and couches.

"Did you get it?" Ariana asked.

Nodding, I extracted the crumpled ball of paper from my pocket and tossed it her way. She snapped it out of the air and smoothed it. I nodded at everyone on my way to the kitchen, hoping some tea remained. After all the bad news at the club, I was delighted to find half a pot simmering on the back of the stove. I turned off the flame and poured most of what was left into a generous mug I plucked from a board studded with hooks.

For good measure, I added a jot from the mead bottle before joining the others. "I'm afraid I don't bring welcome tidings," I began and winced. I sounded impossibly formal.

Ariana's head snapped up from where she'd been studying the crinkled paper. "What?"

"Someone went through your desk, and the club proper is riddled with broken glass and spilled liquor."

Ruby shook her head. "After everything else, that's minor. I'll clean it up."

"Eh, not a good idea," I went on. "I thought I was alone until just before I left. Luckily, my spell was well in hand, and whoever was hiding beneath the floor hadn't expected me to leave so precipitously. Or I might still be there."

"Beneath the floor?" Ariana growled. "Like where that last batch of fuckers with their wasps and pigs came from?"

"Actually, they came through portals," Christa corrected her.

"Yes, but their access point to Earth was beneath that fancy house." Ruby squeezed her eyes tight for a moment; her wings drooped.

"Let's not split hairs," Ariana said and shook the paper. "This isn't anything official. It's just the words 'Shut Until Further Notice.' No seal. No signature. I've seen these types of documents before, and they never look like this."

"I told you," Conan said from where he lay with his head on his paws in front of the hearth.

"Yeah, you did." Ruby angled a fond glance at the wolf. Shifting her gaze to Ariana, she said, "What do you want to do?"

"Good question." Ariana closed her teeth over her lower lip. Her fangs were out, which told me how concerned she was. She turned to me. "You missed two things while you were gone. The short version is the mages pledged to work together. I didn't believe how serious they were until Ruby told me they formed mixed work groups. It must have sunk in if we don't pull together, we're doomed. Their meetings begin today. Everyone set a time three nights hence to get together. By then, they should have strategies in place to kick around."

"What about including Vampires?" I asked.

"It didn't exactly come up again." Ariana made a face. "For now, they seem content with the three of us."

I considered it. We could go trolling for more Vamps, but they'd probably end up being from different clans, so we'd have dominance issues out of the gate. Since I didn't have a ready solution, I asked, "What was the second item?"

Ariana nodded at Christa. "You don't have to go through everything. Hit the high points and call it even."

More than Never flapped his—her?—wings and quorked. Ravens were spirit guides according to legend, so perhaps he was tuned in to Christa's psychic emanations.

Her silvery wings fluttered softly, and she trained her milky eyes my way. "Granted, last night the dark of the moon conferred unusual advantages for scrying, but my vision was duplicated by others in my guild house, and by Fae in two other houses and Witches from two covens."

"Guild houses," Dahlia corrected her. "We adopted modern nomenclature because covens are associated with Witches, and mortals have turned into a bunch of uptight cowards."

"Sorry," Christa said. "I'll try to do better. My point was when seers from several places see the same vision, it becomes inescapable and will become truth sooner or later."

Impatience beat a tattoo through me. I wanted to shout at her to get on with it. I didn't need all the explanations or trimmings. I'd already heard about encroaching darkness after she and the other Fae seers showed up at *Ascent*. She looked distraught enough, though, and her unrest had deepened as I'd described the destruction in the club. So I let her tale unfold in its own time. Urging from me wouldn't make much difference, anyway.

She cleared her throat. "Earth's time is nearly at a close. Darkness approaches from above, below, and every side. We have but two paths open to us. Either we leave mortals to the planet they've destroyed, or we find a way to intervene." Breath rattled from her before she went on. "The first option is cleaner in some ways, although relocating has its own set of challenges, the first of which would be pinpointing a spot where we could live in peace.

"The second alternative is what crops up in my future-seeking, so I believe it is the preferred path. We must somehow convince mortals we are not the enemy. That we are, in fact, their only path to the salvation of their world and their way of life."

I waited, but she fell silent. "Forgive me if this is an indelicate question," I began, "but did your visions offer any clues how we might accomplish that?"

Christa shook her head. A slow, sad smile formed on her face. "It would be convenient if scrying worked that way. It doesn't. What I see are alternative versions of what is to come. The one that pops up most frequently is the likeliest candidate.

Pressure on my lower lip told me my fangs were still out. "Did any of the various groups using divination see anything about dark Sorcery or black witchcraft?" I asked.

"No, but we wouldn't have. What we do is more of a big-picture endeavor, which might mean what you came across at the club isn't much more than a bump in the road."

It hadn't felt that way to me.

"She left something out," Ariana said.

I waited, curious what it might be.

"Thought it might make you uncomfortable," Christa mumbled.

"Yeah, it does," Ariana said and got to her feet. Swinging around, she faced us. "According to Christa, me and Conan joining ranks was foreseen or foreordained or some such mumbo-jumbo. We form the core of the resistance—so it will rise or fall depending on how successful we are defeating enemies and recruiting allies."

"That's why Percy allowed the group to meet in *Ascent*," I said, thinking out loud.

Ruby and Christa nodded.

Ariana muffled a grunt. "Yup. It appears they talked with everyone except me about...everything. I'm not happy about that, but I'll get over it." She extended an index finger and jabbed it at each of us in turn. "No more secrets. Got it?"

"Fair," Christa said.

Ruby stood and dragged Christa to her feet. "We're going to the club to kick some serious ass and clean it up."

"I'm coming," Clive said.

"Bad idea," I told him. "If someone yanks the door open, you'll be badly burned."

The raven squawked again and flew to Dahlia's shoulder. "I'll call in reinforcements from the guild house and join you," she said.

"But I want to help," Clive pressed.

"Teleport to the Sorcerers' guild house," I suggested. "Alert Percy to what's happened, and see if he can't rustle up some Sorcerers to meet the Fae and Witches at the club."

Before I was done talking, the air shimmered around Clive, and he was gone.

"What are you going to do about that bogus notice?" Ruby asked Ariana.

In answer, she picked it up off the table and chucked it into the fireplace, setting fire to it with a thought. "That's what I'm going to do about it," she said succinctly. "Fuck those fucking bastards. I'm not as stupid as they think I am."

Words clawed the back of my throat wanting out so bad they almost caused me pain. Words that said I'd stand by her side, fight with her, protect her, be there in every way that mattered. Instead, I suggested, "Let's have a quick look at that shoulder, shall we? I want to make certain we got all the silver residue."

"Good idea," Conan seconded.

"See you at the usual time," Ruby said just before she, Christa, and Dahlia teleported away.

I drained most of my tea-mead mixture and got up. "About that shoulder—" I began.

"I'll check it. If it needs anything extra, you'll be the first to know. Then I'm going to take a nap. In an hour, we're going into town. *Ascent* is my club. I'll be damned if I stand by and let everyone else fight my battles for me."

Her face had taken on a closed-off expression I recognized from all the other times she'd shut me out. Not sure what to say, I watched her cross the room, enter her bedchamber, and close the door behind her.

"She has a lot on her mind," Conan said from behind me.

I turned to the wolf. "So long as it's just us, do you have any idea how the guardians could have not noticed the ley-lines being violated a second time?"

"*Many ideas,*" the wolf switched to telepathy because he was growling too loud to talk at the same time. "*They think if they chase Ariana off world, I'll return to them.*"

"Why is it so important?" I pressed, wanting to understand.

He shook his head. "*They believe I belong with them. I'm wasting my time with inferior mages. Except they're not doing anything worthwhile.*" He stopped for a bit before going on. "*I was young when I left. So young, it's impossible for me to understand them or their motives. They're like strangers to me, and it makes me sad and angry. And I want them to leave me alone.*"

"You solicited their help," I reminded him.

He woofed once. "*I did. And it was a mistake, but not one I can retract.*" He got to his feet and shook himself.

Before I could come up with something supportive to say, he was gone. I glanced at Ariana's bedroom door. Should I knock or go inside or offer her the privacy she clearly desired?

In the end, I lay on one of the couches, shut my eyes, and did my best to shutter my mind as well. Ariana was like two different people. But I couldn't force her to be anything other than who she was. Either I accepted all of her, or I needed to walk away. Not from doing my part in the battles looming around us, but from my hopes of deepening my claim to her.

Her retreat to another part of the house told me louder than any words I was delusional. The bald-faced truth was I had no claim at all.

CHAPTER FOURTEEN, ARIANA

After I managed to propel myself across the living room and into my bedroom, I took advantage of the momentum to strip off my sweater. While I stood staring at my reflection in the mirror, I brushed hair over my shoulders and examined the hole just beneath my right collarbone.

The black edges had mostly vanished, and the jagged gap had reduced itself by at least half. I probed it gently with my fingertips, gratified the tenderness had receded as well. When Nickolas and Conan had been working on me, the slightest touch had sent waves of agony through me in a cascade of liquid torture.

Not bothering to pull the sweater back on—I'd don fresh clothes before we left—I sank to the edge of my bed. My mind was in a bleak place, circling the drain, and I had to get a grip. I'd been quick to blurt out that *Ascent* was mine. It was, which meant I had to pull my head out of my ass and provide leadership. It wasn't the Faes' job to save my club or the Witches' or the Sorcerers'. Nope. It was mine.

Or, if saving it proved too costly on every front, scuttling it had to be my decision too. Nick complicated everything, but then so did Conan. Everyone from the seers to my longtime companion, who was far more than he appeared, were nudging me to pick up the banner and take my place in history.

Except I didn't want to.

I've mentioned Vamps are far from team players. We work best alone. We might have chosen to live in clan houses, but outside of the daytime fuck-fests, we mostly kept to ourselves. There'd be occasional blood sharing if one of us mowed through too many mortals to consume ourselves. It wasn't right to let food go to waste, so we'd call in our brethren.

But we didn't have team meetings, nor did we go in for group decision-making. The master made the decisions. We went along with them, or not. Rebellions—if there were any —were usually *sub rosa* affairs. Everyone understood the punishment for insurrection was permanent death.

Insight scurried through me. I'd have laughed, except it was only funny in a black humor way. Clan Hawke had been a "don't ask, don't tell," environment. Precisely the same model I'd built *Ascent* on. I dropped my head into my hands. No matter how many years passed, or how far I distanced myself from the Old Country, Mistral would never leave me in peace.

I rubbed my temples. They ached and throbbed from weariness and all the magic I'd expended—and was still paying out—recovering from my near brush with annihilation. I'd been flat fucking nuts when I'd fallen into Nick's arms. It had felt right at the time, and I'd been drawn in by his charisma, his charm, his knock-your-socks-off beauty.

Yeah. I had every excuse in the book, but he'd caught me at a weak moment. I straightened my back and stood long enough to slide out of my trousers. They smelled like sex, like Nick. A bittersweet reminder love wasn't for me. Nope. Not now. Not ever. I was relegated to quickies with mortals for the rest of my immortal life. It depressed the fuck out of me, so I stopped thinking about everything.

I needed rest—and blood. But when I pulled the duvet back and sank onto my pile of feather mattresses, the sleep I craved refused to cooperate. Instead, visions of Mistral and Nick vied with one another until I rolled onto my side and drove a fist into the mattress so hard I split the fabric cover. Feathers flew everywhere, resembling a mini-snowstorm.

I'd have cleared the mess with magic, but I wasn't in the mood.

For fuck's sake, get over yourself, I instructed briskly. *This isn't about me. Earth could be in its final millennium. Magic is in danger of dying out.*

Why should I care? inner voice number two shot back.

Personally, I sided with it. Mortals had never done me any favors. And I wouldn't give two fucks for Earth—except it was my home too.

Rolling to a sit, I shook my head hard. Balanced against a day of reckoning that was fast catching up to everybody, my club—and Nick—paled to insignificance. Conan and I were destined for something. That message rang through loud and clear from multiple sources—including the wolf.

I felt bad about Nickolas. I shouldn't have inched our relationship forward. Another head shake reminded me I was thinking in human terms. Vampires didn't deal in concepts like fidelity or marriages. I nabbed a brush from the bedside table and dragged it through my hair to get rid of feathers clinging to my long locks.

Mistral had tried to warn me. I hadn't listened. Nick had just done the same in my kitchen. He'd said something to the effect that we'd had fun, and he'd always value it. I set the brush down. If his statement didn't smack of Mistral, nothing did. Nick had been more gallant—he wasn't my master, so he didn't have quite the leeway Mistral did—but the underlying message had been the same.

Sex is fun. Playtime. Nothing more.

Relieved to have laid my concerns to rest—no reason to feel bad about Nick—I gave my face and hands a quick rinse at a sink in the corner of my bedroom and got dressed. Nothing filmy. It was still daytime. I needed stout fabrics to block out the sun. Black canvas pants, a gold button-down shirt, and a leather jacket fit the bill. I slid my feet into boots and grabbed one of many sunhats off a hook.

By the time I walked into the main part of my house, ready to leave, Nick was gone. Damn it. I'd wasted more than few minutes shoring myself up with a pep talk, but disappointment still battered me. Despite all my brave words, I had it bad where Nick was concerned. I had to get over myself.

A quick trip to the kitchen to see if any tea remained

yielded a note. Written in a strong hand, black ink on paper he must have found in my desk, Nick said:

Didn't want to disturb you. I've gone hunting. Raise me once you're up. I'll let you know where I'm feeding, and you can join me.

The hand gripping the sliver of paper shook. My eyes flooded with tears. Shit. Fuck. Damn. I dropped the note and curled my fingers around the kitchen ledge. If it had been anything other than granite, it would have crumpled to dust.

An old saying shot through my head. "You can run, but you can't hide." It hadn't exactly been designed for this situation, but it was still true enough. I was falling in love—or lust or possession—with Nick. Nothing I could say or do would change it. Nowhere was far enough away for me to forget about him.

Hell. I'd never forgotten Mistral, and centuries had chugged by.

I bent over the sink and dabbed more cold water on my face. Two choices loomed, actually three because I needed to eat. I could take Nickolas up on his offer, or I could find my own food, or I could teleport to *Ascent* and forget about eating until after whatever blew up in my face at the club.

Door Number Three wasn't wise. My magic hadn't recovered from the silver bullet. If I was going to be anything but a liability in battle, I needed blood. An idea swatted me broadside. As simple and elegant a solution as I was likely to derive, I was surprised it hadn't occurred to me sooner.

To make certain I wasn't about to compound one mistake —intimacy with Nickolas—with another, I forced myself to think through the consequences. No matter which way I sliced and diced things, I couldn't come up with any downsides.

Other than Nick taking Clive and getting the fuck out of Dodge, which wouldn't necessarily be a bad thing. It wasn't as if we had more than a passing acquaintanceship at this juncture. I'd mourn, but I was still mourning Mistral. How much worse could this be?

Decided, I raised my mind voice. *"I'm up. Where are you?"*

His response was so immediate, he must have been waiting for me. I hoped he'd found shelter. And taken something from my house to cover his head. I had no idea where Conan had run off to, but the wolf would find me. I never worried about him.

Before I could chicken out, I settled the floppy-brimmed hat on my head and walked out the front door. It shut behind me, sealed with spells set to recognize Vampires. I might have to change that and re-key it to me and Conan. Easy enough to do.

I knew precisely where Nickolas was, and I set off at a quick pace. I can run as fast as a car traveling at freeway speeds, so I reached him in short order. I'd already decided to feed first and then have the ever-so-brief conversation I planned.

He sat beneath a generous rock overhang and gestured at a still warm pile of squirrels, rats, and raccoons.

"Thank you," I said, keeping my tone formal before I dug into the carcasses. Too bad Conan wasn't closer. I could hide the remains, save them for him, but they were best eaten fresh.

Nick was quiet, but I felt the weight of his gaze on me as I sank my fangs into one animal after the next. "If you're still hungry, I can get more," he offered.

I dropped the last critter—a rat—on the stack of drained bodies. "I'm good," I said, followed by a second thank-you.

He shrugged. "Least I could do. I'm not certain what we'll face at the club, but it's bound to be difficult."

I nodded. "Difficult may understate it by a good big bunch." Walking closer, I rolled my shoulders back and clasped my hands behind me. "Before we leave, there are a few things I need to tell you. Really, only one thing. If you chose to rustle up Clive and leave after you hear what I have to say, I'll understand. The one thing I would ask, if you do go, is that you won't reveal my secret, and you will never return here. Can you do that?"

Nick got his feet under him in a graceful motion that reminded me how supple Vampires are. In defiance of the sun filtering through evergreen boughs, he faced me. "I will never hurt you, Ariana. If you want me to go, I will. Whatever this secret it, it can't be all that horrible."

I tried to muffle it, but a muted snort blew past my lips. "You might want to suspend judgment until after you've heard me out." I shook loose strands of hair behind my shoulders. Now that the rubber met the road, could I actually get the damning words out? They'd never crossed my lips since the awful day I'd beheaded my master.

Nick nodded, and remained mercifully silent offering me as much time as I required.

"This has been my cross to bear since the day it happened," I mumbled, cleared my throat, and tried for a stronger voice. I blew out an unneeded breath. If I was breathing, it told me how nervous I was. I closed my teeth, fangs out, over my lower lip. Either I did this, or I didn't. I'd propped the door partway open, but I feared maybe I was making the wrong decision.

Conan had shut me up, said he didn't want to know.

But Conan wasn't a Vampire.

"There's no easy way to say this," I went on. "You'd have found out sooner or later. I can't sugarcoat it, or make it better. I'm the one who killed Mistral."

I have no idea what Nick was expecting, but that hadn't been it. A combination of horror and disgust twisted his features into an unrecognizable mask. He lunged for me, clearly intent on meting out Vampire justice.

I executed a sideways leap, evading him. "We have bigger problems than something I did hundreds of years ago," I shouted. "I told you because you needed to know. No one else does. They're not Vampires. If they knew what happened—if they'd been there—they'd have applauded my action."

He sprang my way. This time, he caught me and drove me to the ground. Snarling, snapping, growling, he tried to muscle me into position to drink from me. I knew the drill. He'd drain me and then rip my head from my body. If I'd been mortal, I'd have been horsemeat, but I wasn't. Plus, I'd just fed. I rolled around in the dirt with him, punching and tearing. He was stronger than me, but I could hold my own in any contest with another Vampire.

There was something oddly sexual about the aggression. Maybe because I didn't really want to hurt Nick, and the press of his body full length against me reminded me how much I craved his touch.

You stupid bitch, one of my inner mavens shrieked. *Teleport the fuck out of here and write him off.*

It was good advice. I ignored it. He yanked hard on my hair. I buried my fangs in his upper arm and kneed him in the groin. Taking advantage of my momentary victory, I rolled us so I was on top. He slapped me so hard, my head snapped back. I landed a punch squarely in his face and heard the *thwack* of bones breaking.

A blast of magic caught me in the side. I'd been so intent on Nick, I hadn't noticed Conan. The wolf barreled between us doing plenty of snapping and snarling of his own. "What are you doing?" Conan demanded. "Stop it."

Nickolas was balanced on one knee. Blood streaked his hands and face. I'd broken his nose, but it was already healing. "She cannot be allowed to live," he bellowed. "She defiled everything sacred to Vampires."

I rose to my feet. "Ha. Nothing is sacred to our kind. You promised you would leave, you and Clive. I'm holding you to it. Further, you promised to never reveal my secret."

"That was before I knew what it was." Nickolas's face was still screwed into an expression of disgust that made me want to curl into a ball and howl my grief to the world. I'd been right about one thing. Getting Mistral out into the open had been smart. Nick would have found out sooner or later. Better now than when we'd done more than share a couple of orgasms.

Conan had shifted through a few forms while I reminded Nick of the agreements he'd made. When the magic around Conan stopped swirling, a man emerged from the vortex. I'd never seen his human form. Like the other guardians, he was tall and powerfully built. Black hair cascaded to knee level, but his eyes were the same, amber and crackling with outrage.

He shook a fist at both of us. "Get over yourselves. This isn't about some inane rule Vampires lived by long ago. We face unimaginable challenges. Enemies converge from all sides." He turned his next words at Nickolas. "If you leave, walk out on Ariana, I will hunt you and yours until the world ends. It may not be too many years, but that won't deter me. She was kind to you, went above and beyond to help you adapt to a society that had changed, passed you by."

Breath steamed from him, making clouds in the air. "She asked nothing in return, and this is how you repay her?"

Nickolas tossed his head back. "You have no idea what she—"

"I know everything," Conan cut in. "And I don't care. Neither should you. She and I are going to *Ascent*. A battle is raging. Our friends need us. Think about it, Vampire. Friendship is people taking care of one another. Whatever Ariana did—or didn't do—involved someone you didn't know. And it happened long ago. She has suffered for that day for too long. I'll not have you amplify her pain. Take a few minutes, and then make the proper choice."

I was still staring stupidly at Conan. "Why take your human shape?"

"Simpler to find words, and I've never needed them more." The scents of fur and wet rocks intensified. Conan was a wolf again; he swathed me in his particular blend of magic and swept me into a teleport spell. I expected to come out in the nightclub. Instead, he dropped us into an alien landscape. So eerie, I understood we had to be off world. Green sand stretched as far as I could see. No trees. Not even a bush. The sky was pale violet, lit by twin moons. At least it was night in this spot. The air had a sweetish smell reminiscent of gardenias but with undernotes of rot.

"Why did you pick now to confess your sins?" Conan woofed at me.

I nodded. It was a fair question. "Because I like him, and what was between us couldn't go any further with me sitting on such a big secret." No matter which way the cookie crumbled—and it was looking as if Nick was on his way out of here—I was still relieved. Given the chance for a do-over, I'd tread the same path. It beat hell out of keeping tabs on my thoughts and fearing the day Nick would finally figure things out. His reaction would have been far worse several months down the road. I felt certain of it.

I narrowed my eyes. "What's happening at my club?"

Conan barked again, sharp and urgent. "What isn't? The unrest Nickolas sensed beneath the club was a mix of Sorcerers and Witches. None of them are from Earth. I've shamed the guardians into fixing the breach in the ley-lines. Permanently."

"How?"

"I made it clear there was nothing they could do that would force me to join ranks with them. I further told Fairclaw if he did anything to make your life harder, I would personally hunt him down and challenge him to a duel."

"You can't die," I mumbled, "so what kind of deterrent is that?"

"If he loses, he must forfeit his leadership role to another. I remember Fairclaw well. He craves power."

Nick attacking me, Conan's rescue, and his warnings about the conflict at *Ascent* all merged into a confusing mélange, but one point rose to the fore. "It's only a matter of minutes before someone calls in the disturbance, and the cops are all over the club."

"So far, we've warded the place, trying to keep that from happening."

"Why'd you come after me?"

"I was searching for you because your place is beside Ruby and Percy and everyone who suspended their innate dislike of Vampires to work with you." He shook his head; bits of fur flew to the sides. "When I found you, and saw you fighting not the enemy but Nickolas, I couldn't believe the two of you would be so irresponsible."

This time, he shook his whole body from snout to tail tip. "What you did was ill-advised. You're viewing the world through mortal eyes, and you need to stop."

Defensive words clamored in the back of my throat. I quashed them. I'd definitely lost sight of the bigger picture in my desire to square things with Nick.

"I'm ready." I stood tall, fangs on display, eager to kick the Sorcerer and Witch scum back to wherever they'd come from. The domino effect from Nick's reaction was out of my hands. He'd either lend his support—or leave. I wished I didn't care, but I did.

I hadn't expected his reaction. Worst case, I thought he'd

teleport away. His assault had caught me off-guard. It shouldn't have. I'd lived in a clan house. I understood how Vamps thought.

Good object lesson—for me. As Conan transported us away from the green sand and violet sky, I vowed to take absolutely nothing for granted. Not anymore. I'd assumed Nick's caring for me would have stayed his hand. I'd been wrong.

Between dealing with mortals and off-world supernaturals, I couldn't afford to be wrong too many more times. Mentally prepared for damn near anything, I warded both of us.

The din of shouts, squeals, cries, and bodies slamming together reached me before I could see anything. The sweet, coppery tang of blood hung heavy in the air. I inhaled, drinking it in. A small reward before the task that lay ahead. I might not have a nightclub to worry about when this was over, but if we destroyed the invaders, it was a small price to pay.

CHAPTER FIFTEEN, NICKOLAS

 lost it. Totally. Completely. Anger permeated every cell in my body until I couldn't stand to live in it. The guttural sounds blasting from me wouldn't quit. I uprooted small trees and chucked them at crazy angles. Even tried to bring down some huge ones, but they defeated me. My hands were abraded, my palms slick with blood.

I chucked small boulders every which way until my strength faded. A glance at the sky told me the day was fading along with it. I blinked a few times and stared at the destruction I'd wrought. What I'd done was stupid, but I hadn't been able to stop.

My hands were caked with my own blood. Bone showed white through burned places where the sun had gotten to me. My head stung. I didn't need to examine my scalp to know I'd find still more burns. I'd have sent healing energy to tend my wounds except I was tapped out.

I hunkered into a crouch and dropped my head into my

hands. Shame scuttled through me. I'd behaved badly. Like a freshly turned Vampire who hadn't yet learned to control his bloodlust—or his anger. I rubbed my eyes and then dragged the heels of my hands down my face.

Ouch.

Blisters ripped open as I disturbed them, leaving raw flesh beneath.

None of it mattered. I'd heal. Maybe not as fast as if I were rested, but many times quicker than a mortal would. My busted nose was already whole again. One thing was certain, I couldn't stay here. Staggering a little, I got my feet under me and trudged to a nearby stream. Its chilly water felt good on my hands and face.

My feet were still bare. I'd retrieve my boots. Since I was leaving anyway, taking them with me shouldn't matter. I've always viewed myself as strong, determined, afraid of nothing, but my hike through the forest to Ariana's took everything in me.

Her scent grew stronger, the closer I drew to her home. Musk and exotic spices. She wasn't there. If she had been, I'd have bypassed my boots. They were on the front porch where I'd left them, right next to hers. I dusted dirt off my feet and put them on. My stockings were inside. I had others, though.

Time slipped past, maybe five minutes before I realized I was standing staring at her front door like an idiot. It had obligingly opened for me. I could rush inside and break things, but I didn't have the momentum any longer. My anger had run its course leaving a sick, sad, slow pain.

I'd been falling in love with Ariana, been certain she

returned my affections, and then...this. I've run across disappointments and setbacks before. No one lives as long as I have and gets off without the occasional defeat, but this felt worse. Anguish carved deep into my soul—if I still had one, which I probably didn't.

I had my boots. I'd run out of excuses to be here, but I couldn't force myself to leave. Damn it. What kind of deranged bastard was I? Ariana's scent clung to everything. Her house. Me. I had to put a lot of distance between myself and everything here.

Run far away and never look back.

Conan's warning rose to taunt me. I had taken both money and time from Ariana. I'd begun to repay the funds, but I had a long way to go. Leaving the identification documents for her wouldn't discharge my debt. They'd been crafted for me.

My head spun, probably because I'd been outside in daylight for hours. I wasn't any good to anyone in my current state. Blood would help. It had to. It was my go-to place, the only way I knew how to fix things. No self-respecting animal would come within half a league of the spot where I'd uprooted everything in sight. Was I far enough from there to hunt?

Doing everything I could to still the turmoil still dogging me, I sent waves of calm at a passing squirrel. It kept right on running. I stared after it, disbelieving. How could it not have obeyed me? Was I truly that depleted? After two more squirrels and a rat scuttled past, I tried to construct a teleport spell.

It, too, failed. My fangs were out. They'd been out ever

since I lunged for Ariana, intent on ending her for her perfidy to our kind. I retracted them. Even that small action cost me. I had to do something, but my options had narrowed to walking away from Ariana's and falling on my face until my magic recovered.

I combed through my memories, but couldn't come up with any anecdotal tales of Vampires who'd expended too much power and didn't eventually mend. It offered hope, although I wasn't in the mood to accept it. I'd pinned a whole lot on Ariana and me finding our way together. Her disclosure, something I'd encouraged, had soured everything.

I had no dignity left, no pride, little self-respect. I'd behaved abominably, but then so had she. I still couldn't absorb what she'd done. Gathering the shards of my broken honor, I turned and walked slowly away. Not toward the place I'd turned into a one-man war zone, but away from Ariana's.

I didn't care where I went. I had to find a path past today's events, but walking was all I could manage. Night was well established when I stopped by another stream. Thinking perhaps I'd rest, I sat on its bank and stared at the rushing water. Its flow was hypnotic. A marmot settled in to drink on the far bank. I sent a weak thread of magic its way. Surprise flooded me when the animal stopped moving.

Maybe the distinctive scent of aggression had finally faded enough for mesmerism to surpass it. Regardless of the reason, I'd take my wins where I could get them. I splashed through the creek and did everything I could do to ease the creature's passing. Blood helped. I was back on my original side of the stream, carcass in my lap, when I felt the distinctive tang of Vampire magic.

I girded myself for another confrontation. Was Ariana hunting for me? It would be smart of her to do away with me so I couldn't reveal her misstep. Perhaps she'd decided sooner rather than later reduced the odds I'd rustle up more Vampires and form a mob intent on her destruction. I bounded to my feet and positioned myself with two enormous trees to my back. I'd try reason, first. Reassure her I'd leave quietly. If it didn't work, then I'd—

A gateway formed, and Clive shot through. I stared at him and the portal, but it dissipated behind him. "You're alone?" I asked, not understanding why he'd have come looking for me.

He nodded. "Where in the bloody fuck have you been. We need every soldier, and you're here." He narrowed his eyes. "You look like hell. What happened. Why aren't you at the pub with all the rest of us?"

If I'd been the breathing type, breath would have whooshed from me. As it was, I integrated Clive's impromptu appearance with his apparent lack of knowledge about today's events. Evidently, Ariana hadn't said anything. Neither had Conan. Or if they had, Clive wasn't included.

Maybe they'd been expecting him to leave. Ariana would have, anyway. She'd have recognized I'd never depart this area without my clansman. Or without at least talking with him.

Clive walked near enough to drop a hand onto my shoulder. "What happened? Do you need to feed? Christ, mate, you've got blisters all over your face."

"Ariana told me...something disturbing. I—" What to tell him? I hated to admit my teeth-gnashing, breast-beating tantrum, and I felt protective of her secret. What a pisser. I'd been willing to kill her over it, but I didn't want to tell Clive.

"Whatever it was," Clive said, "she needs us. I wouldn't have left if it weren't for you. Been waiting for you to show up for hours. When you didn't, I finally poked around with magic and located you." His grip on my shoulder tightened. "Whatever this is, get over it long enough to return to the pub with me. Things aren't going well for our side."

He let go of me. I felt power jet from his fingertips, and he trotted to collect the results: a respectable collection of rodents. My bleak emotions from earlier roared to life. Shame joined them. He shouldn't be wasting magic to ensure I was hale enough to fight.

"Thanks," I said, my voice so gruff I almost didn't recognize it. "It's enough." Without wasting time, I worked my way through the warm, furry bodies. Before I drained the last one, I was feeling more like myself.

Next to me, Clive was eating too. He'd lured more prey while I was intent on the pile he'd left next to me. "Ready to go, mate?" he asked and swiped a sleeve across his mouth.

It was a two-edged question. I had enough energy to begin healing my abraded face and scalp. And enough to teleport out of here, but could I go to *Ascent*? Be in the same room with Ariana? I had no idea how I'd react. It could go either way from me falling on my knees and begging forgiveness to jumping her, intent on beheading her. Or a whole host of possibilities between those two poles.

Clive angled a pointed look my way. "We need to leave, Nick. Now."

"I'm not certain it's the wisest course for me," I said, skirting the issue.

"Why wouldn't you help Ariana?" he demanded. "She's done a lot for us. She's from a different clan, but she didn't let it stop her."

I grimaced. Clive had just brought up another of the tenets governing Vampires. Our insularity. We never did squat for anyone in another clan. Until they conceded and signed on with ours. Then, and only then, were they afforded all the privileges we extended to our members.

That way of life was dead. It had been on its way out when Clive, Lorenzo, and I caught a ship for the States. During our long tenure in stasis, it had probably finished fading into obscurity. The thing about rules is they only work if people—or Vampires—abide by them.

Magic flickered around Clive. "I'm leaving. We're outnumbered but not quite out-magicked. What shall I tell Ariana if she asks why I didn't bring you back?"

"That you couldn't find me?"

"She'll know I'm lying." He shook blond curls over his shoulders and sent a pointed look my way. "I don't care what she did. You can hold it against her after the battle."

Before I could come up with something to say that didn't cast me in an unattractive light, he was gone. I touched my face. The skin was almost healed, which meant my strength was back to its usual potency. No excuses. Not really. Conan and Clive had said the same thing. I owed Ariana. I'd flirted with telling Clive what she'd done, but hadn't. I had the oddest impression it wouldn't have mattered to him.

So why should it matter to me?

Was it because I'd been raised on whispered tales of Mistral's untimely end? Or perhaps because I'd snuck off, intent on pitting myself against Mistral's killer. Of course, then I'd assumed it had been another man. Just like every other Vampire. No one had ever suspected a female had done him in.

How had she pulled it off? Surely, someone in the clan house had figured things out. I scrunched my forehead in thought. Nah. Probably, no one had fingered her. If they had, she'd have been drained and beheaded. It was the Vampire way. Hundreds of years in the past, when Mistral had been decapitated, we were still clinging to the old rules and rituals.

His death preceded my turning by at least a hundred years.

I shook my head, filled with grudging respect for Ariana. She was smart and gutsy. Principled, but in a way that benefitted her and those she considered her allies. What a dumb sod I was. I hadn't even asked why she'd raised her hand against her maker. She must have had reasons. No one attacked their master on a whim.

I was wasting time wallowing in what-ifs. Clive had been worried enough to return to *Ascent* as soon as he was satisfied I was all right. He enjoyed fighting—we all did—but he'd said we were losing. Twice. It lit a fire under me where nothing else had.

It was stupid to stand on pride. I'd show up and do my

part to protect Ariana and the nightclub and her friends from whatever I'd sensed beneath the club's floorboards. I should have mined for details while Clive was here, but I hadn't. Aye. I hadn't done a whole lot that I should have.

Determined to not make a bigger ass out of myself than I already had, I set a teleport spell in motion, considering my exit point. Perhaps I'd be better served to come out in one of the side streets. Darkness would cover my movements well enough. If I was unfortunate and startled a human, I'd wipe their minds.

I emerged behind the huge store where Ariana's car had been parked, fortuitously between two large, metal bins complete with the infernal labels humans favored: glass and plastic. I resisted punching a hole in them and reshaped my magic into a sloppy ward. Something magical would be able to sense it, but mortals couldn't.

I hadn't gotten ten steps in the direction of *Ascent* when the sounds I associate with battle reached me. Some of them, anyway. Moans, groans, shouts, curses, and the clang of swords crashing together mirrored fights I was familiar with. Gunfire drowned almost everything out, but it came in staccato bursts from weapons I'd never come across before. I crossed one empty street before I came to the first police car, lights spinning in a circle as they split the night.

A long, rolling boom, like thunder but amplified a hundred times, made the pavement buck and heave beneath my feet. What in the hell? Had an earthquake picked this precise moment to strike. Seemed like too much of a coincidence. Damn it. After all my dithering, had I arrived too late?

The closer I got to the club, the more police cars I saw. I'd been planning to come in the back way, but the alley was blocked by some kind of yellow banner and uniformed officers with fancy rifles at the ready. Maybe they were what was making the godawful racket.

The front of the club wasn't any better. Meters of the same thick yellow ribbons had been plastered over both ends of Mercy Street in front of *Ascent*. A cop with a huge cone to amplify his voice stood in the street. Four other police covered him with drawn weapons. The man with the cone was shouting instructions, but none of the police seemed inclined to go inside.

Maybe they remembered their companions who'd been cut to ribbons by hogs and wasps and Sorcerers from another world. I circled the club as best I could—both ends of the alley were blocked by an unbroken line of cops—before deciding teleporting inside was my only avenue. I hated to do that because the burst of power would alert everything magical inside. I'd be a prime target in the moments when I became corporeal again.

Back in front of the club, I remembered a side door Percy and I had used. It was certainly locked, but that was no deterrent at all. Perhaps fortune had me in her thoughts because that entire side of the club was shrouded in shadows. No cops. No mages—good or bad. A hasty shot of subtle magic, nothing like what I'd have had to leverage to teleport, and the tumblers gave way.

After a quick glance in both directions, I slipped through the door, locking it behind me. The first thing that hit me was the smell. It should have filtered outside. The noxious stench of dead mages and spilled blood was strong in my nostrils. Eau de roadkill mingled with decayed vegetation. No one had noticed me yet, so I sent puffs of power in every direction to figure out what we faced and where I could do the most good.

It was dark inside the club; someone had obviously decided lights weren't their friend. Just as well; my vision in full dark is exceptional. It didn't take me long to understand most of *Ascent* was no longer part of Earth. A gateway to one of the other worlds stood open just past the bar. Its energy had incorporated the club, moving most of it...elsewhere. It's hard to describe, but the sensation of otherness was overwhelming. Even the air had a different smell, once I got past the reek of death and decay.

I risked a smidgeon more power, hunting for who was still on this side. Once I located Dee and Clive, I sidled around the edge of the club to the stockroom. After tugging the door open, I strode inside. "You're here." Clive sounded relieved.

"Where is everyone?" I asked.

"Sucked through to the other place," Dee said. Her black eyes were huge and ringed with shadows. Her olive skin had taken on a sallow tinge.

"It didn't get us because we were back here," Clive tossed out.

"How long ago?" I looked from one to the other of them.

"Eh. Maybe ten minutes. We were back here hunting for ammo for one of the guns, when this ungodly noise ripped through the club. It sounded like an atomic bomb hit."

"The suction was so strong, we grabbed hold of the furniture and hung on," Clive said.

"It would have gotten me if it hadn't been for you." Dee angled her black eyes his way.

"Maybe not. You're stronger than you think," Clive said with his usual touch of gallantry.

I recalled the earthquake sensation I'd felt when I was on the move between the labeled rubbish bins and the club. It had to be the same thing Clive and Dee had just described. "Do either of you have any idea where the other end of the gateway leads?"

"No," Clive said.

"Mostly, we were fighting Sorcerers and Witches with weird, twisted charms," Dee added. "We were finally, finally pulling ahead. Lotta bodies out there—mostly theirs, not so many from our side."

"We have to go after the others," I said. "Nothing we can do from this end."

"Same conclusion we came to," Clive said and clapped me across the shoulders. "I am so glad you came to your senses, mate. I was really flummoxed. You needed me, but I was needed here too. In the end, their need outshone yours." He inclined his head. "Apologies. I understand I may not have chosen correctly."

"You did," I said, my tone curt. "Come on. Whatever's happening on the other side of the vortex, we need to be there too."

"The minute you open the door, we'll get dragged into the maelstrom," Dee said.

"I don't think so," I told her. "I saw the opening, but it

wasn't exerting any pull. What I noticed most was a differentness. It suggested *Ascent* had joined wherever the portal leads."

I turned and opened the stockroom door, ready to slam it in case I was wrong. The death smell was still there, but the weird, eerie sensation alerting me the club had moved beyond Earth's boundaries had departed. If remaining silent hadn't been so critical, I'd have shrieked my dismay.

Moving with Vampire speed, I rocketed forward.

Sure enough, the gateway was gone. The bar was, once again, firmly rooted to Earth.

"Where'd it go?" Dee's question was a breathy whisper.

"Wherever it went, it took everyone with it," Clive sounded furious—and unnerved.

I shuffled through our possible next moves, discarding ideas almost as quickly as they came to me. Ariana was gone. Worse than that, she'd been captured, spirited away to who only knew where.

"Dee." I curved my fingers around her upper arm.

She started, almost as if she'd fallen into some kind of trance. "Yeah." She yanked her arm out of my grip.

"Sorry," I said. "Can you take us to the realm of the dead?"

"Of course. What do we do after we get there?"

"Two choices," I said. "We hunt for a break in the ley-lines we can hopefully follow to wherever the vortex led. But it would be simpler to find a guardian or two."

"What will they do?" Clive asked.

"What do you want to bet they know how to find Conan?" I answered him with a question of my own.

"Why would you think that?" Dee frowned. "They left him alone for a long time, presumably because they had no idea where he was."

I nodded. "That was before he revealed himself to them. Anyway, the realm of the dead is our only real lead."

The cop outside with the electronically magnified voice was shouting orders. It sounded as if our window of time to disappear was fast running out.

"Now or never," Dee said and began to chant. When her portal formed, Clive and I jumped through it.

A Few Hours Earlier

Conan hadn't been kidding when he'd said a battle was raging at *Ascent*. The only good thing about it— other than I love tearing into anyone who gets in my way—is it drove my immediate thoughts away from Nickolas. Witches and Sorcerers rampaged through my club, complete with misshapen allies, not unlike the pigs and wasps from one of their earlier incursions. Similar to their first trip, they emerged through a portal system, but I felt them under my feet too, which suggested an opening to some off-Earth locale.

If I ever got a break in the action, I'd investigate, but we were outnumbered. Conan's assessment about things not going well had been spot on. Every once in a while, I made the mistake of sucking in a breath. If there was anything left of it, *Ascent* would need to be fumigated to remove the stench of blood, entrails, and dark magic. It pricked my nose, even when I wasn't breathing, with a mixture of sulfur, ozone, and decay.

This time, rather than pigs, a two-headed beast with rows of snapping teeth mostly obeyed the Sorcerers' commands. The thing looked like a hyena, but whoever designed it had missed the mark. The dual heads were angled in such a way the thing could really only use one of them. Unless someone was clumsy enough to fall into the other mouth, it was useless. Covered with matted brown and black fur, their other downsides seemed to be a short attention span and a stubborn streak. They stopped at everything dead to feed and were tough to spur back into motion. After watching them operate for a short while, I relegated them to annoyances.

Far more concerning were supersized hawks sporting pterodactyl beaks. Gray and black, they honked as they flew. Good thing because their jaws were capable of cutting off heads, arms, or legs. So far, I counted three.

No, two. Percy just brought one down. He fist-pumped the air to celebrate. I silently wished him luck with the others.

Blood smells saturated everything. Witch blood. Sorcerer blood. Fae blood. Sidhe blood. Each had a slightly different tang to me. I noticed when Clive left. When he returned by himself, I melted into a corner ready for him to come for me like Nickolas had, but he didn't. He just dove back into the fray slugging it out with a black Sorcerer. The contest was laughable. Moments later, the Sorcerer's head went flying, and still more blood stench joined all the rest of it.

Losses piled up on both sides. We're mostly only immortal when it comes to human fights. We know how to kill each other. At the point when I started fighting, we weren't exactly holding our own. The word "losing" isn't part of my vocabulary, but Witches—the good ones—and Percy's Sorcerer companions had sustained losses. I heard a shriek from Ruby that was fraught with anguish. I'd never heard her sound like that before. She had to be mourning the loss of one of her own, and it smote me.

Everyone was fighting because of me. If it weren't for my nightclub, we'd have remained invisible. Not a target for wicked magic.

I'd have gone to Ruby, but I was neck deep in wiping out a hyena pack. Like I said, they weren't much more than annoyances, but when they worked in conjunction with one another, they managed to mete out damage. Two of them lay twitching in death throes. The next one I throttled vanished. One minute I had my hands around one of its throats squeezing the life out of it. The next it wasn't there. Ha! Meant some of them were illusions. Tricky of the Sorcerers. I started to spread the word but decided against it. If someone guessed wrong, the animal was plenty lethal.

I was grateful I'd fed. Running balls-out for hours was draining me. I'd have had a much shorter half-life on the battlefield if Nickolas hadn't provided blood. Yeah. Nickolas. Thinking about him was a dead-end street. I wrenched my mind back to front-and-center present.

Hours had passed. I had no idea how many. Sometime in the last maybe thirty minutes, the tide had definitely turned. The hawks were gone. The hyenas had thinned out. I punched one in the neck before slicing through its vessels with a fingernail I keep extra sharp. Nick carried a nasty-looking dirk. He must have had it specially made at one of the smithies in the Old Country because the blend of metals didn't appear to bother him.

Fuck! Nick. Nick. Nick. I had to expunge him from my mind. And my heart and everything else. The hyena writhed in my hands, proving it wasn't exactly out of commission. The feel of its greasy fur was unpleasant. I widened the gash in its neck, shouted, "Die, already," and kicked it aside.

When I glanced around, I felt encouraged. More of us were standing than them. Had we mowed through their ranks? Or had they decided discretion was the better part of valor and left? I edged to where Dee and Clive had just dispatched a trio of Witches. Their faces were smeared with blood and dark, chalky residue from somewhere. We all smelled atrocious.

"It's time for the rifle," I said. "We can finally use it without shooting one of us by mistake."

Dee grinned. Combined with the blood decorating her olive skin and pushing her black hair into garish spikes, the smile made her appear truly vicious. "Bet you want the special ammo, huh?"

I nodded. Clive looked mystified, so I told him, "I had bullets made long ago. They contain a combination of silver and iron filings along with gunpowder."

"Thanks for the warning," he said.

He'd watched his clansman, Lorenzo, die in agony from silver darts shot into his back, but forewarned is forearmed. Besides, Vampires—most of us, anyway—aren't subject to much in the way of feelings beyond anger and lust. Self-preservation is high on the list too.

"Come on." Dee crooked a finger at him. "We're going to have to hunt them down. Boss lady hides shit better than anyone I've ever known."

"They're in the stockroom," I offered helpfully.

"I already knew that part. Could you narrow it down further?" Dee asked.

I shook my head. Dee was right. When I hid things with magic, it often took me a while to unearth them too.

A Sorcerer barreled into me from my blindside. He drove me to floorboards running with blood and yanked my head back. It hurt and pissed me off. I jabbed my knee into his groin hard enough I felt his testicles burst. Not much of a challenge after that little move on my part. While the Sorcerer was bellowing in agony, I dragged my fangs through his neck, partially beheading him. Blood geysered. I was careful not to get any into my mouth. It's deucedly unfair their blood is poisonous for us. Such a waste of resources. By the time I was done rolling around on the floor grappling with him, Dee and Clive had left to find the lethal ammunition I hoped would clear the rest of this rabble out of my club.

The sound of someone shouting through a megaphone told me our warding must have failed. Cops were outside, maybe dozens of the fuckers. I wasn't worried about them coming in. Not after their last sortie where half a dozen had been killed in as many minutes.

A shudder beneath my feet was my only warning before the world caved in around me. A rolling, booming, crashing crescendo obliterated the already unbearable noise level in the large room. Dark magic grew around me forming a pulsing vortex that opened into a portal. Too late, I felt its inexorable pull. I'm strong, but it was far stronger. Maybe if I'd had something solid to grab onto, I'd have been all right.

Furniture flew past me. Heavy tables and chairs broke into matchsticks when they hit the gateway. Apparently, it was keyed to only accept living beings, or those with magic. Conan had been engaged dispatching Witches on the far side of the bar. I yelled for him, but he didn't answer.

Was he already gone?

I was losing ground fast. My attempts to run the other way slowed the inevitable, but only fractionally. My last thoughts before I was swept through the nasty, pulsing hole in the ether were of *Star Trek* and the tractor beam. Stupid, huh?

The gateway spit me into a dark, airless void. The unremitting black didn't so much as allow me to see a hand raised right in front of my face. Frantic to escape, I cobbled a teleport spell together and launched it with as much magic as I could muster. It bounced back, slapping me so hard I feared my neck had broken from the impact.

I yelped with pain, but my words were sucked out of me and swallowed by the void.

What the fuck had happened? Who had this kind of power? Surely not the pack of jokers we'd been fighting. Had Clive and Dee escaped? Presumably, they'd been behind the storeroom's closed door. I was grateful Nick hadn't been part of this debacle. And then I kicked myself for even thinking about him. I'd made my bed, gone into this with my eyes starkly open.

His immediate attack told me everything I needed to know, and I had to move on. But first, I had to somehow get myself out of this mess.

As precipitously as I'd been snatched, the magic holding me shattered and I fell, tumbling end over end as gravity took hold. Still smarting from my last attempt to summon power, I dragged more into place. It was either that or be smashed into a heap of broken bones at the bottom of wherever I was falling to.

This time, magic responded to my call, albeit sluggishly. Big surprise. I'd blown through scads fighting. I'd have taken blood-breaks, but I'd figured if the Sorcerers' blood was toxic to me, probably everyone else's was as well. Didn't figure I could afford to take the chance.

The ground rushed up to meet me. I hit, but not as hard as if I hadn't cushioned my impact. Conan hurried up to me, woofing. Ruby, Christa, and Percy materialized on my other side. I rolled to my feet and looked around. Not Earth, but then I'd known as much the moment I was headed for the vortex.

"Does anyone know where we are?" I lurched to my feet and took in a shoreline. Either a large lake—or an ocean—

stretched to the horizon. At least the water was the right color. It butted onto a spit of orange sand studded with rocks. Cliffs rose behind the sliver of sand. I tilted my head back but couldn't see the top. Gray-black and coated with lichen, the overhanging rocks looked slippery, harder than hell to climb.

My glance upward showed me more bodies catapulting toward us. Who knew if they were conscious or not. I did my best to weave a pillow of air to soften their impact. Conan and Percy shored up my efforts with their own power. Over the next few minutes, Dahlia, Cerys, and a bunch of the Witches from their Guild House joined us. So did several Fae and Sorcerers.

"That's everyone, I think," Conan told me.

Our strip of sand had shrunk by perhaps half. The tide was coming in. I cast another appraising look at the cliff. "We have to get out of here," I said and pointed at the water. As if me noticing it had been some form of encouragement, it sloshed toward us faster. From what I could see, we stood on the last strip of beach that wasn't underwater.

"We could try to teleport up there." I jabbed a finger at the cliffs. I still couldn't see their tops, but they had to be somewhere. I'd never heard of a cliff that extended into infinity.

"Do you have enough magic left?" Ruby asked. "Because I'm not sure I do."

"We'll cross that bridge when it happens," I said, keeping my tone brisk, businesslike. "Everyone try. If you can't, we'll come up with something."

More Than Never left Dahlia's shoulder and flew

around her head, cawing encouragement. Various magics flickered and flared. Some guttered, but about half of us managed to escape. I was standing in water now, and I understood why the vortex had spit us out here. Not to drown us so much as to make us miserable.

Ruby faced away from me, shoulders slumped in defeat. I slopped through water and wrapped an arm around her. "Let's do this," I said and loosed a spell. My directional vectors weren't precise because I'd never seen the top of the cliffs. A rolling snowfield formed around us. I blinked at it for a moment before the other mages came into view. At least we were in the right place. It would make my next trip easier.

"Thank you." Ruby ducked from under my arm and wrapped hers around herself. "Brrrr. If I'd known, I'd have brought a coat."

I snorted. "Yeah, like we had time to pack."

A triple-sized eagle came into view carrying a Sorcerer. Conan had adapted his shapeshifting ability. Excellent. Between the two of us, we spirited the half dozen or so who'd been unable to teleport to the snowfield. Crap. The cliff must have soared 10,000 feet above the beach to have moved from a maritime climate to hardcore winter.

"Does anyone know where we are?" I repeated

"Maybe." Conan's careful reply alerted me he did not bear welcome news.

"If I'm right"—Percy stepped into the conversation —"we're on Omega Two, last of the mapped worlds." He chewed his lower lip, biting hard enough a drop of blood formed. "Whatever we're going to do, we need to be quick about it. Our magic will soon grow too weak to be effective. After that, we'll gradually sink into unconsciousness."

"My assessment as well," Conan said. "The guardians have different labels for these places, but the nearest world is our best alternative."

"Omega One," Percy said. "It's not much better than this one. If we go there, we really won't have enough magic left between us to accomplish much of anything."

Desolation bit hard and deep; I pushed it aside. I'd be damned if all these people—good people who'd moved past their innate distrust of Vampires to work alongside me—lost their lives.

"Is this world constructed like the others?" I asked.

"What do you mean?" Conan replied.

"Its innate magic lies near its core," I clarified.

The wolf looked at Percy, who shrugged. "What are you thinking?" Conan asked me.

"We tunnel downward until we can tap into this world's magic to fortify ourselves. Then we teleport the fuck out of here."

"It's a gamble," Dahlia said.

"Seems like we'd have been in a stronger position back on the beach," a Sorcerer mumbled.

I shook my head. "Water mutes magic, particularly mine. Salt water is the worst. We had no choice but to move away from it. Whoever planned this knows our strengths—and our weaknesses."

Ruby turned to Percy. "This whole shebang happened because Nick, Clive, and Lorenzo pissed off black Sorcerers.

I get it they were angry, but why target all of us. Is this type of reaction common?"

Percy nodded once and shifted from foot to foot, looking uncomfortable. "Aye. Quite common. My twisted kinsmen live for retribution. It's what makes them so dangerous. But I believe today was more about payback for our little visit to Gamma Four where we killed over a hundred of their ilk." He stamped his feet, presumably to warm them without wasting magic.

I took it as a sign we had to quit talking and start moving—before we were all too cold to do anything.

Conan yipped and reared back. The still, cold air crackled with his magic, and the welcome scents of fur and wet rocks reminded me how dear the wolf was to me. In a weird way, I'd raised him, but I've always trusted his instincts. In many aspects, they ran truer than my own.

Snow flew out of the way. A hole formed in the white, undulating surface, expanding into a small crater. Encouraged, I tossed power into the mix and willed the excavation to develop a life of its own. Dream on. It was hard going. By the time we'd cleared a hundred feet, not even past the frozen tundra beneath the layer of snow, I was panting.

Panting.

A bizarre reaction since I don't require air, but it seemed to help, so I kept on sucking it in. Ruby worked next to me. Her magic must have recovered a little bit. The hole grew deeper, but I was lightheaded. How was that even possible? Had some residual silver broken loose from my go round with the bullet?

Was that why I felt like warmed-over dogmeat?

"This isn't working," Conan's voice formed in my mind, and echoed. What was wrong with me?

"Of course, it is," I managed. *"Just slow, is all."*

Voices blurred into an unintelligible gibberish. I could identify who was speaking, but not what they said. My head pounded. My mouth felt like I'd been licking the bottom of a parakeet cage, dry and gritty and sour.

Wind pelted me with chunks of ice. I must not be in the hole anymore. I opened my mouth, tried to protest we couldn't give up, but I couldn't talk. I reached for magic, but I may as well have reached for the moon. I thought I heard Nick's voice, but that more than anything told me I had to be hallucinating. I was in a place Vampires go before we enter stasis, except I hadn't courted unconsciousness.

With the last of my fading resources, I tried to puzzle things through. If this was silver poisoning, I'd hurt more. Maybe. It was possible the cold had mitigated the worst of the burning, tearing sensation I associated with silver. I'd been careful not to ingest any of the dark Sorcerers' blood. But I'd been coated with the stuff for hours. Had enough soaked in through my skin to poison me?

Or was it something else entirely?

I'd been fine until I jumped into the hole in the snow. But I'd been breathing. Was something toxic in the chasm? If so, it hadn't affected anyone else but me. I commanded my eyes to open. They refused. Everything took a million times more effort than it should have.

The buzz of voices continued. I had a feeling they were talking about me, but I couldn't interpret any of it. I wanted to tell everyone how sorry I was. How much I valued them and their friendship, but it was as impossible as opening my eyes.

Because I'd run out of choices. And luck, apparently. I let go and felt myself sliding down a long, dark spiral. Lights flickered, breaking the blackness, but it was probably random neurons firing in my long-dead brain.

And then even they winked out, leaving me falling in the dark forever.

CHAPTER SEVENTEEN, NICKOLAS

Our trek through the realms of the dead hadn't yielded much. They were a seemingly endless tunnel system with passageways at all angles. Those nearest the ley-lines were illuminated by the lines themselves. A form of light-emitting lichen provided enough brightness to see by everywhere else. The odd ghost flitted past, but they left us be.

We found the ley-lines, just like we did last time, but no matter how far we traced them, they extended in unbroken glowing ropes. Try as we might, we couldn't locate a crossroads marking an unauthorized entrance to Earth. Eh, maybe this mess wasn't the guardians' fault after all.

Unlike our previous visit, the guardians didn't stop us right after we arrived. Or if they did, they were so subtle I never felt it. After maybe half an hour of chugging this way and that, I halted.

"This isn't working," I said and asked Dee, "Can you raise the guardians?"

"I don't know, but I'll try." A vertical line formed between her dark brows. "I don't feel as beat up as I did last time we were here. Also, we haven't seen very many wraiths. Usually, they'd be thick because they're drawn to my magic. Not sure what either of those items signifies."

She began a low chant in Gaelic, hands weaving in complicated patterns as she asked the guardians for assistance. Last time, they'd been plenty quick to storm our small group.

Last time, Conan had been with us. He'd been quite the incentive, but presumably he was with Ariana and everyone lost wherever the vortex had spit them out. I sensed Fairclaw before I saw him. His power had the same feel as Conan's. Expecting an unpleasant confrontation, I readied myself to lay pride at the door and beg for his assistance, if need be.

Not that I had anything to trade for his goodwill. I didn't. It left me in a serious one-down position. I can be charming, but I had a feeling charm wouldn't sway the guardian. He hated Vampires and had probably relegated Conan's impassioned speech about Ariana being the only one who'd stood by him to a slagheap.

The silver wolf I recognized as Fairclaw ran lightly along the nearest ley-line. His power mingled with the line's energy; no wonder he used them for transport. They fed his magic, intensified it. When he was a few meters away, he shucked his wolf's body and became the tall mage with knee-length silver hair and amber eyes I remembered. A slender golden band circled his forehead.

"Thank you for heeding my call," Dee said.

He jumped lightly off the ley-line and crossed his arms over his naked chest. "I knew you were here," he grunted. "I had hoped you'd manage to both come and go without fanfare. What do you want?"

He hadn't cursed me or insisted we leave immediately. I interpreted both as hopeful signs. It cost me. Damn, it cost me, but I bowed my head. Vampires bow to no one, but I'd have broken every tenet that bound me to my kind if it meant locating Ariana.

"Apologies for disturbing you," I began, "but—"

"Get on with it," he snarled. "There aren't enough pretty words in any language to atone for your uninvited appearance."

So much for my false show of humility. It hadn't bought me shit. I raised my head and met his unremitting wolf's eyes. Interesting they remained the same from shape to shape.

"I am certain you are aware there was a major battle earlier today." When Fairclaw offered a curt nod, I continued. "I missed the majority of it, but from what I was told we were coming into the endgame, and we were winning, when a portal formed. A vortex paired with it and sucked all who were left into its maw. We"—I jerked my chin at Clive and Dee—"escaped its pull. They were in a back room, and I was newly arrived. By the time I showed up, the gateway was intact, but the vortex was no longer exerting any force."

"We tried to go after our friends," Dee said in a thin, strained voice, "but the gateway vanished."

"We have no idea where they are," I continued. "All I'm requesting is your assistance locating Conan, er Moonwraith. He and our companions could be anywhere. I fear if we systematically check through worlds hunting them, it may be too late to intervene by the time we finally stumble across the right place."

I stopped there. I'd covered the important parts. Begging wouldn't sway the guardian. Maybe not from anyone, but certainly not from one like me.

Another blast of energy unique to guardians told me our conversation hadn't gone unnoticed. Sure enough, a white wolf danced nimbly along the lines, morphing into a female with floor-length white hair and blue eyes. A blue stone suspended from a golden chain sat in the hollow of her neck. Like Fairclaw, she was naked.

"I heard," the woman said. "Everything." She faced off in front of Fairclaw. "If you will not cast the magic to find my son, I shall."

"I did not say I would do nothing." Fairclaw sounded annoyed.

"Shall we work together?" the woman urged. "Two magics are always more efficient than one."

Fairclaw didn't reply, the light brightened around the two guardians until I turned away and shielded my eyes with a hand.

"*So much power*," Clive breathed into my mind.

It was impressive, but would it work? I'd seen a lot of showy displays over my life. Unfortunately, the ones with the most bells and whistles weren't always the strongest mages, only the most manipulative ones.

An hour or better had passed since Ariana vanished down the magical sinkhole. She could be anywhere—or nowhere. For the first time since I'd been turned, I longed for someone to pray to, something bigger than myself that might have a chance of intervening.

I didn't care if Ariana had written me off. After my performance, I wouldn't blame her. And I was still caught up in a host of conflicting mindsets. I loved her, but what she'd done horrified me. I wanted to ask why she'd beheaded her master, but it wasn't a fair question. No answer would offer sufficient justification for such a heinous act.

One thing was certain, even if the guardians were successful—and their power thickened around me by the minute with the same fur and wet granite smells as Conan's —seeing Ariana again wouldn't erase my troubled thoughts. The best I could hope for would be to tell her I was sorry for my actions. Once I'd done that, and seen her safely back to Earth, I needed to go somewhere far away. Come to terms with the impossible—or not.

If I did, I'd return. If not, I'd remain wherever my need for reflection had taken me and somehow build a life for myself, but I was getting ahead of the game. Way ahead. I cracked my eyelids long enough to understand the guardians' spell was winding down.

"Moonwraith is on a place well-known to us," Fairclaw said. "No one has a right to set foot on that world but our kind."

"It is far from here," Conan's mother added. "I shall take you there, and see you safely returned."

"I am grateful," I told her, but felt compelled to add,

"Many others are with your son. Will it be possible to transport them all?"

She turned eyes that looked like polished agates my way. "Surely their own magic is up to the task."

"If it were," I said, "they'd be back by now. The black Sorcerers must have either done something to strip their power or left them in such an uninhabitable spot, return wasn't possible. Maybe both."

"I see." The woman tapped Fairclaw's arm. "You shall come too."

I expected him to demur, but he surprised me. Power built around them. We hadn't moved, but their spell included us. It was still uncomfortably bright, but I wasn't about to complain. The next part happened quickly, so quickly I stopped trying to absorb everything. I'd take time later to sort events into a cohesive whole.

The realms of the dead and ley-lines dropped away, replaced first by endless gray, and then by a blast of intense cold. An arctic landscape took shape, complete with a brisk wind and swirling ice chips. Percy pelted toward us, slipping and sliding on the icy surface. "Thank the goddess," he cried. "We tried to tunnel nearer this world's core, but something in the excavation made Ariana sick. She's alive, but none of us can reach her, and our magic is all but gone."

"She can't be sick," I protested. "Vampires don't get sick."

"Gather everyone," Fairclaw ordered in a refuse-at-your-peril tone. I recognized an order when I heard one. I'd received many from commanders during my tenure as a knight. Master vampires were even worse; they took absolute compliance for granted.

I propelled myself to the tight knot of Witches, Fae, Sidhe, and Sorcerers. Conan and Ariana were in the center of the group. The wolf had laid his body protectively over Ariana, but she was, indeed, in some sort of coma. I wanted to gather her into my arms, but I'd lost that right—if I'd ever had it. Conan snarled at me.

The last time I'd seen him, I'd been intent on Ariana's destruction. He wanted to make it damned obvious he'd protect her with every bit of bone, sinew, and magic at his disposal.

I inclined my head for the second time. "I shall not harm her. You have my word." Turning to the group, I said, "I brought help. We're leaving."

Percy was back. Bending, he gathered Ariana into his arms. Conan whined softly but ceded his post as her protector. Everyone hurried toward Fairclaw and Conan's mother, stumbling on the slick surface as they ran. Even before we reached the guardians, their power surrounded us. Conan's kicked in last. The journey back wasn't as smooth as the trip to wherever the hell we'd been, but even the guardians' power wasn't limitless, and there were a lot of us. Various magics flared as those mages who weren't totally tapped out tried to help.

"Do you know what's wrong with her?" Clive asked me while we transited the gray void.

I shook my head. My mind tracked in endless circles trying to figure it out and getting nowhere. Failure was eating me up. We jolted back into the realm of the dead; the transition far from elegant, but at least we were a simple hop from Earth now.

The guardians cut the flow of their magic. Fairclaw and Conan's mother turned to go, but I ran to catch up with them. "Thank you for all you've done," I began. "I can never hope to repay you for your kindness, and—"

"What is it now?" Fairclaw snapped.

"Do you know what's wrong with Ariana? Vampires never sicken." I stopped before adding we were already dead. It put the brakes on mortal disease, all of which required living protoplasm.

Fairclaw shrugged, but Conan's mother turned to face me. "It was far from accidental your enemies left you on that world. Their complaint is against Vampires, yes?" After I offered a curt nod, she continued, "While Onyx—our name for that spot—would merely have weakened the rest of you, it is lethal to Vampires."

"But I was there. Clive too. We seem to be all right," I protested.

"You did not bide long enough for Onyx to wreak its insidious destruction. Its core is molten silver mixed with many other minerals."

I made a hissing noise. At least I had an explanation, but no solution. I could dig out silver bullets, but Ariana's whole body had presumably been exposed to contamination. "Is there anything you can do?"

"Will you never stop requesting aid from us?" Fairclaw shimmered into a wolf, flicked his tail, and trotted quickly away.

"I'm sorry," I called after his retreating form. I'd done

more apologizing to him than I'd done since I'd been turned, but I didn't care. I'd have groveled if it meant saving Ariana.

"I will see if I can call her back from where she wanders," Conan's mother said, "but then, I too shall follow Fairclaw's path."

Gratitude swamped me. "If there is anything you have need of..." I quit there. Unlikely a guardian would ever require my services.

The mage hurried toward where I'd left everyone. "Bring her nearer the ley-lines," she instructed.

Conan stalked to his mother. "What is wrong with Ariana?"

"She's been poisoned by silver."

"I knew that part," Conan said. "But it's not as if any penetrated her."

"She breathed it in, which is far worse. Will you join your magic with mine, son? Together we might have a chance to roll back the damage before it becomes permanent."

"Of course." Conan added a short, shrill bark to punctuate his words.

Percy laid Ariana next to the nearest glowing rope. Her face had turned the shade of old parchment. Vampires are pale, but her skin had developed an unhealthy translucence.

"The rest of you should leave," Conan's mother said. "Additional magics will only muddy the waters."

"May I remain?" I asked.

Conan growled.

His mother raked me with harsh magic, perhaps

assessing my intent. It burned as it ran from my head to my feet. "Why?" She spat the word.

I stood tall beneath her scrutiny. "Because I love her, and I did something I'm not proud of. I want a chance to tell her I'm sorry."

Percy had herded everyone into a circle. His power formed blue lights flickering on the tunnel walls. When it cleared, only Conan, his mother, Ariana, Clive, and I remained in the realms of the dead.

"I'll stay out of the way, promise." Clive offered one of his best smiles.

"Keep your magic out of this," Conan's mother said curtly.

Clive nodded agreement; I did too and took a few steps toward the curved wall. I wanted to help, but now was a time to remain on the sidelines. Allowing us to stay had been a concession. I'd sensed how close Conan's mother had come to ordering us away. If she had, we'd have had no choice but to leave. The last thing I wanted was to alienate her with still more requests.

Fairclaw was clearly done. He'd performed his good deed for the day. Or the week or the month. Conan's mother might have left as well were it not for the fact Ariana had sheltered her son. Stood in for the mother he'd left behind. Thank all the saints she wasn't the jealous type.

A low hum filled the air, resonating at the same frequency as the lines' vibration. It appeared the mages were borrowing heavily from the ley-lines to reach Ariana. I still didn't understand. At all. Silver poisoning sends us into seizures, followed by bones breaking, skin sloughing off, and permanent death.

So far, all it had done was render Ariana unconscious. Did it mean she was holding the toxin at bay?

Her pallor deepened. A low moan rose from her throat. It smote me. She was in pain. What they were doing was making it worse. My fangs showed up out of nowhere. I pushed them back. No matter what happened, I refused to make Conan's mother regret permitting me to remain.

I might not know her at all, but I did know Conan. His loyalty to Ariana was unquestioned. He would never stand by and let his mother do anything that wasn't in Ariana's best interest. I repeated that assurance over and over in my mind as Ariana's groans grew louder, more strident.

Conan and his mother were chanting in earnest in a language I'd never heard. Hands extended, they wove a canopy of filmy, iridescent strands that draped over Ariana's inert form. Time slid past. It felt like hours, but it was only minutes. Long ones.

The mages' chant was faster now. They'd definitely picked up the pace. I felt the bite of their power from four meters away, harsh and urgent. Magic was never a long process—for anything. Their spell had to be reaching its zenith; pressure from its energy sent shock waves bouncing off the tunnel walls.

Ariana's back arched. Her heels drummed on the sandy floor. She shrieked, a heartrending sound that made me want to tear into both mages. They were hurting her, killing her.

Fangs out again, my vows to remain out of the way forgotten, I started forward. Clive gripped my upper arm and dragged me back. *"No!"* He screamed it into my mind to get my attention. I fought against his hold, but he's strong.

Fuck everything. I had to get control of myself. My hair-trigger reactions had ruined everything between me and Ariana. If I didn't put a lid on them, I might wreck her only chance at recovery. So far, neither Conan nor his mother had glanced my way.

I nodded at Clive to let him know he could let go of me. Hands balled into fists, I sank to a crouch. If these were Ariana's last moments, I wouldn't sully the dignity of her passing. She'd moved from pounding her heels against the floor to full-body seizures. They rippled through her, contorting her limbs at odd angles. Her screams came nonstop, and they made my heart hurt. Tears formed in the corners of my eyes.

I hadn't believed it when I'd seen Ariana cry, hadn't thought Vampires could. The same pain I remembered from when I'd been human, grief where anguish carved so deep the only thing left was tears, shot holes in my dignity.

I didn't care.

Conan's mother grabbed Ariana's head and turned it to the side. A dull gray stream of vomit splattered on the sand, followed by several more. Ariana made a gagging noise. Conan propped her head up with a paw. He continued to chant.

Finally, the spasms first slowed, and then ceased. Conan's mother lifted Ariana to a clean place. The glistening streamers that had formed a canopy over her lowered, wrapping around her body. I focused intently on the woman I loved, willing some color to return to her face.

She was still unconscious, but she didn't seem as deeply submerged as she'd been. The only sound in the tunnel was the gentle humming of the ley-lines and Conan's rough panting. I pushed upright but remained in place. Questions rampaged through my mind. Would Ariana be all right? Would she recover fully? How could we best support her?

I didn't ask any of them but waited for Conan and his mother. Eventually, they turned and walked to where Clive and I stood.

"The next hour will tell the tale," Conan's mother said. "I have done all I can. Purged the toxin. Fairclaw already said as much, but that world, Onyx, is ours. It is where we originated." She curled one hand into a fist. "No one has a right to touch it except us. You will not have any further problems with off-world Sorcerers. We shall see to it."

Conan's ears pricked forward. Some part of his mother's message had been news to him.

"Thank you. For everything," I told the mage.

She shook her head. "Never thought I'd see the day when I leveraged magic to save a Vampire, but life is a strange journey."

Conan snarled, probably annoyed by his mother casting aspersions on Vampires.

His mother dropped a hand onto his thick neck ruff. "I appreciated being able to blend my magic with yours, son. If anything can save your friend, it was our efforts."

The wolf quieted. I expected him to shake off his mother's hand, but he didn't.

"Can we move her?" I asked.

"I will take her home," Conan told me.

"May I accompany you? I won't remain. I just want to make certain she wakes."

Conan regarded me. I held myself still beneath his review. After so long, I'd been certain he'd say no, he nodded.

His mother folded her hands together. "Until next time."

Conan jumped up and put his paws on her shoulders. He swiped his tongue across her face. "Until next time...Mother."

A soft smile illuminated her face. Conan settled his front paws on the ground again. His mother walked into air and vanished.

We flanked Ariana. Clive on one side, me on the other, and Conan at her head. I welcomed the feel of the wolf's power as it enveloped us, and we traded the realm of the dead for Ariana's living room. Clive picked her up and placed her on one of the sofas. I tucked a pillow under her head. Her color was definitely better, and the gossamer remains of the spell were sinking into her body.

"She's improving," Conan said.

It matched my assessment, but I appreciated hearing him say it.

"That didn't look like any silver poisoning I've ever seen," Clive spoke up.

"Nor me," I added. "Until the part where she started seizing."

"Probably because the core of that world is made of many elements," Conan said. "By the time I recognized silver, it was too late. And I had no idea fumes would hurt her." He shook his shaggy head. "I didn't know anything about Onyx. When I ran from the guardians, I was too young to have learned much about our history."

Another head shake ran through his body. "This is my doing. I should have been more careful."

"You couldn't have known," I said.

But the wolf just trained despondent eyes on me.

Ariana made a mewling sound. I sprang to her side, gratified to see her usual skin tone. Like all magical beings, she had decent recuperative ability. When I touched her hand, she turned it over and wrapped her fingers around one of mine. I bent close to her ear. "Ariana, darling. Take all the time you need to grow strong again." I hesitated before plowing on. "I love you, but I have things to think through. I'll return if I can."

She turned her head toward the sound of my voice, battering my resolve to leave. Before I weakened, I gently uncurled her fingers from mine and stood.

"Where are you going?" Conan asked.

"Not sure," I said. "I have a lot to figure out."

The wolf stalked in front of me. "You will not sic a pack of Vampires on her for what she did."

I met his gaze. "You have my word. Any soul-searching I have to do will be an individual pursuit."

"Do you need me to come with you?" Clive asked.

I walked to him and dropped a hand onto his shoulder. "I owe you thanks for stopping me before I made a mistake back in the tunnel."

"None needed," he said. "You'd have done the same for me."

It was true. I would have. "You're welcome to

accompany me if you want," I told Clive, "but you can remain here as well. Or go where you will. Up to you. Our old ways are no more. We will have to discover new ones as we move forward."

Clive rolled his shoulders back. "If it's all the same to you, I believe I'll stay, but I'm as close as telepathy unless you travel far from here."

"And I'm as close as this damn thing." I tugged my cell phone from a pocket. "So long as I can find somewhere to plug it in."

"Nick?" Ariana called weakly.

It decided me. If I was leaving, I had to go now. "Tell her I'll return if I can," I repeated, and set a spell in motion. Her living room faded, replaced by the walls of the cave I'd taken refuge in for stasis. I fought the desolation sweeping through me and lost.

Dropping my head into my hands, sobs ripped through me as my entire being vibrated with grief. Once it ran its course, I'd go home to northern Italy. Maybe somewhere along the way I'd find peace and a way to return to Ariana.

EPILOGUE, ARIANA

ix Weeks Later
It took a month for my strength to return, which is a ridiculously long while for a Vampire. During that time, my friends did all the heavy lifting making *Ascent* habitable for customers again. I kept expecting to hear from the cops, but I never did. They'd been outside the club that afternoon; I'd heard them shouting through their bullhorns. My guess was there'd been bunches of them. After a few weeks passed, I quit expecting any fallout but still puzzled over it. Something must have scared them so thoroughly, they'd written my club off their hit list of hot spots.

When I was feeling well enough to do more than loll around on the couch waiting for Clive and Conan to bring me blood, I got hold of my lawyer. He's done quite a bit for me over the years, making certain my business was up to snuff for all the local codes. He's where I dump my taxes every January too. As a preemptive strike, we filed a lawsuit

"

against the City of Kirkland for not providing adequate protection to keep *Ascent* safe from incursions—human and otherwise. And for the extensive damages the club had suffered. My insurance gleefully jumped on board. Insurance companies love to spread the pain to someone else's bank account. I didn't expect the suit to go anywhere. Neither did I expect to collect a dime. Best case, it would keep whoever manned the paranormal task force from breathing down my neck.

Speaking of which, despite having everyone scouring the papers and social media, I never caught a whiff about Riteway and Hernandez. Surely, the cop shop had expended resources—probably a lot of them—to hunt for their own. Normally, when an officer goes missing, there's a huge brouhaha about it. From what I could tell, there wasn't even a public memorial. It was as if the two detectives had never existed.

If new principals had been assigned, the media was damned quiet about that too. I asked Percy to do some digging. What he came back with was heartening. At least for now, the city had decided their resources were best used elsewhere. They'd disbanded the paranormal task force.

It was a start, but it was small potatoes. Our much-larger next-door neighbor, Seattle, had one of the best-staffed, best-funded forces in the country. I was sitting at my desk in a corner of my living room running numbers when I felt Fae magic and glanced up from my spreadsheets. For the first time maybe ever, I was caught up with *Ascent's* financials. The Witch ensemble had begun playing two nights a week.

So far, we'd made enough extra those nights to more than justify their wages.

My front door swooshed open, and Ruby walked in, flanked by Dee and Clive. "Top of the evening." Clive mimed a bow, and then dropped a wad of cash in front of me. He'd been paying off both Nick's debt as well as the one he'd incurred for his own set of identification documents. Dee jabbed him in the side. The two of them had been looking pretty cozy. I wondered if they were fucking, but their sex lives were none of my business.

"Club did great tonight," Clive said. "Cerys and the Witches really packed them in."

Ruby sent a meaningful look at him and Dee. "Yeah. Yeah," Dee said. "We'll make ourselves scarce."

"Going hunting," Clive said.

"You'll probably run into Conan out there," I told him. "He showed up an hour ago to check on me." I grinned. "After all these catered meals, I'm not sure I even remember how to find my own food."

"It will come back to you," Clive said and laughed. Hooking an arm with one of Dee's, he guided her back through the still-open door, shutting it behind them.

I liked him. He had a dry, understated sense of humor that took me back to my roots in the British Isles. Pushing my chair back, I walked around my desk to where Ruby stood. Full on Fae, her red wings were on display, and her eyes glowed golden in the candlelight.

"I assume the three of you worked this out beforehand," I said.

"That obvious, huh?" Ruby smiled warmly. Somewhere

along the way, my illness and recovery had shelved the last dregs of everyone's residual distrust of me.

"Yeah. What's up? I'll make tea for us."

"That would be lovely. I'll tend the fire. It's dying."

It was, indeed, but then I'd only lit it for ambience not warmth.

Ruby waited until I brought steaming mugs of mulled wine—with a bit of tea—to the couch that sat across from the hearth. Once I'd settled in a chair cattycorner from her, it was my turn to wait.

She cleared her throat. "When will you be coming back to work? Or are you?"

I winced. Leave it to a Fae to get right to the point. No beating around the bush. No cunningly crafted questions—or jabs—about my overlong recovery.

Opting for honesty, I said, "I've been wondering the same thing. Every afternoon, I get myself ready, but something doesn't feel quite right, so I tell myself I'll go the next night."

Ruby skewered me with her eerie eyes. Absent her habitual glamour, she appeared wise and ancient. "Is it Nick?"

I dragged my gaze away. If I'd been the blushing type, I'd have turned red.

"Aw, honey." Ruby wrapped her long fingers around one of my wrists. "Still got it bad, huh?"

A spate of denials clawed at the back of my throat, but they were lies.

"Have you heard from him?" Ruby pressed.

I shook my head.

"Clive hasn't, either," she told me, which settled one unknown. I'd been itching to quiz Clive but had restrained myself.

"Conan told me what happened," Ruby said. "Some of it. I pieced the rest together. Christa filled in some bits. Apparently, peering into the past is far simpler than scrying the future."

My head snapped up, and I looked square at Ruby. "You know about Mistral?"

Ruby shrugged. "Only that he was your master and you killed him. You're pretty levelheaded. I figure you had a good reason." She exhaled noisily and slopped down half the mulled wine in her mug before continuing. "Between Clive's explanations and what I dredged up, I understand Nick's reaction. Vampires don't have very many rules, and you broke the only one that actually mattered."

Annoyance shaded to anger. I shot to my feet. "If you came here to lecture me, you can fucking get out of my house. I'm appalled the lot of you were talking about me behind my back. Judging me. Fuck all of you."

Standing still wasn't in the cards. I turned on my heel and bolted out of the house.

Ruby materialized in front of me, forcing me to a halt. "For fuck's sake get hold of yourself," she sputtered. "I'm your friend, goddammit. You need to pull your head out of your ass and get back to work. Beyond *Ascent*, all the mages have been meeting regularly about our next steps. Because of you"—she thumped my chest—"we've come up with some workable strategies we're going to try first.

"Things that just might work."

I was still so furious, my body quivered. Mixed with the anger was shame. I'd turned into an object of pity. Poor, jilted Ariana can't leave her house...

Another chest thump. "None of that is true." Ruby had somehow made herself taller, and she was yelling right in my face. "Yup. I helped myself to your thoughts. No privacy among mages. Suck it up, doll. We talked about you because we're worried about you. Because we *care* about you."

She stopped there. Wise Fae. Sometimes less is more, and the part about her and the others caring about me broke through the dam I'd constructed around my heart. Some would tell you Vampires don't have hearts, but I do. I'd done so much crying since my brush with death on Onyx, I wasn't surprised to feel the hot gush of tears.

I brushed them aside. "I'm sorry," I told Ruby. "I don't know what's wrong with me."

Back to her normal height, she wrapped an arm around me. "I do. You fell in love. The guy left. You're in mourning, but you'll get over it. And you know what?"

I swept more tears aside. Sheesh. I was turning into my own daytime soap. "No. What?" I snuffled.

"Have a little faith. I think he'll come back."

"Nah. He won't. What you said earlier was right on. I broke a huge taboo. If I'd been caught, I wouldn't be here now. Clan Hawke would have decapitated me and burned my bones and spit on them."

"How long ago was it?" Ruby asked, her voice soft.

I tried for mental math, but came up short. "At least five hundred years," I said at last. "Maybe as many as six."

"Don't you think you've suffered enough?"

My tears yielded to gulps of laughter. "Fuck yes, I have. More than enough, but I brought the whole house of cards down on myself when I told Nick."

"You had no choice." Ruby nodded sagely. "How can you begin anything with someone special if it's built on lies?"

"Thank you," I murmured.

"For what?" She arched her dark brows.

"Saying what you just did. It's why I told him. I didn't see how I couldn't. The only other choice was culling him out of my life, and I couldn't do that, either. So I was stuck. But when he launched a full-on attack, I questioned the wisdom of what I'd done. And wished I hadn't."

"No good time for the truth. Ever," Ruby agreed. "Come on back in so I can finish my wine."

With her arm still around me, we walked inside and sat in companionable silence. When the mugs were empty, I said, "It's time."

"For?" I felt the subtle prick of Ruby's magic as she prepared to dig beneath whatever came out of my mouth and reminded myself it was good to have friends. Good to be cared about.

"I'll be back at *Ascent* this afternoon. It's past time for everything to get back to normal."

"Good choice," Ruby said and stood. "Don't write Nick off. I truly believe he'll come back. See you later on today."

I got to my feet too. "Thanks for not giving up on me."

"What are friends for?" With a smile and a wave, she trotted out the door. A small jolt of Fae power told me she'd teleported away.

I wandered around my house for a few minutes,

returning the mugs to the kitchen, before I walked outside. It would be dawn soon, the start of a new day—even if my part of it wouldn't technically begin until late afternoon.

The implications of what Ruby said sank in. Seemingly, everyone knew about Mistral. No one held it against me. Maybe it meant there was hope Nick would come around after all. Meanwhile, I was done putting my life on hold.

Conan loped out of the shadows and dropped a freshly killed young deer in front of me. The blood scent was rich, heady, and I sank to my knees to feed. When I looked up a short while later, Conan had shifted into his motorcycle form. A muted, "Vroom, vroom," made me laugh. I was still laughing when I dropped a leg over the bike, and we took off down the driveway into what remained of the night.

You've reached the end of *Warped Line*, second of the Cataclysm books. *Cracked Line*, next in the series will be along shortly. Keep reading for a sample. While this book is still fresh in your mind, please take a moment and leave a review. I'd very much appreciate it.

Until next time.

BOOK DESCRIPTION: CRACKED LINE

Vampires don't fall in love. Except I did.

Not the best decision of my long life. I definitely cracked an unspoken line, but Ariana trounced me as far as line-crossing went. Very few acts constitute crimes in Vampire circles. Hers was the worst. I fled to the Old Country to buy myself thinking time.

I still loved her, but what she'd done was so vile I couldn't set it aside.

The world is a very different place from when I went into stasis. I woke to wars on every side. Vampires are scarcely strangers to battle. No one's ever accepted us, but they've mostly let us be. It's different this time. Very different. Mortals won't rest until they've wiped out magic.

Normally, their efforts would be laughable, but they've coopted help from magic-wielders. Ones they've imprisoned and systematically stripped of power until the poor sods would agree to anything in exchange for their freedom.

We face huge problems, but I'm tackling them one by one. I'll return to Ariana's side, but perhaps only as her comrade-in-arms. Time will tell if we can be more to each other.

Time and circumstances. In a world without magic, Vampires will wither along with every other mage. I cannot let that happen.

CRACKED LINE, CHAPTER ONE, NICKOLAS

*S*cottish Highlands

So far, the plastic cards that passed for money in this strange modern world hadn't failed me yet. Someone must be paying the bills back at *Ascent*, a nightclub owned by the woman I love. I truly hope she wasn't underwriting my expenses. One of my Vampire associates from Clan Giovanni is there too. I don't feel much better sticking him with my overhead, but I'm still working things out.

I arrived in Ireland a fortnight ago after crewing on a fishing vessel that was crossing the north Atlantic. I couldn't force myself into an airplane. I can teleport if the distances aren't overly long, but something about flying makes my skin crawl. I spent time at a couple of airports, and all it did was solidify my uneasiness.

I'm a Vampire. That says everything—or it should. Luckily, the night shift on fishing boats isn't popular. When I made it clear the dark hours were my preferred assignment, I had my choice of crafts. I picked the one that looked the most seaworthy and was shocked how little time it took to cross the choppy Atlantic. My journey from east to west a century before had taken weeks. This trip was over and done with in a matter of a handful of days, spitting me out in Galway, Ireland.

The captain wanted some electronic something-or-other to transfer my wages, but I insisted on cash. It irked him, but I'd been a hard enough worker, he didn't dismiss me without my money. It wasn't much, but it was enough to rent a room at some point. I had no intention of remaining where I was. Thank all the demons Ireland is perpetually gray, otherwise leaving the ship would have been much more difficult than it was.

I holed up in a squalid pub for what remained of that day. It's allure was it only had one very small window, and it was so dirty not much light filtered inside. The place was empty enough, the proprietor seemed grateful for the brews I purchased. I kept expecting him to insist I buy more, but he never did. Judging from the appearance of his establishment, he was used to patrons who were barely hanging on.

Once it grew dark, I scuttled through the door and hunted for a spot I could teleport from. I wasn't at my best. Fish blood is near the bottom of my list of preferred food. Even obtaining that was a challenge on board the ship because I was rarely by myself.

Tonight, my destination was the Scottish Highlands. My hopes were high I'd find swathes of deserted forest where I could hunt. I ended up in the Northwest Highlands not far from Loch Shin where I retained lodgings in a down-at-the-heels boarding house. While far more populated than I remembered, the region met my needs well enough. I'd been born not far from here in a humble shepherd's cottage around five hundred years ago. After cleaning up—I still smelled vaguely of fish—I went hunting. My sense of humor returned after draining a sixth rabbit, and I laughed at my expectations naught would have altered during my long absence. The lush forests from my memories had been reduced to not much more than the odd tree here and there, but they were sufficient to meet my needs.

I had no idea what to expect in Castelrotto, but my plan was to locate my Vampire clan and demand my share of its wealth. It wouldn't go over well, but once I'd been master of the clan. I might have to do battle with the current master, but it could be arranged. I wouldn't stand by and let them fuck me out of what was rightfully mine.

Assuming Clan Giovanni still existed. It could have fallen to ruin in the century since I'd left, with its members dividing the spoils and running for cover.

Throughout my days crossing the United States and still more on the boat, I'd made up my mind to return to *Ascent* and my friends there. And to repay my debt to Ariana. I'd signed on to be a soldier in the supernatural army squaring off against mortals who wanted to crush everyone with magic. I wouldn't welch on my commitment.

I'd been one step up from destitute when I'd left; returning with money would ease my way on many fronts. And then, I'd be able to contribute to the war effort with more than my supernatural strength, speed, and affinity for killing.

The part that was still murky as hell was whether or not I'd try to mend things with Ariana beyond apologizing again for trying to kill her. Not that she didn't deserve death—or she would have if the old rules still applied. She'd beheaded Mistral, master of Clan Hawke and her maker. Vampires don't have a whole hell of a lot of rules, but we have clung to that one. The punishment for killing a master Vampire is permanent death.

Ariana has gotten away with her crime, probably because everyone assumed a male had murdered Mistral. Centuries had passed, and she'd ended up halfway around the world from where she'd committed her transgression. I'd known something ate at her, and I'd urged her to confide in me. Perhaps if I'd known I'd have kept my mouth shut.

Nah. Knowing would have made it all the worse. The second I found out, my innate vampiric reactions kicked in, and I tried to end her. I might have succeeded if her dire wolf companion, who was far more than he appeared, hadn't intervened.

Before her revelation, Ariana and I had grown close. Close enough, I'd fallen hard for her. It was why she'd told me about Mistral. Once I was thinking clearly, I understood we could never have developed true intimacy with her guarding a secret like that one.

As usual, when I thought about Ariana, my head grew fuddled. Vampires did not select mates. We didn't "fall in love." Neither did we develop proprietary interests in our sex partners. But she cared about me. And I returned her interest, lust, and affections. That she'd laid aside her longstanding silence about Mistral told me how important I was to her. She'd divulged her secret with full knowledge I'd have every right to demand her execution.

I couldn't think about her for very long without feeling like a rat treading water. I never got any closer to a solution, but I didn't quit trying. I needed to settle on a path before I returned to the nightclub. Even if I vowed I was done hungering for Ariana, I wasn't at all certain I'd be able to follow through and keep my distance.

Every time I shut my eyes, she rose in all her dark-haired glory to tantalize me. Lush curves graced her tall, sinuously muscled body. With her acres of legs and full breasts, she was the stuff wet dreams were made of. And then some. Her eyes were a rich, mysterious blue that shaded from azure to lighter colors depending on her mood.

I spent my nights hunting. Days, I retreated to my lodging, thought about Ariana, and brought myself off to a stunning variety of fantasy images. Every evening, I swore I was done, but the following dawn found me with my cock in my hand dreaming of all the things I wanted to do to pleasure Ariana.

After a week in the north of Scotland, I'd run out of excuses. My strength had returned. If I was going to go to Castelrotto and hunt for the remnants of my clan, I needed to get on with it. I timed my arrival to coincide with dusk and warded myself because I couldn't think of a single spot it would be safe to wink into view.

It didn't take long to locate a modest pension that advertised breakfast along with their room rate. Not that food is any kind of draw, but I needed a base to operate out of. I did not want to give the authorities any reason to look too closely at me. Ariana had showed me pictures of Castelrotto on her computer. If she hadn't, I'd have been in shock. The medieval town had altered beyond recognition. Even the ancient buildings had taken on new coloration, new fronts.

I waited until night was well underway to make a trek to the imposing Catholic church on the outskirts of town. Other cathedrals took up part of the town square, but we'd established a clan house beneath the Catholic church's graveyard, taking advantage of multiple crypts. Because the town was so old, excavations to build family tombs were common. We'd simply knocked out the earthen walls between several of them and created a commodious underground catacomb. Mortals had a healthy fear of the dead, so they never ventured into the tombs during nighttime hours.

We made a practice of nabbing the occasional human who entered the crypts during the day. It kept us safe by spreading rumors of ghosts and demons.

And Vampires.

Aye, there was a time when we were feared. Respected, even.

I closed off my thoughts of an era that would never return and merged with chattering crowds cluttering the narrow streets. Why weren't all these people at home, eating their nighttime meal and reading bedtime stories to their children? Music drifted from several cafés along with the smells of everything from roasting meat to decadent sweets.

I can eat if I choose, but there's very little point since I derive zero nutrition from anything that isn't blood. The layout of the streets was the same—tough to alter something as basic as that. The odd person bid me a good evening. I replied in kind as I worked my way past the square and into darker side streets. I still felt the press of thousands of mortals, packed into the ancient city like mackerels in crates on the fishing boat I'd just left.

The comparison made me smile. The stark truth was I viewed humans about the same way I viewed fish: not terribly bright and subject to the whims of their companions. If one fish swam into our nets, others were bound to follow it. The lemming effect in action.

I'd passed the worst of the crowds, and I welcomed the darkness as I left the brilliantly lit square. Two more turns and the dark, imposing bulk of the Catholic church came into view. First constructed around 1300, it had been completely rebuilt in the middle of the 1800s. Workmen had been so ubiquitous, we'd had to leave the clan house for several months.

I paused in the shelter of a stone overhang and risked a thin thread of magic. It ran forward unimpeded, and I redirected it to both sides. Not so much as a quiver disturbed my seeking spell. If anyone magical was nearby, they were deeply warded.

I hadn't exactly expected Clan Giovanni to still be in residence beneath the church graveyard, but I had no idea where to hunt for them, either. Determined to hunt for clues, I started forward. No one saw me clear the fence around the cemetery. In the years since I'd left, someone had replaced the old wooden staves with chain link that stood taller than my head. Signs suggested entry to the cemetery was controlled by a single gate toward the front.

Graveyards are strange places. I sensed the departed far more strongly here than I had in the realms of the dead. Perhaps many of them had chosen not to cross over. Just like with every other creature, living or dead, there's not much love lost between corpses and Vampires. We have no further used for them, and they hate us because while we're dead—like them—we're still living the life they crave.

I glided to the Giovanni crypt. Our clan name is as common as Smythe or Jones in the U.K. We'd picked that crypt as a joke, but its entrance had served us well. Someone had slapped an official looking proclamation on the door, along with a rusty padlock. The paper was badly weathered, but I could still read enough to get the gist.

Closed to entry—by anyone.

I hit the lock with the flat of my hand, and it clattered to the dirt. Apparently, keeping riffraff out had been important once, but not so critical anyone kept up with maintenance. I pushed the door open and ducked inside, pulling the door shut behind me. No one would see the broken lock, and I may as well maintain the illusion the crypt had been abandoned.

A quick sniff told me there hadn't been Vampires in this place for a long time, perhaps fifty years or more. I dialed in my night vision and strode down the long set of steps into the top level of the tomb. Raised biers lined both sides, like always. Atop them sat a variety of coffins that still stank of embalming fluid.

One more flight of stairs brought me to the stout oaken

door that had once led to our clan house. Or the remains of it. The planks bore ax marks, and then someone had nailed crosspieces over them. My earlier caution yielded to anger. I made short work of the cheap, plywood sealing the door to what had once been my domain, and kicked it open.

Mortals had dared intrude on Clan Giovanni. I smelled them. Who would have done such a thing? More importantly, why weren't they dead and drained? I hadn't gotten two steps into the clan house when the unmistakable odor of silver burned the inside of my nostrils. I built a hasty ward. Nothing lived down here. I'd checked, and silver couldn't hurt me as long as I limited my exposure and didn't breathe it in. The latter is simple enough since we don't breathe anyway.

Over the next hour, I searched every last cranny of my former home. My heart grew heavier with each dead Vampire I uncovered. Most were nothing but piles of bones. Why hadn't they teleported out of here? I didn't understand why they'd remained until they died from silver poisoning. Maybe some had escaped. Not everyone was here, but that didn't necessarily mean anything.

Our census could have changed in the years since I'd left.

I punched a wall in frustration and was rewarded with the rumble of unstable dirt ready to cascade onto my head. I latched my fingers together after that. I did not want to waste scads of magic digging myself out from beneath a cave in.

How long ago had all this happened?

My first guess was it coincided with the notice tacked to the Giovanni crypt. If it was dated, I'd missed it, but I'd look again. I dragged Vampire remains into the main room. The least I could do was immolate the remains. My fire burned quick and clean. I crouched off to one side. If I'd still been human, I'd have paid lip service to some kind of prayer, but Vampires don't do things like that. The only deities we believe in are ourselves—and perhaps our makers.

It didn't take much to drag my thoughts back to Ariana. I knew her well enough to understand she must have suffered for her decision to decapitate Mistral. But she hadn't let it get in her way. Maybe when she'd done it, she'd been too young to fully appreciate the ramifications.

A rustle snagged my attention. It might have been the pop and crackle of my dying fire, but I didn't think so. Expecting anything from a nefarious boobytrap to a human with a silver dart gun, I shot to my feet and barked, "Show yourself."

If no one was there, I'd rather feel like an idiot, than have missed a critical clue that spelled my doom.

Shadows thickened, shifted, and reformed. When they quit undulating, Roseann walked out of them. "You're finally back," she said. The Vampire I remembered would have rushed into my arms and given me a hug, but she just stood watching me out of wary eyes.

"Aye. I'm back."

"Naught to return for." She ground out the words. Her flame red hair had developed rust overtones. Her green eyes were dull. A patched skirt and stained white jacket covered her tall frame.

"What happened?" I asked.

"Pfft. What does it look like?" she countered. "A nosy priest led a mob of Vampire hunters right to us."

"Why didn't you fight back?"

She skinned back her upper lip, fangs on display. "What makes you think we didn't?"

"Because we're better than this." I swung an arm wide. "Since when can a passel of mortals kill so many Vampires?"

The anger that had glistened around her like a prickly cloak broke apart. She shook her head until strands of hair fell in her face.

"Did any of the rest of us survive?" I pressed. I didn't want to pillage her thoughts, but I would if she didn't start talking.

Roseann nodded dully. "Aye. A dozen. We left, obviously."

My fires were out but for glowing coals. "We should too," I told her.

Moving more like a very old woman than a Vampire, she lifted her head until her sad, green eyes bored into me. "I set a snare, so I'd know if anyone disturbed this place. The spell is so old, it shocked me when it chimed today." Pushing her shoulders straighter, she kept talking. "It's best if I leave. The others won't want to see you. They believe your lengthy absence was why we failed. A clan requires a master. If we'd had one, perhaps we'd have known some of our own led a double life."

My mouth fell open. "We were betrayed by our own?"

She nodded. "Fools. We were fools. We didn't pay attention until the poison had already taken hold. 'Twas subtle at first, so faint, we chalked it up to the drugs humans had begun imbibing by truckloads."

"If you deem it wise," I said, "tell the others I am deeply sorry. I was forced into stasis. It never occurred to me the clan wouldn't replace me."

Her eyes narrowed. "What of Clive and Lorenzo?"

"Clive is well. I left him in the northwestern United States. Lorenzo made some bad decisions. Humans killed him with silver darts."

She shrugged. "He always was too impulsive for his own good. Never cold tell that boy anything."

I resisted wincing. Her description was accurate enough, yet I still blamed myself for his unfortunate demise. And now I had still more death on my conscience—or whatever passes for one in my kind.

Roseann turned to go.

"Wait. Please."

"Why?" She didn't turn around.

"Did you at least lay claim to our hoard?"

She twisted to face me. "You make us sound like a fucking flight of dragons." Her words might have been harsh, but a ghost of a smile played around her mouth.

"Well?" I raised my eyebrows into question marks.

Roseanne spread her hands in front of her, the nails cracked and broken. "We were all sick when we teleported out of here. So weak if we hadn't helped one another, we'd never have escaped." A tear formed in the corner of one eye and rolled down her face. "We did the best we could. Even tried to spirit more of us away, but we knew we were done in." She shook her head. "We had to conserve what little ability we had to shield ourselves from discovery. It took months, maybe a year, before we regained enough strength to make a difference. By then, everyone here was..."

"It's all right." Her tale was almost as painful to hear as it was for her to tell it.

"No." She curled her fingers into fists and punched the air. "This will never be all right. The only good to come out of it was the perfidious scummy mortals killed our two-faced kinsmen."

"Damn. I'd been hoping to do that."

"They beat you to it." Roseann dropped her hands to her sides. "We'll never be the same, but we're alive, able to feed, and in a safe spot." She stood tall, the first show of spirit I'd seen since she materialized. "You'd asked about our money, our gold. Most of it was in that bank vault. Once the officials knew what we were, we were denied access. One of us tried to use a different name and barely escaped. If he hadn't been ready to teleport out of there, they'd have nabbed him."

I sucked air through my teeth. The bank had been my bright idea. It had seemed modern at the time. So much more civilized than burying gold bars and gemstones and hoping no one dug them up by accident.

"One more thing for me to apologize for," I mumbled.

"Eh, you couldn't have known."

"Same bank, right?" At her nod, I went on, "I'm going to teleport in there and take what's ours. Where can I leave your share?"

Her faint smile had returned. "Right here, Nickolas. I'll be watching and rooting for you."

"Will you tell me who survived?"

She shook her head. "Better if you don't know."

"Will you tell them you saw me."

"Aye. I will do that."

Before I could list all the things I wanted her to relay from me, magic glistened around her and she was gone. Probably for the best. My days as master of this clan were over. And then some. I raked my hands through my hair. If I'd been here, would it have made a difference? I liked to believe it would have, but I might have been just as clueless as the rest of my clan.

I could dissect this later. My current task was to take back what was rightfully ours from the bunch of bastards who'd stolen it. More than furious enough to kill first and ask questions later, I set a teleport spell in motion aiming for the basement of the Castelrotto branch of the Bank of Italy.

ABOUT THE AUTHOR

Ann Gimpel is a USA Today bestselling author. A lifelong aficionado of the unusual, she began writing speculative fiction a few years ago. Since then her short fiction has appeared in many webzines and anthologies. Her longer books run the gamut from urban fantasy to paranormal romance. Once upon a time, she nurtured clients. Now she nurtures dark, gritty fantasy stories that push hard against reality. When she's not writing, she's in the backcountry getting down and dirty with her camera. She's published over 80 books to date, with several more planned for 2020 and beyond. A husband, grown children, grandchildren, and wolf hybrids round out her family.

Keep up with her at www.anngimpel.com or http://anngimpel.blogspot.com

If you enjoyed what you read, get in line for special offers and pre-release special reads. Newsletter Signup!

Demon Assassins

Witch's Bounty

Witch's Bane

Witches Rule

Dragon Heir

Dragon's Call

Dragon's Blood

Dragon's Heir

Dragon Lore

Highland Secrets

To Love a Highland Dragon

Dragon Maid

Dragon's Dare

Dragon Fury

Earth Reclaimed

Earth's Requiem

Earth's Blood

Earth's Hope

Elemental Witch

Timespell

Time's Curse

Time's Hostage

Gatekeeper

Shadow Reaper

Rebel Reaper

Untamed Reaper

GenTech Rebellion

Winning Glory

Honor Bound

Claiming Charity

Loving Hope

Keeping Faith

Ice Dragon

Feral Ice

Cursed Ice

Primal Ice

Rubicon International

Garen

Lars

Soul Dance

Tarnished Beginnings

Tarnished Legacy

Tarnished Prophecy

Tarnished Journey

Soul Storm

Dark Prophecy

Dark Pursuit

Dark Promise

Underground Heat

Roman's Gold

Wolf Born

Blood Bond

Wolf Clan Shifters

Alice's Alphas

Megan's Mates

Sophie's Shifters

Wylde Magick

Gemstone

Lion's Lair

Unbalanced

STANDALONE BOOKS

Branded, That Old Black Magic Romance (paranormal romance)

Edge of Night (short story collection, paranormal and horror)

Grit is a 4-Letter Word (nonfiction)

Heart's Flame (post-apocalyptic romance)

Icy Passage (science fiction romance)

Marked by Fortune (post-apocalyptic coming of age story)

Melis's Gambit (historical paranormal romance)

Midnight Magic (paranormal romance)

Red Dawn (post-apocalyptic paranormal romance)

Shadow Play (historical paranormal romance)

Shadows in Time (Highland time travel romance)

Since We Fell (contemporary romance)

Warin's War (paranormal romance)